The Old Men of Omi

The Old Men Of Omi

An Akitada Novel

I. J. Parker

I · J · P

2014

Published 2014 by I.J.Parker and I·J·P Books
428 Cedar Lane, Virginia Beach VA 23452
http://www.ijparker.com
Cover design by I. J. Parker.
Cover image by Toshikata Mizuno

The Old Men of Omi, 1st edition, 2014
ISBN-13: 978-1500851958

Praise for I. J. Parker and the Akitada Series

"Elegant and entertaining . . . Parker has created a wonderful protagonist in Akitada. . . . She puts us at ease in a Japan of one thousand years ago." *The Boston Globe*

"You couldn't ask for a more gracious introduction to the exotic world of Imperial Japan than the stately historical novels of I. J. Parker." *The New York Times*

"Akitada is as rich a character as Robert Van Gulik's intriguing detective, Judge Dee." *The Dallas Morning News*

"Readers will be enchanted by Akitada." *Publishers Weekly* Starred Review

"Terrifically imaginative" *The Wall Street Journal*

"A brisk and well-plotted mystery with a cast of regulars who become more fully developed with every episode." *Kirkus*

"More than just a mystery novel, (*THE CONVICT'S SWORD*) is a superb piece of literature set against the backdrop of 11ᵗʰ-cntury Kyoto." *The Japan Times*

"Parker's research is extensive and she makes great use of the complex manners and relationships of feudal Japan." *Globe and Mail*

"The fast-moving, surprising plot and colorful writing will enthrall even those unfamiliar with the exotic setting." *Publishers Weekly,* Starred Review

". . .the author possesses both intimate knowledge of the time period and a fertile imagination as well. Combine that with an intriguing mystery and a fast-moving plot, and you've got a historical crime novel that anyone can love." *Chicago Sun-Times*

"Parker's series deserves a wide readership." *Historical Novel Society*

"The historical research is impressive, the prose crisp, and Parker's ability to universalize the human condition makes for a satisfying tale." *Booklist*

"Parker masterfully blends action and detection while making the attitudes and customs of the period accessible." *Publishers Weekly* (starred review)

"Readers looking for historical mystery with a twist will find what they're after in Parker's latest Sugawara Akitada mystery . . . An intriguing glimpse into an ancient culture." *Booklist*

Characters

(Japanese family names precede proper names)

Characters in the Capital and in Otsu:

Sugawara Akitada	Senior official in the Ministry of Justice
Yasuko & Yoshitada	his children
Tora	his senior retainer
Genba	another retainer
Saburo	a third retainer, a former spy.
Mrs. Kuruda	Saburo's mother
Fujiwara Kosehira	Governor of Omi Province
Yukiko	his eldest daughter
Takechi	Police chief in Otsu city

Persons connected with the case of the warring temples:

Abbot Gyomei	chief priest of Enryaku-ji
Kanshin	prior of the temple
Kojo	a warrior monk
Master Cricket	a hermit
a poor porter and his wife	
a wood gatherer and his family	

Persons connected with the Jizo murders:

Wakiya & Juro	two old peasants
Masaie	village headman in Okuni

Nakano	a retired judge in Otsu
Tokuno	a sweeper
Fumi Tokiari	a rice merchant in Otsu
Taira Sukenori	nobleman; deceased
Taira Sukemichi	his son
Hatta Hiroshi	Sukenori's *betto*, deceased
Hatta Takashi	his son
Mineko	a maid in the Taira family,

1

Old Man Wakiya and the Spring Festival

They staggered from the neighbor's farm followed by laughter and shouts: "Watch out or the *kappa* will jump out of a paddy and snatch ya."

The two old men, white-haired and white-bearded, were drunk out of their skulls and hooted with laughter.

Juro raised a jug toward the moon. "Bring on yer *kappa*! We'll fight'em."

His friend Wakiya snorted. "Me, I'd rather have a woman than a *kappa*. I'd even take a fox."

They bumped into each other, laughing and holding each other up.

"Yer drunk!" Wakiya said. "Gimme the wine. Yer gonna drop it."

"Never! Come to poppa." Juro kissed the jug. "Better'n a child any day. Children are a pain."

Wakya burped. "That bitch my son married. She's waiting at home with a broom to beat me. Gimme that jug."

Juro passed the jug over and stood swaying as his friend raised it and drank, spilling wine all over himself. "Pah," he spat. "Yer kid peed all over me." He threw the jug back and giggled.

Juro caught it by some miracle. "Watch out, ya almost killed him," he grumbled.

This struck both of them as hilarious, and they set off down the moonlit load, arms about each other's shoulders, singing. They were singing different songs, which led to another argument about who had the correct words, and the jug changed hands again.

By the time they reached Juro's farm, the jug was empty. They embraced tearfully, and parted.

Wakiya staggered onward, weaving this way and that, nearly falling into an irrigation ditch once or twice, and talking to himself.

"What a day! I'm beat. Been dancing like a boy! Ha,ha. And the women! Rokuro's wife's got big titties. Got a feel, but she slapped me. Amida, I wanted to give her one! He, he. He's not dead yet . . ."

He broke off when he saw the figure of a man sitting beside the narrow road. He squinted. The man looked familiar. But a cloud passed over, and he shook his head. "What's he doing out here anyway?" he asked himself.

The man waited patiently as Wakiya zigzagged toward him. When they were finally face to face, he asked, "Are you Wakiya?"

Wakiya swayed and nodded. "Tha's me. I know ya. What's yer name?'

"You don't know me."

"Mmm. Maybe I do and maybe I don't." Wakiya took a stumbling step and halted again. "Got my own place th'other side of the woods. " A thought occurred to him. Perhaps he could avoid his daughter-in-law's ire. "Ya want to come? There might be a drop of wine?"

The other man got to his feet. "Thanks. I'll walk with you and give you a hand. It's dark under the trees. You might take a fall." He laughed.

Wakiya chuckled. "Yer not a *kappa*, are ye?"

"No. Come along," the stranger said impatiently, taking his arm. "They must be waiting for you at home."

"Yeah, that bitch of a daughter-in law's gonna beat me. An old man! There's no respect for old people these days." He hiccupped. "Yer not from here, are ya?"

"Not anymore."

They were in the trees now. It was too dark to see the stranger's face, but he was looking about him as if he were searching for something. Wakiya said, "See any foxes?" and giggled.

That was when the stranger turned and took Wakiya by his scrawny neck. He shook the old man violently. Wakiya waved his arms and gurgled. He managed to knee the man in the groin. The stranger cursed under his breath and relaxed his grip a little.

Even in his drunken stupor, Wakiya knew his danger. He shouted in his thin reedy voice.

"Shut up!" snarled the stranger and squeezed again.

Wakiya kicked and scratched and made hoarse sounds until the stranger pushed him away with another curse.

The old man fell to his knees. He wailed and struggled into a stumbling run trying to get away.

But the stranger was not drunk, and he was younger and faster, and he had a rock in his hand. The rock smashed into Wakiya's skull before he had taken four steps. Wakiya arched back with a choking cry, then sank to his knees. "Wha . . . wha . . ." he mumbled, as the rock hit him again, and again.

Wakiya, finally silent, fell forward on his face. His white hair now made a red patch on the dark road.

2

The Visit to Otsu

It was spring again.

A blue sky hung over the mountains, birds of prey circled in the clear air, touches of pale green shone brightly from among the deeper green of pines and cryptomerias on the mountain side, and all along the broad highway, paddy fields had been flooded in readiness for the young rice plants.

A time for high spirits and optimism.

The small procession of officials from the capital rode along at a sedate pace behind a front rider with a white banner. The two riders who followed him wore fine clothing, one of them a green brocade hunting coat and white silk trousers tucked into his boots, the other a red coat over black trousers, plus blue trimmed half armor. Behind them followed six men in more sober black robes and hats, while a sedan chair, carried by four bare-legged porters, and a series of pack horses managed by servants, followed.

They traveled sedately because of the sedan chair. The black robes belonged to government officials traveling on the emperor's business, while the two men in front seemed to be on an outing.

All but the man in green brocade enjoyed the fresh air, the green rice fields, the budding cherry trees.

His companion had been watching him anxiously for a while and now said in a bracing tone, "You'll have a grand time, sir. His lordship's been looking forward to your visit. I'm sure he'll do you proud."

Akitada started from his abstraction and looked across. "Yes," he said. "Yes, Tora. I imagine so. It will be good to see Kosehira again. I'm very glad he got this appointment."

"He's much closer to us now. You'll both have many other chances for visits back and forth."

"Hmm." Akitada looked about to gauge their progress. They were more than halfway between the capital and Otsu on the shores of Lake Biwa.

"Are you feeling all right?" Tora asked. "We can rest if you like."

Akitada frowned. "I'm well enough, Tora. Don't forget that I have ridden this distance and much more many times in my life."

"That was then, sir. You haven't really been this far since you were wounded."

"That was eighteen months ago. I'm perfectly well."
He said it sharply to hide the fact that he was tired and
that his back and backside both hurt from the unaccustomed time in the saddle. To prove that all was well, he
leaned forward and patted his horse. The gray, beautiful
though he still was, had also slackened in his energy.
They were both past their prime.

Tora glanced back at the straggling procession behind them. "I'll try to get them to speed up a little," he
said, swinging his horse about. "We'll be in Otsu by
sunset."

Akitada glanced after him. Tora was still as agile and
energetic as ever, yet he, too, had suffered serious
wounds in his master's service. Akitada had taken him
on many years ago when they were both young men.
Tora had been a deserter, a peasant who had been con-
scripted for the wars in the north and had ended up
beating an officer. When they met, he had claimed the
name Tora for "tiger," and proved his right to it. But to
Akitada's amusement, he had lately taken to using his
birth name and ennobled it by linking it with the village
Sashima where he had been born. He was now Lieutenant Sashima Kamatari. Neither the double name nor
the rank were strictly legitimate. They had become
necessary in Kyushu where Akitada had struggled with
the governorship of Chikuzen province. After years of
disdain for the "good people," Tora clearly enjoyed his
new status these days.

The highway between the capital and Otsu was always crowded. Akitada's entourage shared the roadway
with mounted messengers, farmers' carts, pilgrims and

other travelers, both on horseback and on foot, as well as contingents of soldiers and of heavily armed *sohei,* warrior monks belonging to one of the temples on Mount Hiei.

They had been passed quite rudely by these soldier-monks a mile or so back. In spite of the fact that their flag marked their convoy as on imperial business, the *sohei,* their heads shrouded by white cloth, but their bodies wearing full armor, had forced their way past with shouts of "Make way! Make way!"

Akitada had glowered at their leader, who had stared back impudently as he passed. His followers had laughed and added some rude shouts that "slow old men should stay home."

He could not be sure whose *sohei* these were but guessed they belonged to the mountain temple complex of Enryaku-ji.

The government was becoming very nervous about the warlike preparations at Enryaku-ji. The temple now hired mercenaries and trained both lay monks and regular members of the monastery to fight. They claimed they had to do this for their own protection, but Enryaku-ji owned an enormous amount of land in the area and was turning its manors and villages into armed camps. His visit to Otsu was an effort to avert a war between the monks of Onjo-ji and those of Enryaku-ji by settling land disputes legally.

Akitada sat his horse with slumping shoulders, bleakly taking in his surroundings. This journey added to his sense of futility by bringing back memories that were painful. Ten years ago, he had been here, mourning the death of his firstborn during the smallpox epidemic. In a way, he had also mourned losing his wife's love. On that occasion and in his distraught state, he had thought to end his loneliness by raising a silent child he found wandering near the highway to Otsu. This had been in vain, but somehow he had found his wife's love again. They had clung together more closely than ever before.

But now he had lost her for good. It had happened in another spring two years before, and this time he had found no way to cope with this loss except through work. To make things worse, he was in poor health, having suffered a knife attack some time later.

His health was part of the reason for this excursion. It was thought he needed to get away for some pleasurable and relaxing days or weeks as the guest of his best friend Kosehira, currently governor of Omi province.

The other reason was the assignment, but the real work was to be done by the men in his entourage with minimal supervision on his part. Much of it would be in the hands of the man riding in the sedan chair. Yoshida Kunyoshi was the imperial archivist. The other officials served in various offices and bureaus of the government, but they all had one thing in common: they were very familiar with the contentions of   two immensely powerful Buddhist temples in Omi province: Enriyaku-ji and Onjo-ji.

Kunyoshi was well over eighty and had occasional memory lapses, but no one else had his experience. Akitada knew him well and had frequently consulted him in the past. Their relationship went back to the very early years when Akitada had been a student at the university and sought information for papers assigned by his professors. But this had been a very long time ago. Nowadays, Kunyoshi suffered from all the aches and infirmities of old age and had become ill-tempered.

Akitada, though only in his forty-third year, felt like an old man himself.

Tora returned, muttering about city people being unable to ride horses. Akitada sympathized with them but said nothing. He looked forward to getting off his horse and relaxing his sore body in a hot bath.

He also looked forward to seeing Kosehira again. It had been years now; they had both been sent to opposite ends of the country. Kosehira had regained the favor of the court after a punitive assignment for having supported an imperial prince suspected of treason.

"Look, there's the lake!" cried Tora. "It's beautiful. Oh, sir, you'll see we shall have a wonderful time. Very little work and no tangling with murderous villains this time. We'll go hunting, fishing, riding, and visit famous spots, and in between there'll be delicious food and a good rest."

The lake *was* beautiful. It glistened like a polished silver mirror between the hills up ahead, but Akitada could not hide the irritation that Tora's cosseting caused. He hated being treated like an invalid, especially when he felt like one.

∞

Kosehira and two of his sons were waiting outside Otsu. Akitada dismounted, somewhat painfully, and embraced his friend as the two young men and Akitada's retinue looked on. Akitada was nearly moved to tears to see his closest friend again. He released Kosehira, blinked, and looked with astonishment at the two young men. Kosehira introduced them as Arihito and Arikuno. Akitada remembered them as small boys. They bowed with smiling faces while he marveled that so much time could have passed in the blinking of an eye.

Kosehira studied Akitada's face with a worried frown. "You look ill," he said. "Are you? Is something wrong?"

Akitada grimaced. "No, no. I'm well enough. I'm not used to traveling long distances on horseback any-more."

This did not reassure Kosehira. He said, "We must get you home right away. A hot bath and a good meal, and then it's bed for you."

"Thank you, honored Mother." Akitada smiled at him fondly.

They chuckled, but Kosehira simply overruled Akitada when he tried to protest the arrangements. The officials and some of the servants and porters would proceed to Otsu and the tribunal, where quarters were waiting for them. Akitada and Tora, however, would turn off to ride with Kosehira to his private villa in the foothills overlooking the town and the lake.

The villa was a sizable property with gardens and outbuildings, but Akitada saw little of it. After the prom-ised bath and a fine meal that Akitada did little justice to, Kosehira said, "If I recall correctly, you already know Otsu."

Akitada nodded. "Yes. I thought I might look up a few acquaintances. The Masuda affair, though it's been ten years, is still fresh in my mind. I wonder if Warden Takechi is still here. I really liked the man."

"I'm glad to hear you say that. Takechi is indeed still here, and a most reliable man indeed. He's police chief now."

Akitada was pleased and searched his mind for other names, but he was getting very sleepy. Kosehira noticed.

"More time for talk tomorrow." he said. "I look forward to introducing the rest of my family, and then we'll make some plans for your entertainment." He rubbed his hands, glowing with pleasure. "I have such plans! You'll see. I've dreamed of seeing you again for such a long time."

Akitada grew speechless at this and embraced his friend again before seeking his room.

∞

He slept well and for a long time, waking to bright sunshine and feeling quite refreshed. A small amount of soreness remained, but the hot bath had done much to deal with the effects of the long journey. Perhaps, he thought, I haven't quite become an old man yet. He resolved to do more riding while he was here and also to practice swordsmanship with Tora to get himself back into shape.

But first things first: he was to meet Kosehira's family and see more of the villa and then accompany his friend to provincial headquarters in town. He planned to talk to the team that was to work on the temple documents and witness statements.

As he made his way to the reception rooms, he could see that Kosehira had made his family comfortable. There were several wings facing a large garden and ample service buildings. From the galleries that linked the pavilions, one could catch enchanting glimpses of the lake and the city below while surrounded by trees and fields of rice and other crops.

He discovered that he shared the eastern wing with the male members of Kosehira's family when he nearly collided with two small boys chasing each other. The first one merely ducked aside and kept going, but his brother stopped and bowed, flushing with embarrassment.

"Your pardon, sir. We were in a hurry because my brother forgot to wear his good robe this morning."

"Quite all right, son," Akitada said, smiling and wondering if some special occasion was taking place. "Where would I find your father?" he asked, as the boy started inching past him.

"Oh, he's in the North Pavilion."

That was awkward. The northernmost wing of a mansion was usually reserved for the owner's wives. Akitada resolved to explore the gardens until Kosehira emerged from the company of his ladies, but the boy added over his shoulder. "He's waiting for you. We're to have a grand meal today."

Akitada looked after him and shook his head. Puzzled, he left the gallery for the garden and wandered along moss covered stones in a generally northern direction. He passed a pretty pond with budding water lilies and lotus and saw trees and shrubs blossoming here and there between the pale green leaves. The greenery opened suddenly, and he stopped below a veranda with red lacquered railings and pretty lanterns suspended from the rafters. Children could be heard inside and the softer tones of women's voices. Akitada turned away, unwilling to offend by entering his friend's women's quarters.

But then one of them, a very young and pretty one, looked out and saw him. "Here he is, Father," she cried, and came out on the veranda, giving him a brilliant smile.

No blackened teeth, Akitada noted with approval, but also regrettably no shyness around strange men. He resolved to have a talk with his own daughter about proper manners for young ladies.

Kosehira joined her, also smiling brightly and waving. "There you are at last. Good morning, Elder Brother," he shouted. "I was about to go and get you. Come up and meet my ladies and my worthless children. And then we'll have a proper feast in your honor."

Akitada's heart warmed at this invitation. He was being treated like a member of the family while he was here. He went up the steps to the veranda, embraced Kosehira and then walked eagerly into a large room which was filled with women, children, and maids, and where many places were being set with pillows and food trays. When he arrived among them, they all stopped what they were doing and fell silent.

"Hatsuko, Ayako, and Chiyo, come meet Akitada," Kosehira said. "This is the man I've been telling you about all these years."

Akitada blushed and bowed to three ladies in pretty silks, the oldest his own age, but with a pleasant mother-ly face, the next perhaps five years younger and plump, and the third a bit younger again and elegantly thin.

Lady Hatsuko, Kosehira's first lady, wished him welcome, apologizing for the large, noisy family. The other two bowed and smiled.

Then came the introductions of the children, start-ing with the handsome young men he had met the day before. "Arihito and Arikuni you remember. Arikuni is now at the university. This little one is Arihira, a very good boy, and the baby is Arimitsu." The "baby", somewhat out of breath and with his silk robe untied, made a face. He was at least ten and insulted.

Kosehira had not noticed. His face softened as he said, "And these are my little ladies." He waved five young girls of assorted ages forward. "They are Kazuko, Masako, Motoko, Yoshiko, and Yukiko. No need to mark their names. You'll see plenty of all my children while you're here."

Akitada was still amazed that Kosehira should have grown children. The oldest of his daughters was the one who had announced him, and she looked marriageable. He did remember her name. She was Yukiko and, giv-en her pretty face and sparkling eyes, Akitada guessed that Kosehira would soon see her married off. Or per-haps she already was married. In many of the great families, sons-in-law moved in after marriage. But if she had a husband, he was not here this morning.

Unlike her sisters, who had bowed prettily and silently, Yukiko said, "I'm honored, sir. Our father has told us many stories about your adventures. You have become a hero to all of us."

Akitada blushed, more furiously than earlier, and gave Kosehira a look. He said, "Thank you, Lady Yukiko, but you mustn't believe everything you hear. I'm really a very dull fellow."

And so he was, in truth. But so friendly was Kosehira's family, and so lively was the children's chatter, that he soon overcame his awkwardness and joined in the conversation as the maids, assisted by two of the younger girls, brought in a delightful meal of rice gruel with fish and vegetables, a number of elegant side dishes, as well as *mochi*, nuts, fruit, and chilled juices.

Akitada tried to remember the children's names and talked to them about his own two and about the games they enjoyed.

Kosehira and his wives smiled as they listened. "You know, Akitada," Kosehira said, "you should send for them later this month. The great Sanno-Sai Shrine Festival will take place then. There will be a fair, and processions, and a boat race. They'll love it and can watch with my brood."

His first lady joined him in urging Akitada to let his children come.

It was a kind invitation and one that Akitada accepted with heartfelt thanks. Yasuko and Yoshi should get along well with Kosehira's younger children. They had had little joy in their young lives.

It was only later, as he and Kosehira were riding into Otsu to the provincial headquarters, that the conversation turned to matters of provincial security.

"We met a large number of armed monks on our way here," Akitada said. "I didn't like their looks. Are they causing problems for you?"

Kosehira rolled his eyes. "Are they! The monks of Enryaku-ji have invited every feckless lout and deserter to join them. Their recruits call themselves lay monks, but they're just hired thugs. You can't imagine what they get up to when they spend an evening in town."

Akitada could. He foresaw awkward meetings with the representatives of the temple. Not that he had much greater respect for Onjo-ji. The whole war had started many years ago when the two religious communities competed for the title of most important Buddhist center in the country. They had busily acquired land and whole villages, all of it tax free, and now had money, power, and influence even beyond those of the prime minister and perhaps the emperor himself. He felt ill-equipped to deal with their current squabble.

But ultimately, he reassured himself, it was just a matter of interpreting the legal documents they would furnish and double-checking the archives. Somewhat cheered he turned his mind to putting the men who had travelled out with him to work. After that, Kunyoshi would be in charge, and he would be free to enjoy his visit with Kosehira and his family.

3

Old Man Juro and the Gorge

They almost arrested old man Juro the next day. That was after they found Wakiya dead in the woods. He had been battered so viciously that he had died in a pool of blood. Animals had gathered to lap up this blood, and crows were waiting in the trees, ready to swoop down for their meal.

But he was found early by his daughter-in-law who had expected him to be lying drunk in a ditch. She had carried the broom with her, intending to make him pay for the inconvenience. Instead, she found his corpse.

The local headman had arrived with his assistant to study the corpse and listen to the daughter-in-law's complaints about the drunkard's lack of consideration for his family. She wanted to know who would pay for the funeral and was there perhaps a chance to collect some blood money?

The headman grunted and sent her for a ladder. They put the corpse on this and carried it back into the village. By then, they knew most of the story of Wakiya's celebration and paid a visit to Juro.

Juro was thunderstruck. "He was going straight home," he said. "He was fine." Then he frowned. "But he was really afraid of that daughter-in-law of his. He said she'd beat him. Did she do this? "

The headman considered. "Don't think so. She was shocked. She thinks you had a fight and you killed him."

Juro was lucky. His old lady had woken when the two friends had staggered homeward, singing at the top of their voices. She had watched Wakiya weaving off toward his own house after Juro had come in to face her wrath.

The headman and his people left, none the wiser about Wakiya's killer. This did not trouble them unduly, however. After a decent wait of a day and a night in case someone volunteered information or the killer decided to confess, they let Wakiya's daughter-in-law arrange for his funeral.

It was a poor enough affair, even after she had made the rounds asking for donations from his friends. Juro had sacrificed his drinking money for the week. After all, poor old Wakiya had been his best pal for onward of twenty years or more. They had both worked for the same landowner, doing much of the heavy work like cutting trees, plowing, and digging irrigation ditches. It had paid off in the end; they could both stop working and farm their own plot of land.

Juro would miss Wakiya.

But he wasn't one to refuse a cup of wine after the funeral, especially not when he had donated his drinking funds to the pathetic affair the two monks had provided. And so it was only days after his drinking bout with his dead friend that Juro found himself tipsy again.

Halfway home, the thought crossed his fuzzy mind that there was a killer loose and that it was night again, and that he was walking the same road again. He came to halt and considered. The sky was moonless, being clouded over. He was still on the outskirts of the village and looked anxiously about him. All seemed quiet and peaceful. Here and there lights glimmered from a house, but no one was out and about.

Still, better safe than sorry, reasoned Juro. He would take another path home, one that he rarely used because it skirted a rocky gorge. In rainy months it was treacherous, because the water could wash away parts of it. But it was spring and had been dry. Besides he would be careful.

Whistling softly to give himself courage, he turned off the road and followed the path. When he got close to the gorge, he could hear the stream gurgling below. He stopped whistling and slowed down. The ground beneath his feet was rock and loose stones, and he walked close to the hillside.

Somewhere along the way, he thought he heard some stones fall. He stopped and listened. There was not a sound, except the rushing water below. Perhaps an animal had crossed the path, he thought, and started up again, moving a little faster, anxious to get home now.

Just before the blow fell, he heard another sound behind him, but by then it was already too late. A blinding pain exploded in his head, and he tumbled forward.

4

Monks and Old Friends

Akitada woke with a heavy head and a sour taste in his mouth. The pain in his head came a moment later. He grimaced. Sitting up late with Kosehira and drinking too many cups of his good wine had been a mistake.

Well, the wine anyway.

Kosehira had been a pleasure as always. No one else had his cheerful disposition and kindness. No wonder his family was such a happy one. The next thought, however, was an unfortunate comparison. Perhaps his own family life had once been as happy, or at least harmonious, but it was so no longer. Tamako was gone, and the children could not fill that void. Akitada was deeply lonely, perhaps more acutely lonely than he had been after her death, when grief had blotted out all other emotions. He found himself wishing for such a family as Kosehira's. He too wanted laughter and the cheerful noise of women and children around him.

He sat up and held his aching head. Well, it was not to be, and he might as well enjoy such pleasures vicariously while spending time with Kosehira and his brood.

But unlike the day before, Kosehira was all business this morning. A servant had brought Akitada his bowl of rice gruel and some fruit juice, announcing that his Excellency would be leaving for the tribunal as soon as Akitada was ready.

A governor of Kosehira's stature traveled with a large retinue between his home and the tribunal. Akitada compared this to his recent post in Chikuzen province in Kyushu where they had found an empty tribunal with neither staff nor horses. Of course, Kosehira was a very wealthy man and closely related to the ruling Fujiwaras. It made it all the more surprising and endearing that he was a man without the slightest touch of arrogance, a simple, cheerful, friendly soul, and a very loyal friend.

The Omi provincial headquarters, unlike those in Chikuzen, once again impressed by their size and the large number of soldiers , officials, and clerks who occupied them. Greeted by salutes and fine displays of cavalry and infantry, they rode to the main hall and dismounted.

To Akitada's surprise, Tora was already there and waiting for him.

"Did you see the guard, sir?" he asked Akitada, after having saluted Kosehira in the military fashion his new rank inspired. "That's what I call a guard. It made me wish we'd had more time in Chikuzen. I could have whipped that ragtaggle bunch of peasants into great shape."

Akitada said drily, "If you may recall, we barely made it out alive. I doubt if they would have taken kindly to your methods."

Tora grinned. "Only a matter of time and the right methods. I'd like to look around here, if you don't need me."

Akitada glanced at Kosehira. "What are the plans?"

"I'm told Enryaku-ji is sending a delegation to bid you welcome. Meanwhile you may want to see if your people have everything they need. Let me know if I can send you some of my staff."

Akitada controlled his irritation with Enryaku-ji. "Thank you, brother. Tora, you may look around, as you call it."

He found that Kunyoshi, for all his advanced age and poor memory had a talent for organization. When he was shown to the large hall that contained the tribunal archives and now also Akitada's staff and documents brought to Otsu from the imperial archives, he saw that desks had been set up for all the clerks and that each had a particular task. The senior officials in charge of the separate aspects of the case were gathered on the dais, where they would put their heads together to discuss the various problems. These gentlemen were Kono from the Bureau of Buddhism, Aikawa from the Bureau of Taxation, Kanazawa from the Censors Office, and Shiyoda, a recorder for the Council of State.

Shiyoda outranked the others, but even he was one step below Akitada in rank. Akitada was to supervise all of these men, and his clerk from the Ministry of Justice was to supervise all of the other clerks. It was a good arrangement, provided all of these people got along and none showed undue favoritism toward either temple. Akitada could have wished none showed any favoritism toward the Buddhist faith and instead put their minds to preserving public lands that would pay taxes. Anything owned by a temple was tax exempt, and therein lay a problem.

He gathered the papers pertaining to the claims made by Enryaku-ji and carried them to an empty desk. There he rubbed some ink and then began to read, making notes in his tidy script. There was no need for him to do this. His clerk could as easily have done it, but Akitada wanted at least a working knowledge of what the situation was. Having finished with the documents, he returned them to his clerk and collected documentation pertaining to the disputed properties from the local files. The more he studied these papers, the more he became convinced that both temples had rashly and illegally appropriated land belonging to taxpaying individuals. How they had got away with it was not clear. He decided to ask Kosehira when a servant arrived to tell him that a deputation from Enryaku-ji awaited him in the reception hall.

Akitada sighed and made his way there.

Three monks awaited him. All seemed to belong to the upper ranks of the order and wore black robes and silk stoles made of colorful patches. They had sandals on their feet and their heads were shaven. Two appeared to be middle-aged and one elderly.

When he came into the room, they rose to their feet but did not bow. Instead they placed their hands together and inclined their heads slightly.

One of the middle-aged monks took a step forward. "I think you are Lord Sugawara?"

Akitada nodded.

"My name is Kanshin. I'm the prior of Enryaku-ji. With me are Josho, our Venerable Teacher, and Seisan, Master of the Law. We have come on behalf of our superior, Abbot Gyomei, to bid you welcome. It is our hope that you will visit Enryaku-ji as our guest."

Akitada smiled. "That is very good of you and His Reverence Gyomei. I shall give myself the pleasure at my earliest convenience."

It was a very short speech, given an invitation by so illustrious a figure of the faith as the head of Enryaku-ji, and he could see that they were displeased.

"May we trouble you for a small amount of your time?" Kanshin asked. "We have come a long way."

Not so very long, since Enryaku-ji hovered on the mountainside above Otsu, but given the terrain and their elevated status, perhaps it must have seemed so. In any case, Akitada gestured to the dais, where a few cushions awaited important visitors.

They settled themselves, the oldest with several small groans. Akitada asked, "May I send for refreshments?"

"Very kind," nodded Kanshin. "The way was hard and we're no longer young."

Akitada rose again, went to a door and clapped his hands. A servant appeared with commendable speed and was sent for fruit juice and snacks.

Akitada returned to his place and looked expectant.

But Kanshin waited also.

The servant returned with juice and trays of nuts, rice crackers, and dried fruit. The monks sipped sparingly and ignored the food.

When Akitada had said nothing for a longish spell, Kanshin sighed. "We have been told that His Majesty has sent you and various experts to look into the outrageous claims made by Onjo-ji monks. It is our hope that the strongest steps will be taken against them. They have threatened our people, and in several instances they have driven them off our land and put their own peasants in their place."

Akitada smiled. "I'm aware of certain claims by both temples against each other. Rest assured that we will use due diligence in clearing up contested land claims."

Silence fell again as they looked at each other. Their faces became more glum. Kanshin said, "There can be no doubt for whose side the decision will fall. We have uncontestable documentation. Our rights have been confirmed by several emperors."

"No doubt," said Akitada, still smiling. "But you see, Onjo-ji seems to be equally well prepared to argue their case. I'm very much afraid you'll have to be patient while we weigh the various claims. It shouldn't take too long. And then perhaps I can give myself the pleasure to visit your magnificent temple." He emptied his cup of juice and waited.

THE OLD MEN OF OMI

They bit their lips, or glared, or muttered, but one by one they got up, folded their hands and inclined their heads, then stepped down from the dais and walked out in single file.

Akitada heaved a sigh of relief, and left also, turning toward the back of the compound. Here he wandered about a while, peering into several small courtyards. Most were empty of vegetation but in one he saw a large earthenware container with a small wisteria tree. The wisteria had buds already. It was a white one, but even so it reminded him of Tamako's purple wisteria, dead now and a symbol of his greater loss. He went over and bent to the drooping panicles which gave off a hint of the delicious scent. It seemed spicier than that of their purple vine. This plant was still young, or else had been pruned severely to make it fit into a planter, but in the back of his memory rose another image of a lush white wisteria in a walled garden, a plant and a scent that had come to represent another loss.

Once, only once, he had fallen in love with a woman who was not his wife, and parting from her had been the most painfully wrenching experience. She was Hiroko, Lady Yasugi, a married woman who had come into his life at a time when Tamako had turned against him. In the end, his love had come to nothing though he had offered her marriage. He wondered what had become of Hiroko and her children. It was more than ten years now. Would she be very changed?

Idle thoughts, born from loneliness. For some reason, this journey was stirring up many painful memories. He shook off his gloom and decided to get his horse and visit the town. Perhaps Chief Takechi would be in and they could renew their acquaintance while he probed for information about the two warring temples.

∞

Otsu had changed. It was a bustling town of substantial buildings, filled with inhabitants who had become wealthy from doing business at the juncture of two major national highways and in the proximity of two great temples. There was also a busy harbor where goods from the northern provinces arrived by boat and either continued via the Seta and Yodo Rivers south or unloaded for the overland journey to the capital. Such business and wealth attracted all sorts of people. Pilgrims arrived daily, itinerant entertainers plied their trade at markets and fairs, prostitution prospered, day laborers abounded, and many members of the great families chose to retire here, either because they had shrewdly invested in Otsu's businesses or because they wished to end their lives close to the great temples but somewhat removed from court business.

The last time Akitada had visited, it had been the week of the O-bon festival and some days beyond. The crowds thronging the streets and watching performers had been large and boisterous, but even today there was an atmosphere of celebration. At a shrine he passed, a small fair had attracted families with their children, and it was market day.

He remembered the way to the warden's office, but when he reached it, he found it was now an official post station. Leaning down from his horse, he asked one of the men loitering at the gate what had happened to it.

The youth pointed down the street to a large roofed gatehouse belonging to the new police headquarters.

Takechi had moved up in the world. His office was now in a substantial hall inside a compound which also held stables and a proper jail.

Akitada dismounted, turning his horse over to a red-coated constable and asked if Takechi was in.

He was, and Akitada soon walked into his office, a large room similar to the one occupied by Superintendent Kobe in the capital. Here, as there, the office holder had a large desk for himself and a secondary desk for a scribe, and here, as there, several constables awaited orders.

Takechi had aged and changed in other ways. Akitada almost did not recognize him. His hair was quite gray by now, and his face more deeply lined. He had trimmed his large mustache into a more fashionable style and wore the uniform of a police officer and the traditional black cap. But when he looked up, frowning and then staring for a moment, his face relaxed into a wide smile of pure pleasure. He rose quickly and came toward Akitada with outstretched hands.

"My Lord! What a surprise and pleasure!" At the last moment, he dropped his hands and, blushing a little, made Akitada a bow.

"Thank you, Chief. The pleasure is equally mine. It's very good to see you again."

"Yes, sir. But is something wrong? What brings you?"

Akitada chuckled. "Nothing at all except a desire to see you again. This is just a friendly visit."

Takechi relaxed. "Wonderful!" He turned to the constables and the scribe, saying, "Get started on your assignments right away. We'll discuss the details later." They left the room, closing the door behind them.

"Please don't let me interrupt your work," Akitada said, looking after them. "You have risen in the world and must be very busy these days. I'll be in Otsu for a week or so. We can easily find another time to chat."

But Takechi shook his head. "No, no. I have some time. But that doesn't mean we cannot share a meal another day. I'd like you to be my guest. We have a very good restaurant down at the lake shore. Their noodle soup and seafood dishes are praised throughout the land."

"Thank you. I'll look forward to it. How have you been?"

Takechi placed a cushion for Akitada and poured them some wine. "I'm very well, as you can see. Just getting on in years. My body expands and my agility lessens. But there are compensations. Both the governor and the local people have honored me with their trust. I enjoy a good income and, as you see, my office is quite resplendent." He chuckled, then added, "Otherwise I'm afraid I'm just the same old peasant's son trying to keep his wits together while putting the bad fellows behind bars."

"I'm happy to see your success. As I told the governor a little while ago, you have earned that respect. I remember how you stood by me and that poor child when I was universally distrusted and maligned and he would have died at the hands of those monsters."

Takechi grinned. "Ah, you should see him now, the young Lord Masuda! It would please you greatly. He's grown into a fine youngster."

"Good! I take it his grandfather is no longer alive?"

"No. He died a few months later, but he died happy."

"And the ladies?"

"Quite well, both of them. Lady Masuda resides in the mansion, and the younger lady has remarried."

Akitada nodded. It was what he would have expected of both. "But I'm keeping you from your work," he said, emptying his cup. We'll talk some more when you're free. I'm staying with the governor and will spend some time at provincial headquarters, looking into legal squabbles between the temples here."

Takechi nodded. "Onjo-ji and Enryaku-ji. Yes, a pity that. The local people take sides and we have much trouble keeping them from getting into fights. The monks are stirring it up. But it's not too bad. Otherwise, things are fairly quiet, except for one death that puzzles me. Come to think of it, you may know the dead man. His name is Nakano. He was a judge when you were here."

"Nakano? Dear me, yes. The man confiscated all the gold I had brought with me to buy out that child. He would have sentenced me to hard labor if he hadn't learned who I was. And he returned my gold very grudgingly."

Takechi nodded. "Yes, that's pretty well in character. In any case, it may be a natural death—he was an old man— but I don't quite like the look of things.

Would you be at all interested in joining me when I have a look at the body?"

Akitada raised his hands. "Judge Nakano is in very good hands. I'm here to deal with the temple case and have a brief vacation. I'm looking forward to some hunting or fishing."

Takechi nodded. "Yes, of course. Forgive me, sir. I had no right. Especially when I'd heard about your lady's death. Please accept my condolences."

Akitada thanked him and fled. He knew he was fleeing from his grief and his memories and was ashamed, for Takechi was a good man, and at one time he would have enjoyed working with him.

5

Tora Meets the *Sohei*

Tora was whistling again. Sometimes things worked out perfectly. His master had looked rested and pleased to be with his best friend, and he, Tora, had been given a day off to have a good time in a place that promised all manner of entertainment.

To make things perfect, he had found a friend. Having taken the opportunity to study the workings of the provincial headquarters, he had paid a visit to the provincial guard, introducing himself as Lieutenant Sashima, formerly commander of the Chikuzen guard. The local commander, a native son belonging to provincial gentry, turned out to be haughty and short with him. Tora decided the fellow felt threatened and became reserved himself. The soldiers were decent enough, but that was probably due to their sergeant, a cheerful older man with twinkling eyes and a ready laugh.

When Tora mentioned that he planned to have a look at the town, Sergeant Okura offered to join him, since he had some business to attend to in the harbor area.

Okura lost no time apologizing for his commander. "He's a dry old stick," he said, "but fair enough. We have to put up with the local gentry who snap up all the best jobs in a province. This one at least tries."

Tora nodded wisely and told the tale of their arrival in Chikuzen and his confrontations with the police captain. Okura volunteered that his own background was the army. Tora responded by calling him "Comrade" and asking where he had served.

"In the north. Horrible snowfall," said Okura.

"Tell me about it. My master was governor of Echigo a few years back. Another miserable assignment. We were attacked by the local warlord."

Okura stopped and goggled at him. "You don't say? When was that?

"More than fifteen years ago. Time flies."

"The Uesugi affair! Brother, we must talk more!" They had reached the harbor area and Okura pointed to a large wine shop. "We'll have a few cups there after I take care of this business. Give me half an hour. It seems we have much to talk about."

Tora laughed. He liked the idea and Okura himself. "Take your time. I'll watch the boats."

Okura headed for the harbor master's office, and Tora wandered along the waterside.

Otsu's harbor was large like those of Naniwa and Hakata, and yet very different. All three were busy, but while large ocean-going ships docked in Hakata and Naniwa, traffic on Biwa Lake consisted of huge numbers of smaller boats carrying anything from lumber and tax goods to passengers who by-passed travel by road for a leisurely boat voyage.

Tora strolled about, attracting curious stares because of his silk-laced half armor and sword. The unloading of barges and boats was done by laborers wearing only loincloths and bandanas tied around their heads. They were cheerful enough on this pleasant spring morning, and Tora smiled at some of the crude jokes they passed back and forth when two slatternly women sauntered past. The women gave back as good as they got.

The amount and types of materials unloaded and reloaded for the land trip to the capital amazed him. He expected the rice bales from the Northern provinces; these were stacked into huge piles by a steady stream of the half-naked bearers. Elsewhere barrels of oil awaited transport, as did huge sacks of silk floss and rolls of fabric. But there were also many horses, and large containers of paper, lacquer ware and clay utensils, as well as all sorts of food stuffs. The capital absorbed it all and asked for more.

When he decided it was time to meet Okura and was about to turn back, he noticed a disturbance near one of the larger boats. The steady line of bearers walking down the gangway with their burden of rice bales had come to a halt and a group of people seemed to be struggling and shouting on the quay. Tora investigated. To his surprise, he saw several armed monks like the ones they had seen earlier on their journey. They seemed engaged in a threatening argument with some people.

As he got closer, he counted four *sohei,* and three were armed with *naginata,* those long handled halberds with sword blades at their ends. The fourth had a sword. All were big men, wearing the usual black armor and white headgear. They had seized one of the laborers who struggled in their grip. Two men, who appeared to be the harbor master and his clerk, objected to this. The harbor master was shaking his fist angrily. "Let him go and stay away from our workers," he shouted. "There are laws around here!"

The monks laughed. One said, "The laws are ours. And so is this man."

The laborer cried, "I'm a free man. I'm a free peasant. They drove me off my land. Help me!"

One of the *sohei* who had a grip on him, snarled, "Shut up, you dog!" and shook him. The other brute punched him viciously in the side. The laborer sagged to his knees and vomited.

Tora clenched his fists and was about to intercede when the clerk in his sober, dark gown and black cap said sharply, "Stop that! He told the truth. He came to us and proved he was free. I signed him on. He's an honest man who has served in the northern army. You've got the wrong man."

The monk who had punched the worker laughed. "If he's a soldier, he'll get to fight again." He turned to the laborer. "Tell them! You know what's good for you, don't you, fellow? You've got a family, haven't you? What's to become of them if you don't obey the temple?"

A look of fear passed over the laborer's face. He nodded and got to his feet. "I'll go with them," he said dully. The *sohei* grinned. The one with the sword said, "See? All is well. He's one of ours all right."

When they turned to leave with the man, Tora stepped in their way. "Halt!" he snapped. "That man stays here. If you have a claim, you can take the matter up with the governor. It's against the law to kidnap people."

The *sohei* stared at him from their white head cowls, taking in his half armor and sword. Their spokesman said, "No need to interfere, Officer. He's one of our peasants. A run-away. It's our business to round up such men."

Suddenly the worker flung himself to his knees before Tora and clasped his legs. "Don't let them take me, sir!"

One of the bullies snarled, "Up, shitface!" and clenched a fist to strike him again

Tora pushed him back. The monk stumbled, but his companion cursed and came at Tora. He was huge, with fists like sledge hammers, and he was fast. Tora tried to jerk aside, but a glancing blow landed on his cheek. His head snapped back and for a moment he saw stars. When his eyes cleared, he saw that two of the monks had lowered their halberds.

Tora was badly outnumbered and he had no doubt that all four of them were trained fighters. Besides, a sword is at a disadvantage against a halberd. But he drew his sword anyway and stood his ground, crouching slightly and balancing on the balls of his feet, ready to move in any direction when the attack came.

Nothing happened for the space of several breaths. Then the monk with the sword said, "Leave him be. His time will come."

There was some foot shuffling and a good deal of glaring, but eventually the three *sohei* with halberds obeyed and all four stalked away. The laborer still knelt on the ground and sobbed.

Tora asked him, "Will they come back for you?"

The laborer wiped his eyes and blinked up at him. "Maybe, maybe not. Are you with the provincial guard?"

"No, but I know the governor." Tora's cheek started to hurt. He looked around. "What's going on here?"

The overseer came up and said, "Thank you, Officer. Please tell the governor that those bastards come down from their mountain whenever they need more slaves. They help themselves to the best workers and claim they escaped from temple land and owe them labor or money. Somebody should put a stop to this. He was the third man they tried to grab this week."

"He seemed willing enough to go with them in the end," said Tora, frowning.

The laborer said sadly, "I've got a wife and children. They might get them, too."

Tora's eye was throbbing. He wondered if he had made things worse. "I take it you prefer to work here. But if you really left their land, they have a right to make you go back."

The overseer looked disgusted. "You can believe what you want, but around here we've learned not to trust those hooded bastards." With that he turned and shouted orders at the other bearers, who had stood at a distance, watching the encounter. Soon the line formed again and the rice moved out of the boat and onto the land. The laborer got to his feet, nodded to Tora, and joined them.

The clerk shook his head and walked away.

Tora stood for a moment longer, then walked back to the wine shop. He did not like what he had just witnessed. Even if the monks had the law on their side, they should not be allowed to enforce it themselves. What was the world coming to, if every landowner simply arrested his people without taking the matter to the governor or prefect?

Okura was sitting at one of the outside tables. Also waiting was a flask of wine and two cups. Tora cheered up.

"The next round is mine," he said, emptying the cup Okura handed him. He smacked his lips. "Not bad. You know your suppliers." He held out the cup for a refill.

Okura obliged, then asked, "What happened to you?"

"A small disagreement with some fractious monks. Four of those *sohei* raided the laborers unloading a boat and tried to take one of the men away. I interfered. What's going on here?"

Okura's face fell. "Those cursed *sohei*," he muttered. "They're always at it. They're either recruiting new soldiers or arresting men for hard labor on their land. They own just about all the land in Omi."

Shocked, Tora said, "Surely not."

"Well, close to it. Onjo-ji and Enryaku-ji between them own or control hundreds of hamlets. The peasants and landowners signed over their estates to gain tax-free status. The temples allow them to keep their harvest and buy their rice at a discount. That way, both profit."

"That should be against the law."

"Who's going to oppose a powerful temple? The court always decides in favor of the monks."

"Surely the governor can put a stop to what I just saw?"

Okura shook his head. "He's a good man, but he will not tangle with either temple."

"Well my master's here to do just that," Tora said angrily. "I'll let him know what's going on."

"Good luck!" Okura grimaced. "I'd like to see it. We've had too much trouble, and it's been getting worse lately. But drink up. You owe me some stories concerning that warlord Uesugi. We heard about it in our camp, but it was winter and the news was hard to come by."

The wine was good and Tora complied.

6

In a Spring Garden

Akitada returned to provincial headquarters to check on the progress of the temple dispute and found the work progressing to his satisfaction. Then he went to Kosehira's office. His friend was deep in paperwork, three young clerks standing by and a scribe scribbling furiously as the governor dictated.

"Akitada!" said the governor, emerging somewhat dazed from a document. "Dear me, is it time already?" He glanced through the open doors. The sun was well past midday. "Forgive me. A sudden press of work. Would you mind going back by yourself? Tell my people that I expect to get home by sunset. I have neglected you shamefully."

"Not at all," said Akitada. "I've had a very pleasant time with Chief Takechi. We were doing a bit of reminiscing. I'll see you later then."

He got back on his horse and enjoyed the short journey back up the hillside. At the villa, he turned the animal over to the stable boy and then went to deliver Kosehira's message. He found the younger children romping in the garden with Kosehira's eldest daughter.

They greeted him eagerly. Yukiko, in a charming red embroidered jacket and pale green gown over white trousers, claimed he looked tired. "Come, Cousin Akitada," she said, taking his hand and leading him to a small summerhouse overlooking the shimmering lake, "you must rest and admire the pretty view. I love it here."

Made uncomfortable by the familiar way she treated him, Akitada withdrew his hand and said stiffly, "It's very beautiful, Lady Yukiko."

And so was she, truth to tell. The light green silk gown with the embroidered Chinese jacket suited her slender figure perfectly. Her hair was thick and glossy and tied in back with a white silk bow, a hairstyle that Tamako had also favored as more practical than loose hair. But she was nothing like Tamako in other ways. Yukiko's movements were quick, and her laughter frequent. She had a disturbing way of casting smiling glances at him from the corners of her eyes.

"Oh," she said now, blushing rosily. "Forgive me for calling you 'cousin.' It was very forward of me. But you see, Father calls you 'Elder Brother' and I thought 'Uncle' would make you feel like an old man. What may I call you?"

Akitada had been more shocked by her touch than by being called cousin and felt himself redden also. "Not at all. I like being called 'cousin' by such a pretty young lady," he said awkwardly. "You are very kind. The fact is I *am* an old man, and you made me feel young again." When he realized that this had sounded not only flirtatious but also encouraged more reassurances that he was not at all old, he flushed again.

She looked at him, wide-eyed. "You old? But that's silly. You're my father's age—I know because I asked. I've asked a million questions about you—but you look much younger and you have had such an exciting life that no one could possibly think of you as old."

"You flatter me, Lady Yukiko. I don't know what to say, except that your father must have grossly exaggerated."

"Please call me Yukiko. You seem like a part of my family. If you're going to be formal, you force me to be formal also. I'll have to start carrying a fan and hide my face whenever I see you. Do you want that?"

Her eyes twinkled, the soft lips smiled, and, yes, she dimpled when she said this. Feeling foolish, Akitada smiled back, gazed into her pretty face, and said quite honestly, "Heaven forbid!"

She laughed. It was a very pretty laugh, natural and light-hearted, and it fell like music on his ears. There had been too little laughter in his life. Kosehira was a lucky man. He lived surrounded by happy people.

As he thought this, Akitada realized that Kosehira himself was surely the cause of such a joyous home. Kosehira's wealth and influence had perhaps made it easier for him to be cheerful, but there were more fundamental differences between them than status. He had never been able to laugh spontaneously like that. Even when he had been Yukiko's age, he had been intense and forever worried about what people thought of him. These days, he was bitter and cynical, having found little in his experiences to lighten his mood and give him hope.

She still studied him. Perhaps he should have made her a compliment, but he shied away from this.

"What is it?" he asked.

"You looked absolutely crushed. What were you thinking about?"

He turned away. "Please show me your beautiful garden. You don't want to know my thoughts."

"Forgive me," she said softly. "I'm always saying the wrong thing. You must still love her very much."

Akitada sighed. Young women could be very difficult. "I wasn't thinking of my wife, but yes, I did love her very much. And there is nothing to forgive. I'm a crabby old fellow and you are trying hard to raise my spirits. That is a great kindness." He added a smile when he saw the uncertainty in her face.

She smiled back. "You're not crabby, just very reserved and a little shy. Come along, then. It's a very lovely garden, better than our other ones in the city or the country."

Kosehira had two primary residences. Akitada was familiar with the mansion in the capital, having attended many parties there and also been Kosehira's only guest. It was typical of the homes of the ranking noblemen and imperial princes. But he had to admit that this villa was prettier and the garden more interesting. Some of its attractiveness came from the fact that they were in a mountainous area and so the paths dipped and turned and climbed again, often via stone steps. And at every turn, there was some pleasure: a stone lantern among flowering azaleas, a sudden overlook revealing another glimpse of the lake, a rustic stone garden seat, a water basin where they disturbed some birds, and a small rill that flowed into a pond.

They came to a halt beside the pond. "Oh," he said, delighted, "you have *koi*. So do I, in a much smaller pond outside my room. They have given me much pleasure."

"I wish I may see them someday," Yukiko said and knelt on the mossy stones without regard to her pretty clothes. "Look, there's Black Dragon, and over there Silver Star. And that spotted one is Glowing Embers, and the solid red one I call Setting Sun."

"You've named them all?"

"Most of them. Sometimes when I get lonely I come and talk to them."

"How could you get lonely in such a lively family?"

She rose and turned to him, her eyes suddenly sad. "You can be lonely in a large crowd. You see, there really is no one to know but yourself in this world. I think we try to forget that by seeking out others to distract us from ourselves."

He was struck dumb. It was a profound insight for someone so young. And she was a mere girl. How odd! It made him uneasy, and he told himself that perhaps she had read this someplace. "Do you enjoy books?" he asked impulsively

"Oh, yes. I love them. I have read all of *Genji.* And also many diaries and some Chinese poetry. But that is just another way of distracting yourself. It passes the day."

But Akitada was surprised by something else this time. "You read Chinese."

She blushed. "Don't tell Father. I've been sitting in on my brothers' classes with their Chinese tutor. It's not at all suitable for a lady. I know that, but . . ." She paused, then added in a rush, "You see, I've always wanted to know what a man's life is like. I already know about women and their lives, but I know next to nothing about the lives of men when they are away from home."

This young girl was full of surprises. Akitada did not know what to say. Was it natural for a girl to want to know how men lived and thought? Surely females had more pleasant occupations among their silks and brocades, their fans and mirrors, their picture books and musical instruments, their charming lives playing games. He did not know what to say and looked down into the pond where Black Dragon emerged from the depth to snatch a gnat and disappear with a flip of his tail that scattered the other fish.

"Will you tell me about your adventures?" she asked. "About Sado Island and Echigo? About the monks in Kazusa and that mad painter in the capital, about the lost boy and how you got buried in an earthquake?"

He looked up, startled. Her eyes were bright with excitement and she glowed with rosy color. He did not think he had ever seen anyone look so beautiful and so alive.

"And how you were fighting the pirates in a burning warehouse . . . ?" she added but faltered when she saw his face.

Akitada silently cursed Kosehira for filling his children's heads with such tales. All of the events she had cited had been terrifying and some were tragic. He looked at her without speaking. Her lower lip began to tremble.

"Oh," she said. "I did it again. I'm sorry." And the next moment, she had gathered her full trousers and run back up toward the house.

Akitada stood bemused, watching her slender legs in their white silk stockings and her small feet in black slippers skipping away, jumping over rocks and tree roots, until she disappeared from sight.

Extraordinary!

And strangely moving. He was not used to such admiration. Indeed, he hardly thought he deserved it. Whatever happened had not been by his choice. Those dangerous events had been forced upon him, and he still bore the scars and deeper wounds in his soul. He rubbed the leg which a brutal policeman had broken by beating him with a cudgel. It had somehow healed in the weeks he was a prisoner in a gold mine, but he shuddered at the memory. And this child, this girl who was not fully grown yet, wanted him to tell her all about it.

Of course he could not do anything of the sort. For one thing such a telling would require privacy, and he feared that being alone with his friend's daughter had become far too unsettling.

But he was secretly pleased that she thought so well of him.

∞

Kosehira arrived that evening looking tired, but the eager greetings from his children, who had watched for him, and the sight of Akitada cheered him instantly. Making an apologetic gesture to Akitada, he listened to the excited tale his youngest son was bursting with—it involved the capture of a lizard who had escaped again— and he admired a drawing by his youngest daughter, then laughed out loud when the next daughter's kitten took exception to the dog and lashed out. The dog squealed and ran, and the kitten chased after it.

Only after greeting his wives and enquiring about the time of the evening meal did he take Akitada by the arm and walk him into the garden.

"What a day!" he said. "You must forgive me. There were so many callers with complaints, petitions, reports, invitations, and suggestions that I couldn't get away sooner. Have you been bored?"

Akitada smiled. "Not at all. Your daughter Yukiko showed me your beautiful garden." He made this admission half fearfully, wondering what her father would make of it.

Kosehira shot him a curious glance. "Good, Yukiko has made herself useful. What do you think of her?"

"She is quite beautiful and charming. And I take it she's a clever girl also."

Kosehira chuckled. "Did she tell you she studies Chinese?"

"You aren't supposed to know."

"I knew all along. Yukiko has her own mind. She always gets what she wants. Since she's also sweet and affectionate and loves people and animals, I don't have the heart to deny her. I'm afraid I've always doted on her and she knows it. Don't tell her."

Akitada smiled and promised. There was something wonderful about the bond between a father and a daughter, he thought. He loved his children equally, but Yasuko could melt his heart with her smile. Still, the subject of Yukiko made him uncomfortable and he changed the subject. "Any interesting business in Otsu?"

"Oh, nothing. Though we do seem to have a crime or two. Someone may have killed an old judge in town, and up in the Echi district, two old men have been attacked on the road. Both are dead."

"I suppose," said Akitada slowly, "that this isn't bad, given the very busy highways passing through your province."

Kosehira sighed. "You're right, of course, but when a judge is involved, I have to pay attention." He cheered up. "Now come and let's see what cook is surprising us with. My first lady sounded very mysterious about their plans this morning."

The surprise was roasted pheasant. Normally prohibited to devout Buddhists, pheasant tended to make people bend the rules. The traditional hunting skills still thrived among noblemen who enjoyed hunting the birds both with bow and arrow and with falcons. Kosehira's table had been provided with several birds as a gift to the governor from a friend who owned a pheasant preserve and supplied the imperial table with the birds.

Akitada enjoyed the meal, but the sight of Yukiko, her head bent over her tray, eating little, and never once raising her eyes to him, made him feel guilty. He wished now that he had been friendlier. She had taken time to amuse him because he was a guest, and he had made her feel ashamed.

Well, he would find a chance to reassure her.

7

Death of a Judge

When Akitada woke the next morning and thought about his encounter with Lady Yukiko, he panicked. The whole conversation had been most uncomfortable and improper. Not only must he not seek her out to reassure her, he must do his best to avoid any more private meetings.

Having made this decision, he felt better and got up. He would start his day with some exercise and then ride into town with Kosehira. There he could look in on the progress of the temple case, and then . . . well then surely something would offer.

Slipping on his hunting trousers over his undergown, he tied them at the waist. Then he put on his boots, stuffing the trousers inside. Taking his sword, he went to look for Tora.

Tora was at the well in the service area, splashing water on his face and using an end of his shirt to dry himself.

"Good Morning, Tora!" Akitada called out. When Tora turned, he gaped. "What the devil has happened to you?"

Tora grinned and touched his left cheek. "You mean this? Does it show?"

"Yes. You have a black eye. What have you been up to now? You know we have to behave ourselves while we are guests of the governor."

"Not my fault. I got a fist in my face when I asked a bunch of monks what they were up to."

Akitada raised his brows. "Oh. I don't suppose you feel much like a work-out then?"

Tora snorted. "What makes you think that, sir?" He grinned. "About those monks . . ."

"Later! Get your sword."

He followed Tora to his room in the guest quarters and was astonished to see that he had tidied up the place. His bedding was rolled up neatly, and he had placed his clothes carefully over a stand with his sword hanging from its end and his empty saddle bag folded underneath. Akitada had expected something quite different. Had Tora's wife taught him so well? He watched as Tora tucked his jacket into his trousers, put on boots, and took down his sword.

"We could go outside, but there's gravel. In the stable yard we'd have more solid ground," Tora said.

"I don't relish being watched by the grooms. As for the gravel, are you trying to make excuses again?"

Tora grinned. "Never! You'd better watch yourself, sir!"

They laughed and jumped lightly down into the small courtyard outside Tora's room. The area was small and private, being fenced in. Akitada felt surprisingly well and immediately went into the familiar crouching stance. Tora followed suit, and with a mutual shout they began their practice. This consisted of a series of set exchanges to remind them of the appropriate responses to each move. Tora took the lead. He was clearly more familiar with the sequence. Akitada bit his lip: he had forgotten too much.

Worse, he was soon out of breath and his reactions slowed. Sweat started trickling down his face and back.

"It's getting warm. Let's shed these shirts," he proposed.

They stripped to their trousers and continued. For a while, the cool air on Akitada's wet skin felt wonderfully refreshing, and he got in a few good moves. But soon he tired again and made mistakes. Ashamed of his poor performance, he kept on a while longer until a badly handled move made him slow to respond to the next attack, and Tora's sword almost sliced into his arm.

They stopped. Akitada was bent double to catch his breath, and Tora wiped more perspiration from his face.

"You need regular practice, sir," Tora said, eying Akitada's exhausted stance.

"Yes. That was a shameful performance," Akitada acknowledged, straightening. "I had no idea that a few months of doing nothing could ruin a man so completely." He stretched. "I'm past it, Tora. I'm an old man. I don't think I'll ever be as good again as I was."

"Hmm," said Tora judiciously. "I've slowed down a lot, too, but a man should never give up. We'll practice every day. And I'll get hold of a set of staves. I like using *bo* for a smoother movement. How about it?"

Akitada smiled. Tora had taught him the use of the fighting stick many years ago. At the time it was the only weapon a man like Tora was allowed. His sword fighting skills, acquired during a brief military stint, were mediocre, and Akitada had traded lessons with the sword for those with the *bo.* The memories cheered him, and he said, "Very well. It shall be as you say. I'm in your hands. Now tell me about your eye."

Tora did so, concisely and with a good deal of anger. When he was finished, Akitada nodded.

"I share your anger, but there's nothing I can do. If this man is really one of their peasants, they have a right to order him back to his fields." He put on his shirt again and thought for a moment. "I suppose you could look into the matter, because they may well come back. From your description, they recognize no master but their own superiors. It's despicable. But be careful. By all accounts those *sohei* are vicious."

Tora grinned. "They don't scare me, sir. Though I did notice something. One of those bastards had a weird tattoo on the back of his right hand. A circle with a triangle inside it. Doesn't that mean he's a convicted criminal?"

"I don't know what strange practices the warrior monks may have. But you're right. Some provincial governors still encourage tattooing repeat criminals. Besides this sort of thing is frequently done to members of a gang of highway robbers."

"How can the monks take in convicts?"

"No doubt the man claimed that Buddha has saved him from a life of crime. Or perhaps he's only a lay-monk. Many of the *sohei* are simply hired thugs. Anyway, be careful. Oh, and before I forget it, when you have the time, ride home to make sure all is well. And tell the children that they will attend the great shrine festival later this month. That will cheer them up."

Tora's smile broadened. "Will do, sir. Umm, suppose I leave late, spend the night, and return early tomorrow? That way I'll be available to you during the day."

Akitada suppressed a smile. "Excellent idea."

∞

The exercise had certainly done nothing for Akitada's self confidence, and he was determined to stay out of Lady Yukiko's way. After washing at the well, he changed into formal clothes and joined Kosehira on his ride to the tribunal.

He had a vague notion of paying a visit to the Masuda mansion to see how the young heir was getting along, but Kunyoshi was eager to show him what they had found in their search of the provincial archives. Since the papers related to dubious transfers of land from private owners to Enryaku-ji, Akitada sat down and started to go through them. The illegalities had been hidden rather cleverly, he found, and congratulated Kunyoshi on noticing that all was not as it should be.

In the end, however, there was not enough evidence to put pressure on the temple, and Akitada decided to put the documents aside until they could build a bigger case.

It was nearly midday when he got up and stretched. The unaccustomed morning practice had made him sore again, though he thought this a better soreness than the back pain from his ride to Otsu. He had just decided to eat in town and then climb up to the Masuda place, when Kosehira put his head in the door.

"Akitada! Am I glad you're still here. I need a favor."

"Gladly. What can I do?"

"Come, I'll tell you on the way." Kosehira noted belatedly that everyone had risen and was bowing to him. He said, "Oh, forgive me, gentlemen. Please don't interrupt your work. I hope I see you all well this morning. Can you spare Lord Sugawara?"

They straightened and smiled, and Kunyoshi, always the spokesman, assured the governor that his lordship had permission to leave."

Akitada chuckled when they were outside, but Kosehira looked distracted. "Listen," he said. "Chief Takechi has sent a messenger. Something is wrong about that judge's death. I can't possibly leave. I have to meet with the prime minister's secretary to account for the fact that I have given no support to Onjo-ji in their case against Enryaku-ji. As you may guess, the prime minister and his immediate family are supporters of Onjo-ji."

"But surely you cannot be expected to act for one or the other before my delegation has sifted through the documents and the Ministry of Justice has decided on guilt or innocence?"

"Naturally, but that doesn't mean the prime minister can't try to muddy the waters."

"Of course I'll go to talk to Takechi, but you need merely tell this secretary that your hands are tied until the official investigation is complete."

Kosehira sighed. "You're too logical, Akitada. I must find some other method."

Amused, Akitada went to have a horse saddled. It struck him for the first time that Kosehira did not always have an easy time of it in spite of being a member of the ruling family.

At police headquarters, Takechi was out, but they directed him to the judge's house.

Nakano had done well for himself. His house aspired to mansion status. Nakano had built outbuildings, added a wall and a roofed gate, and laid out a garden in the back. The gate was open but two constables kept an eye on a group of onlookers in the street. It was a familiar scene that Akitada had encountered many times. A violent death drew the curious, and the law had to step in to protect the investigation.

He identified himself, telling the guards that he had come from the governor. Very properly, one of them went to notify the chief who was inside the house.

Takechi came out and greeted Akitada enthusiastically. "How good of you to come yourself, sir," he said as Akitada dismounted and a constable took his horse. "This looks suspicious after all. I'd be very glad to get your opinion."

They walked into the late judge's residence. Akitada saw immediately that Nakano had spared no money on furnishings. The *tatami* mats were thick and hardly worn; the cushions looked plump and were of silk; numerous scrolls of scenes around the lake hung on the walls; and here and there, folding screens stood about with pictures of mountain temples and hermitages.

Akitada asked, "Did he belong to a wealthy family?"

"No. His father was a mid-level official in Aki province. I think he owned some land there, but nothing impressive. He earned this himself by investing in business."

"You don't say." Akitada remembered the way Nakano had confiscated the large sum of gold he had carried in order to buy the child's freedom. Nakano had relinquished it eventually when he realized Akitada's background, but it had been done with great reluctance. No doubt he had "earned" some of his wealth in his capacity as judge.

Takechi took him to the judge's study. This, too, was furnished well. Nakano had a large library and his desk was elegant and heavily carved. The writing utensils on it were made of jade or lacquer. Some sheets of paper with spidery handwriting lay on the desk. In a corner, his bedding lay spread out on a thick mat.

"He was lying here," Takechi said, pointing to a place in the middle of the room. The floor was bare and showed scuff marks from many feet. The body was gone.

"Where is he now?"

"Back at headquarters. The coroner is in a quandary."

Akitada raised his brows. "Why?"

"Because he thought it was a natural death and is no longer sure about it now."

"Ah!" Akitada looked around. "What about the servants? Have they been questioned?"

"There are only two. A young couple. They swore nobody came during the night. It must have happened at night. The wife found him in the morning when she brought him his gruel."

"You saw the body here. What did it look like to you?"

Takechi scratched his head. "Well, he was lying just there. On his stomach. His legs were drawn up a little and his arms were out like this." He spread his arms wide. "There were no wounds. It looked as though he'd become faint and fallen down. His bedding hadn't been slept in." Takechi gestured toward the neat quilts. "I figured he'd been working at his desk and got up to go to bed when death overcame him. He was an old man after all."

"How old?"

"In his eighty-second year. When a man gets that old, death isn't a surprise. It can happen any moment."

Akitada went to look at the papers on the desk. The judge seemed to have written down details of a legal case. "Any idea what he was working on?" he asked the police chief.

Takechi shook his head. "It's something to do with the imperial pheasant preserve. I couldn't make it out. The two servants can't read, but they thought he was writing down a record of his cases. Reminiscing, you know."

Akitada nodded. Old men were prone to doing that. He'd found himself remembering events of the past since Lady Yukiko had asked him to tell her about them. It was strange, this connection between past and future. The young wanted stories, and the old spent their declining years telling them. And so the past was likely to color how the next generation would think and act.

Suddenly depressed, he put such reflections from his mind and admired the fine writing utensils, picking them up one by one and turning them in his hands to study the decorations. Among them was a small wooden carving, a contrast to the delicate workmanship of the other items. It appeared to be a figure of Jizo, the Buddhist divinity who was variously the protector of children, women, and travelers. Such figures, carved from wood or stone, abounded in the land, being found along roadways everywhere. More than any other divine representation of the Buddhist faith, Jizo seemed to belong to the people.

This figure was roughly made. Unlike the stone statues beside the roads, it was small enough to hold easily in one's hand.

No doubt it had had some special meaning for the judge or he would not have kept it on his desk beside the pretty objects. He replaced it and turned to look about the room but saw nothing else of interest. "Have you spoken to the servants?"

"Yes. If you've seen enough here, perhaps you'd like to talk to them yourself, sir?"

As it turned out, the young couple occupied roomy quarters in the former stable. The judge had evidently no longer any need for horses. They were greeted by the wife, who was holding a baby and trying to control a half-naked toddler at the same time. She bobbed several bows, looking distracted and gesturing for them to come in.

Akitada saw that they were quite poor. The room was bare except for some worn bedding, a few chipped utensils, and an iron cooking pot over a meager fire.

They remained standing. Though the floor had been swept, there were no cushions or reed mats to sit on. Such abject poverty was unusual for a couple who clearly served as the main servants in a large household.

The chief smiled at the frightened-looking woman and tickled the toddler's neck. He asked, "Where is your husband, Tatsuko?"

She looked vaguely guilty. "Kiyoshi went to the harbor looking for work. We have no money and no food."

"Ah," said Takechi, "the judge forgot to pay you?"

A glint of anger appeared in her eyes. "He's always slow, and then he takes back some of our earnings for rent. There's two more of us now." She nodded toward the children. "What will happen? He owed us wages. I don't even have enough for the children to watch a puppet play."

"I don't know." Takechi glanced at Akitada, who was already searching his sash for some money to give her.

Akitada said, "I take it Nakano was a tightwad. I will never understand how anyone can treat his people this way. I expect they worked hard for what he paid them." He passed several silver coins to the young woman. "Here, this should help for a while. Do you know who inherits?"

She shook her head. "He never married." She was staring at the silver in her hand, then looked up. "Thank you, your honor," she cried and fell to her knees, bowing so deeply that the child at her breast sent up a loud squalling.

"Never mind." Akitada gave her a hand to help her up. "Did you or your husband hear anything last night?" he asked.

"Nothing. We're too far from the house and sleep soundly. Did he cry out or something?"

Akitada said, "We don't know. I wondered if you might have heard a visitor come or leave."

She gazed at him, shaking her head. "A visitor? He had no visitors. He had no friends either. I don't think anyone liked him, and he didn't like people."

The loneliness of old age. Neither family nor friends. But in this case, Akitada could not dredge up much pity.

Takechi said, "There's a cousin in the capital and a niece or two in Nara, daughters of a sister he lost touch with. I assume one or the other will claim the property."

"What will become of us?" she asked again, holding the child more closely.

Takechi patted her shoulder. "I'll keep you in mind and will try to get you your pay, but I think your husband had better look for other work. And a place to stay."

She nodded and started to cry.

8

Dead Men Don't Speak

They returned to police headquarters and the adjoining jail. This jail was very different from the one Akitada remembered, where he had occupied the single cell in the old office. Now he found a separate building with an astonishing ten cells and assorted other rooms. Eight of the cells were occupied.

"Do you have this much crime in Otsu now?" he asked Takechi.

"This time of year we have more transients than at other times, and outlying districts send us their most serious criminals. Three judges reside in Otsu now, and our provincial headquarters can handle crimes much more efficiently than in the past. It's a good thing, but it means more work for me."

He headed for a door at the very back and opened it. Within lay a simple room, well lit by several open shutters to the outside. The floor was scrubbed wood, and rolls of bamboo mats were stacked against a wall.

But Akitada's eyes fell on two men crouching over a body that rested on one of the mats near the opened shutters. One was young with a slender body and an intent expression on his face. He looked up with a frown at the interruption. Then his face cleared. "Ah, it's you, Chief."

The other was elderly and apparently an assistant or servant of the younger.

Takechi made the introduction. "This is Doctor Kimura, our coroner. Kimura, I brought Lord Sugawara along in hopes of clearing up this case quickly."

Kimura stood and bowed. "An unexpected pleasure, my Lord. And an honor to meet the famous solver of crimes."

Akitada said drily, "Thank you, but my interest isn't personal. I'm here on behalf of the governor who could not come himself. I'm merely to report. Have you finished your examination?"

"All but the study of the dead man's organs, sir."

Akitada eyed him with considerable respect. Few coroners bothered to cut bodies open. "Does that mean you cannot tell how he died?"

The young coroner smiled. "Not with certainty. Though I should warn you that his organs may not offer much information either. Still, one must be thorough, right?"

"Right." Akitada approached the corpse to peer more closely. The judge was not a pleasant sight. Naked and considerably aged since they had met ten years before, he was no longer merely well-nourished; he was fat, and the fat hung off his bones in ugly rolls. His skin was mottled, though Akitada saw no wounds of any sort. His face, marred by jowls and deep lines running from below his eyes to his chin, resembled that of a demon. The white hair was thin and showed the scalp underneath. His topknot, tight though it was, failed at keeping his features in place. Akitada straightened and asked, "What can you tell us so far?"

"As you can see, there are no obvious wounds to the front of his body. The back is similarly unmarked. Except for this." He bent to raise the dead man's head by the topknot and gestured to its back. "Feel just here."

Both Akitada and Takechi felt. Akitada detected a slight swelling.

Takechi said, "It isn't much. Did it bleed?"

"No. The skin isn't broken."

"Hardly a fatal wound then?" Akitada asked.

"No. But there is something else." The coroner lowered the head and raised an eyelid. Takechi and Akitada bent to look.

"His eye appears to be bloodshot." Akitada shook his head. "That can happen to a living man and is fairly common among the old, I think."

"It isn't just bloodshot," Kimura said. "If you look closely, sir, you may see that the white part of the eyeball appears to have many small red dots in it."

The others knelt to study the dead man's eyes. The coroner raised the second eyelid. Both eyes were indeed as he had described.

Akitada sat back on his heels. "What does it mean?"

Doctor Kimura spread his hands in a gesture of helplessness. "I don't know . . . or at least I hesitate to say."

"Speak up, man," Takechi urged. "We can always decide later if it's significant."

"Well, I've seen this once before. On a murder victim in the capital. The corpse—it was a middle-aged woman—had died of strangulation. Her husband was her killer. I was a student at the university then and for once our professor, who normally lectured, took us to the police morgue, so that we might observe a female body. The secrets of the female are normally hidden from physicians who must diagnose and treat illnesses based on book learning." He blushed a little when he met Akitada's surprised eyes.

Akitada smiled. "I would think that a man with your intellectual curiosity would have remedied this by visits to the willow quarter."

The blush intensified, but Doctor Kimura said, "Yes, but I was very poor in those days. I found that such education seemed well beyond my reach."

Akitada and Takechi chuckled at this, and after a moment, the young coroner joined them. The moment of amusement over, Akitada pointed out, "The woman was strangled. I assume her killer left marks on her throat?"

Kimura nodded. "That is so."

"But the judge's neck bears no marks of strangulation. How then can the two cases be related?"

Again Kimura made the helpless gesture. "I cannot account for it. I only mentioned it because the spots on the eyes were the same."

Akitada bent over the corpse and examined his face and throat carefully. When he straightened, he shook his head. "Nothing. How do you account for the bruise to the back of his head?"

"He could have fallen backward and hit his head."

Takechi said quickly, "He was not lying on his back when we found him. He was on his side, almost on his front."

"It is possible that the fall merely stunned him and he moved, perhaps in an effort to get up." But Kimura looked worried.

"You think something is wrong," Akitada said. "That someone may have caused this death?"

Kimura stared down at the judge's body. "I don't know, sir. I have no proof. We will cut him open, but I may not find anything useful. He was an old man, and not very healthy. He could have become dizzy from an excess of blood in his head, or its opposite. That would have caused him to fall. Death came a little later. Alas, dead men don't speak."

Takechi nodded. "I get it. It's a natural death after all. Very well, finish the examination and let me have the report."

Kimura bowed, and they left.

"What do you think, sir?" Takechi asked when they reached his office again.

"The coroner appears to be a very careful man. You're lucky."

"Yes. I think so. But I meant about the judge?"

"I think you've done all that was required, and so has Kimura. I shall tell the governor."

∞

Something nagged at Akitada after he parted from Takechi. Perhaps it was simply the fact that he had known Nakano and learned more about the man today. The judge had not been a likable man. The way he treated his servants proved this, as did the fact that he appeared to have no friends and that any family he had stayed well away from him. He had also been a miser and was probably quite rich by now. As a judge he had been corrupt. Such men make enemies and are likely to end up murdered.

On an impulse, he returned to the judge's house where he found that the housekeeper's husband had returned. He was playing with the toddler, carrying him on his shoulder while galloping around the courtyard. The child shrieked with delight and his father looked happy.

Akitada stopped. Just so he had carried his own children. And Yori had shrieked exactly like that. Yoshi was more given to giggling, and Yasuko had cried, "Faster! Go faster!" and belabored him with a small, pudgy hand. He missed the children and looked forward to having them come for the shrine festival. He would send Tora home today to carry the invitation and spend a night with his wife. That part of normal married life, Akitada missed most of all.

During the past year, he had gradually sought relief from several women who obliged for silver or a length of silk. They were discreet and pleasant—indeed one or two had been well educated for such women, and one had confessed to coming from a good family. This last had shocked him, but she had been matter-of-fact about her life. Her father was land-poor and had to feed a large number of children. She had become tired of never owning a silk dress, rarely having enough to eat, and not attracting any suitors except the most unsuitable ones. She liked her present life much better.

But such visits were not the same as the comfort a man found with his own wife.

The father made another turn and caught sight of Akitada. Startled, he stopped and put the child down. The boy wailed his protest.

"Don't stop on my account," Akitada said and went to pick up the toddler. The boy stopped crying to stare at Akitada.

"Forgive me, sir," stammered his father. "I didn't see you. Let me have him back. He'll get your fine robe dirty."

"I don't mind. He's a handsome boy. I used to do what you just did with my own children." The boy got hold of Akitada's ear and pulled, chuckling. Akitada was tempted to put him on his shoulders and start galloping but decided that his father would think him mad. He lifted the child up and down a few times, enjoying his delight, then handed him back.

"You must be Kiyoshi. The chief and I spoke with your wife earlier. I'm Lord Sugawara."

Kiyoshi bowed deeply. "Tatsuko said a gentleman gave her silver. Was it you?"

Akitada nodded. "You have not been paid. It seemed wrong that the children should suffer because your master died."

"We're very grateful for this kindness. I can perhaps repay it by doing some work for you? You can see I'm very strong."

He was indeed muscular, but Akitada had no need for more servants. He thanked him. "Perhaps instead you might talk to me about your late master?" he suggested.

"I'm at your service, but let me take my son back to his mother."

Akitada wandered into the house, peering into rooms as he passed them. They were all empty, though furnished with thick *tatami* mats and amenities like candle holders, oil lamps, braziers, and small screens. Here and there, he also saw clothes racks. All of those things were of good quality and everything was very clean. The wooden floors shone. He thought of the poor young couple. Judge Nakano had certainly got his money's worth from their services. Given the fact that Otsu provided many opportunities to earn a living, he began to wonder if Nakano had used some sort of threat to keep them in bondage.

And that, of course, would give them a motive. But a motive for what? Nakano's death was most likely due to his age and ill health.

He returned to the study and cast another glance at the desk with its papers, fanciful writing implements, and that odd carving of Jizo. He picked it up to see if it might have an inscription, making it something like an amulet, but saw nothing.

"I'm ready now, sir."

Akitada turned, startled. The young man was back. He was barefoot; that accounted perhaps for his silent movements. He looked curiously at the little figure in Akitada's hand as he waited.

This room was the only one that was not painfully neat. The floor still bore all the marks of recent activity by constables and others.

The violent intrusion of strangers after a death.

"Any idea why your master had this little carving of Jizo?" Akitada asked, holding it up.

The young man shook his head. "I never saw it before his death, sir. It's not the sort of thing the judge would own. It was on the floor when we found the master dead. My wife put it on his desk."

"Strange. Where did it come from? Did he have any visitors recently?"

"No, sir. No one."

"Well, then, did he go out the day before he died?"

"No, sir. My wife and I do the shopping."

A brief silence fell while Akitada looked at the young man thoughtfully. If he had indeed worked against his will for the judge, he could not be trusted to tell the truth."

The young man shifted nervously, then said, "If you'll forgive me, sir, but the figure looks like the sort of cheap stuff people sell at markets and fairs around here. Travelers buy them for good luck, and we have many travelers passing though."

"Hmm. Yes. But that doesn't explain how it got here." Akitada replaced the carving on the desk and looked about again. "I'll mention it to the chief. Meanwhile it will be best if you and your wife stay out of this room. The police will seal the doors until the investigation is finished."

The young man bowed. "Is there anything else, sir?"

Akitada noticed that the servant's eyes wandered to the desk, and he glanced at it again. This time he noticed that the stack of notes had been shifted aside a little. "Have you or your wife tried to clean up here?"

"No! The police chief said not to touch anything."

It came too quickly and with a furtive expression.

"Very good. That's all for now. You may leave. I'll see myself out."

As soon as the young man was gone, Akitada scooped up the judge's notes and put them inside his robe. Then he left, closing the door behind him.

9

The *Sohei* Return

Tora arranged to have a pair of staves sent to his room, then he, too, rode into Otsu. He was uneasy about the man he had rescued and wanted to check on him. His first call was at the harbor master's office.

He dismounted and tied up his horse, then went inside. The clerks stared, but the harbor master saw him from his backroom and came to greet him.

"How may I assist, sir?" he asked with a nicely calculated bow, and a glance at Tora's black eye.

"You recall the incident yesterday?"

"I do indeed. Please accept my deep regrets for the monks' behavior toward you."

Tora blinked, then got it. Touching his eye, he said, "Oh, this? That's nothing. I came to check on that worker. Those bastards threatened him."

"I haven't seen him today. If he's smart he'll have left Otsu with his family. North of here, at Hikone, there's also good work and it's much safer."

"Hmm." Tora pondered this. It made sense, but he had a bad feeling about the man's absence. He had not been eager to leave on the day of the incident, so why now? "What's his name, do you know?"

"Kinzaburo. He comes from someplace near Awazu."

"He was worried about his family, you said? Did he bring them to Otsu with him?"

"That's what I thought. He lost his farm. They couldn't have stayed behind."

"And where would they live here?"

"There's a workers quarter over there." The harbor master pointed. "Most of the men employed in the harbor live there. It's poor housing, but the rents are cheap."

Tora thanked him and walked along the harbor looking at the teams of bearers and porters and scanning the area for armed monks. All was peaceful this morning. The unloading progressed briskly, and the men sang as they trotted back and forth between the quay and the bowels of the boats. Kinzaburo was not there.

The workers quarter seemed a safer bet for finding him. In Otsu, this looked not much different from all the poor housing wards in other cities. The capital had several of these in its western part, and Hakata's had borne a strong resemblance to Otsu's. Here as there, the harbor provided abundant work to unskilled men who had nothing to offer but a strong back and nimble feet. They labored as porters and bearers, carrying heavy loads on their backs, or as sailors, taking boats up and down the shores of Lake Biwa, or they took cargo by land in wagons or with pack horses. It was poorly paid work and very hard, but it was abundant and they all hoped to save a little by living in shacks or in one room in row houses so that some day they might buy a little bit of land.

Tora was familiar with them. Their dreams invariably came to nothing as the years passed and a large family, or drinking, or gambling consumed their savings. But a poor peasant whose land had been stolen by greedy monks and who was about to be put in bondage with his family might prefer even this hopeless existence.

The poor, mostly women, children, and the old, treated Tora with respect, and his questions eventually led him to one of the row houses. The last unit of this was the home of the porter Kinzaburo.

He walked into tragedy.

Children squalled inside. When Tora lifted the rag that served as a door and looked in, he saw two small children and a screaming baby lying in its mother's lap. The mother cowered in a corner, her face bloodied and her body shaking. When she became aware of him, she started wailing. The small space looked as though a battle had raged in it. Broken crockery, torn clothes, and blood stains covered the dirt floor.

He was still staring, aghast, when a shrill voice behind him demanded, "Haven't you done enough, you filth? Leave her alone."

Tora turned and saw a bent old woman peering up at him from dim eyes. She held a stick in one trembling hand and waved it in threatening manner.

"Go away! And may the gods smite you!"

"What's happened here, grandmother?" Tora asked, raising his hands to show his innocence.

She lowered her stick a little. "Who are you? What do you want?"

"Lieutenant Sashima, in the service of Lord Sugawara. I came to talk to Kinzaburo. Where is he and what's happened?"

"The animals came down from the mountain and got him. And that's not all those assholes did." She shook her stick. "Look at her!"

"You mean the monks? From Enryaku-ji?"

"I don't mean Onjo-ji. They're holy men." She peered past him into the room. "See what they did to her, poor girl? And her with a small babe." She poked Tora with the sharp end of her stick until he stepped aside and let her pass. Waddling over to the cowering woman, she said, "Come, come, Keiko. Pull yourself together. They're gone and the children are hungry."

The woman responded with another heartrending wail.

"All right, Keiko," the old one said firmly. "Enough of that. Get up now and let's see what the bastards did to you." She bent over the sobbing woman and pulled her up.

Tora turned away. It was clear that Keiko had been raped.

The old woman muttered softly, and gradually Keiko answered. There had been four of them. Kinzaburo had tried to fight them. Three of them had beaten him unconscious and dragged him out of the room. The fourth had told her to get the children ready. They were to return to their farm and work there. Then he had left. She had started to gather their few things, weeping all the while. When the three who had beaten up her husband returned, she was ready to go with them, but they had other things in mind and had taken turns raping her. Then they had left again."

Tora cleared his throat. He was hoarse with anger. "Is she decent, grandmother?" he asked.

"Yes, yes. What do you want from her? Hasn't she suffered enough?"

Keiko knelt on the floor, her face bowed.

"Forgive me, Keiko," he said and cleared his throat again. "I came to help. I'm sorry I was too late. Do you have somewhere you can go with the children? Somewhere where those animals won't find you?"

She shook her head. "We've only been here for two weeks. We don't know anyone."

The old woman said, "Well, you know me. Leave it to me. I'll find you another place." She turned to Tora. "But what will she do without her husband. How will they live?"

Tora fished around in his belt and counted out two pieces of silver and twenty coppers. "It's all I've got, but I can get more. Make sure she isn't robbed of the money. I'll try to get Kinzaburo back."

Keiko gave a little cry, laid the baby down and crawled to him, knocking her head against the dirt floor and murmuring, "Thank you, thank you, thank you."

Tora was embarrassed. "Stop that!" he said roughly, then recalled what she had gone through so recently and added more gently, "You're welcome. I blame myself for not warning your husband about those bastards. I'll do my best to make them pay for it."

She sniffled and sat up. "You're a good man," she said softly.

She was quite pretty, he thought, even with her swollen and bloodied face and with disheveled hair. She was also very young to have already given birth to three children. He thought of his own, only, son. Hanae had not expressed any desire for more children, and he had not pressed her. Having children did something to women's bodies, and his Hanae was still as slim and desirable as ever. But sometimes he wished he had a houseful of little ones, like his Excellency Fujiwara.

He thanked her for her good opinion of him and pressed the money into her hand. "Now best get away, or they'll come back for you."

∞

Tora returned to provincial headquarters and went to look for Okura. He found him at the guards' barracks, playing *kemari* in an open area outside. He and eight of his men had formed a circle and were passing the ball from one to the next by kicking it. Hands could not be used, and the ball must not touch the ground. It was a difficult game that required concentration and agility.

Tora watched for a moment and saw they were good. Disposing of his sword and half armor, he joined the game. They played for half an hour, and when they finally stopped and washed the sweat off their faces at the well, Okura said, "You show promise, Tora, but you're sadly out of shape."

Tora chuckled. "True enough, and in more ways than one. This morning, the master and I took up sword practice again."

Okura raised his brows. "You expect trouble?"

"Well, it has a way of finding us. Take my run-in with the *sohei,* for example."

"I told you, you can't do anything about that. It's hopeless. We tried."

"Well, things got worse today." Tora dried his face and hands with his robe and then told Okura about Keiko and her children, and about the way they had beaten and abducted her husband."

Okura listened. "Terrible," he said, shaking his head. "There've been rumors about those soldier monks behaving like hoodlums and raping women. Each time someone complains, someone else stops the rumors. But even so, Tora, you can't do anything about it."

Tora glared at him. "You surprise me. I thought you were better than that. I tell you what I'll do about it. First I'll tell my master. He'll know how to handle the bastards. And then I'll make it my personal duty to bring Kinzaburo back."

∞

He found Akitada at the governor's villa. He was sitting on the small veranda outside his room, reading some documents. "Sorry to interrupt," lied Tora, still filled with righteous outrage.

His master looked up and shook his head. "You really should do something about that eye," he said. "You'll frighten Hanae half to death. She thinks we're safe from violent encounters on this trip. I assume you stopped by to tell me you're leaving for home?"

Tora was so upset that he had actually forgotten about that. He rearranged his plans. Surely Keiko and the kids were safe enough for the night. He said, "Yes, sir. Though there's another matter on my mind. Something happened that we cannot allow to go unpunished."

Akitada raised his brows. "You haven't got into another scrape already?"

This calm and gentle rebuke irritated Tora, who thought it typical of the "good people" to remain unmoved by the plight of the poor. He scowled. "No, sir. This is about those monks again. Of course if you've decided you don't want to be bothered, then no more is to be said."

Akitada sighed. "What have they done this time?"

But Tora had his pride and outrage reinforced it. "Never mind, sir. I'll take care of it myself." He turned on his heel. "I'll be back tomorrow."

"Tora!"

The tone was preemptory and Tora stopped. "Yes, sir?"

"Tell me!"

"I suppose it's not really important, sir. It just involves some poor people. Nobody else cares, so why should you?"

"Tora!" His master's voice and expression signaled danger.

"It's just that they came back and got the poor bastard. First they beat him unconscious and dragged him off, then they came back and took turns raping his wife. They'll make her go back to their land and work the family as slaves."

His master's face lengthened. "How did you find out?"

"I went to check on him with the harbor master. He hadn't come to work. I found out where he lives and went there. An old crone told me what happened, and the poor wife confirmed it. The old one's taken them to a safe place, but we need to get Kinzaburo back from those bastards." He paused, remembering the scene. "There are three small children, one a babe. They have nothing. And those animals even destroyed their few pots, clothes, and bedding."

There was a long silence. Then Akitada asked, "Does the governor know about this?"

"No. I told Okura. He's the sergeant of the provincial guard. I liked him, but he's just like the rest of the people here. Nothing to be done because it's monks from Enryaku-ji. Okura says the governor will not touch them." Tora sniffed angrily. "I must say I'm surprised at his Excellency, sir."

"Well, there are special difficulties about Enryaku-ji. The temple and monastery are of extraordinary importance in the capital. And it has been this way for centuries." Seeing Tora's angry glare, he went on, "Over time, the temple bought land to support itself and its community. Such lands are considered tax free because of the services performed by the temple and its monks. As for the peasants who work the land belonging to someone else, they are legally bound to that land. If it weren't so, peasants could leave their fields whenever it suited them, and then where would we be?"

Tora came of peasant stock himself, and old resentments rose within him. "That makes slaves out of free men," he snapped. "That's usually only done to people captured in war, or those who sell themselves. It's evil to force Kinzaburo to work for the temple when he doesn't want to. But I suppose it's all right for the officials and holy monks to do it. After all, they're better than ordinary folk."

His master snapped, "Don't be ridiculous. It's not the same at all. They've been given land to feed their families in return for a small share for the landowner. That's a fair contract. And for that, they owe the landowner the cultivation of the fields. If peasants don't work the paddies, the land returns to wilderness and nobody eats."

Tora bit his lip. "Right. I'll be leaving now, sir," he said dully and turned. He half expected to be called back. After all, the master had not really commented on the brutality of the beating and the rapes. But there was nothing. He walked out, slamming the door behind him.

10

An Unwelcome Visitor

On the way back to the capital, Tora considered his options. Given his master's surprising and disappointing indifference to the actions of the *sohei*, he could either forget the matter or try to help the unfortunate Kinzaburo and his family himself.

Forgetting about them was out of the question. For one thing, Tora hated brutality, especially toward women and children. For another, for all his elevated status as Lieutenant Sashima, trusted retainer of Lord Sugawara, he was a peasant by birth and at heart. He could not deny this bond with Kinzaburo and his family. And thus his choice was simple and quickly made. He would find a way to free Kinzaburo and return him to his family. In the process, he hoped to deal out some punishment to the *sohei.* But this he did not insist on. It would merely be an extra satisfaction. He had served his master long enough to know he must guard against making trouble. It was bad enough that he would have to go against orders in this case.

Or if not orders precisely, then implied refusal of permission.

Having settled matters to his satisfaction, he hurried homeward, thinking with pleasure of surprising Hanae and spending the evening with his family and the night in her soft arms.

The gate was opened by the stable boy. Tora rode in, tired and dusty, and snapped, "Don't you know that you must check who's at the gates before throwing them wide? What if it had been armed robbers?"

The boy grinned impudently. "That would've been something to see. Nothing ever happens around here."

Saburo came up behind him and cleared his throat. "I wouldn't say that."

Tora swung himself out of the saddle and tossed the reins to the boy. "Watch your mouth, kid. You're not too old to be put over my knee." When Tora turned to Saburo, the boy stuck out his tongue and took the horse away.

Saburo's face wore a peculiar expression, half sheepish and half dejected. "So, what's been happening, brother?" Tora asked.

Saburo grimaced and glanced over his shoulder. "A terrible thing's happened. I don't know what will come of it."

"Spit it out." Tora was getting impatient. Hanae was waiting.

Saburo opened his mouth, but a sharp voice cried, "So!" A woman's voice. It added, "And you are who?" Saburo shrank into himself as if he expected a beating.

Surprised, Tora turned his head. A small, round, elderly woman in black had appeared around the corner of the stable. She waddled closer, surprisingly quick on her feet for her size. In fact, she seemed to glide across the gravel as if carried by invisible animals under her full skirt. Her face was sharp-featured for one so fat, and her expression was ominous.

"Who the hell is she?" Tora burst out.

"Language!" cried the woman, waving a finger at him. "A man is judged by his manner in the presence of ladies. Keep it in mind for the future! Hmmph! Lost your voice? You must be Tora, the handsome one. What happened to your face?"

Resentment evaporated. Tora treated the little woman to one of his brightest smiles and an exaggerated bow. "I am Tora. My apologies, auntie. Your ears are too sharp. You weren't meant to hear that."

"I'm not your auntie. You will address me as Mrs. Kuruda." She stopped before him and looked him over. "A pretty face and a smooth tongue, but you're a troublemaker. Your wife must have her work cut out for her."

Tora saw Saburo flinch and looked at him. "Mrs. Kuruda?" he asked.

"My mother," murmured Saburo, hanging his head.

"Speak up, son," the little woman instructed him. "And always stand up straight, look people in the eye, and speak clearly. Have you forgotten everything I taught you?"

Saburo straightened. "No, Mother," he said more loudly.

She returned her attention to Tora. "What brings you home? I thought you were with your master in Otsu."

"Umm, I had some free time and thought I'd look in to see that everything is all right." Tora shot another glance at Saburo.

"Not necessary. Now that I'm here, I'll make sure of it. A good thing I decided to look in on Saburo. Everything's at sixes and sevens without your mistress. Saburo told me she died in childbed, poor woman. A woman's karma is a terrible thing. We bring our children into this world in pain and suffering. We raise them in the sweat of our brow, going without food so that they may eat, we slave for them, teach them, watch over them, hold them when they're sick, and never ask for anything in return. We give our lives to see them live, while men just go their own ways without a care in the world."

Tora gaped at her. "That's not really what happens," he protested.

"Pish pash! What difference? She died giving birth, and now the household is left without a mistress."

"Well, my wife and Genba's are looking after the children and the house. And there's a cook and a maid."

"All very well, but it's not the same, is it?"

There was no denying that, so Tora said nothing.

"Right," she said. "Now you'd better get cleaned up. You missed dinner, but I'll have the cook reheat something. Off you go now. I have things to do. I can't stand here gossiping." She waddled away as briskly as she had come.

"I'm sorry," Saburo muttered.

"That's your mother?" Tora was still looking after her. "You never said anything. Where'd she come from?"

"It's a long story. Come, you'd better do as she said or it'll make things worse."

Tora frowned. "She's not *my* mother, and you look like you wish she wasn't yours. You have a lot to explain, brother."

Saburo sighed. "I was sent to the monks when I was ten. She had some crisis of faith and thought making me a monk would save both our souls."

"That doesn't explain her sudden appearance. You've never talked about your family. What about your father? Is he going to turn up, too?"

"My father died. By that time I was in training as a spy and not allowed to see my family. Not that I wanted to."

"Out with the whole story. How is it that she's suddenly here after all that time?"

Saburo looked at the house, then gazed at the gate, the stables and the kitchen buildings beyond almost as if he were trying to memorize them. "I'll have to leave," he said sadly. "I can't throw her out, and therefore we'll both have to go. I'm sorry."

Tora regarded him, his eyebrows raised. "Why should you go? Surely she'll return to her own home after a visit with you."

"My sister's husband threw her out. She has no place to go." He added bitterly, "They helped her find me."

"They threw her out? That's terrible. But don't worry. The master will make her welcome just like he made Hanae and Ohiro welcome. She's your mother, man."

Saburo gave him a desperate look. "I could never inflict my mother on his household."

"Don't be silly. Look, I want to see Hanae now. Why don't you get Genba and Ohiro, and we'll put our heads together about this matter."

Saburo nodded and walked off.

He walks like an old man, Tora thought, shaking his head—and all because his mother came to see him. What's the matter with people?

He did not bother to ponder this question but went straight to his own small house, where Hanae squealed with joy and threw herself into his arms.

When they both emerged from the joyous reunion, and Tora had explained his black eye, he spared a thought for his son. "Where's Yuki?"

"With the schoolmaster. Oh, Tora, he's making such good progress. You must be proud."

"Hmm." The fact was that Tora did not approve. His secret fear that his son would be smarter than his father had already come to pass when Yuki had dared correct Tora's speech and offered to read him a story he had written.

Hanae said, "It was most generous of the master to educate our son. And I think he'll do the same for the others."

Of the "others" there was so far only one, and she arrived wailing in the arms of her mother Ohiro. Genba, all smiles and solicitude these days, walked behind. His first words typically concerned his daughter. "Tamiko's cutting another tooth," he said proudly. "What do you think of that?"

Tora thought it an unfortunate nuisance when they were to have a family council, but Genba's joy in his child was so great that he did not have the heart. Genba was in his early fifties and had not expected to have a family. His changed life struck him as miraculous, and he assumed others shared his feelings.

Saburo trailed in, looking more dejected than before.

"What's this about?" asked Ohiro, jiggling the baby.

"Saburo's mother," Tora told her.

"Oh!" Her face fell.

An uncomfortable silence ensued, then Hanae said brightly, "She's a very helpful lady."

Saburo snorted.

"Saburo's afraid the master won't like it," said Tora.

Another silence fell.

Saburo sighed. "My mother makes trouble. She's not your usual mother."

"Well," said Hanae practically, "I don't think she means to make trouble. It's just her way. She wants to make things better."

Saburo snorted again.

"He can't tell her to go away," pointed out Tora.

"I can go with her," said Saburo.

There was an immediate outcry against this. Genba said stoutly, "I think she's a fine woman. You have to make allowances. She comes from a family with money. Now she's fallen on hard times. It must be dreadful to have your own children dislike you." He glanced worriedly at his own offspring.

Hanae looked at her husband. "I think Tora should go back and tell the master about Mrs. Kuruda. When he hears that she has no other place to go, he'll welcome her. We can manage."

Saburo shook his head. "You don't know what you're saying, Hanae. I cannot inflict my mother's tongue on anyone else. A fast tongue is sharper than a fast sword. The gods know how I fear it myself. She'll tell a praying monk he's doing it wrong."

"I'm surprised at you, Saburo," Tora said with a frown. "Filial piety demands that we honor our parents and serve them all their lives. This is your duty. Really, brother, I'm shocked."

The others nodded their agreement.

Saburo hung his head again. "I said I'd take her with me. It's my problem."

Ohiro, who had been occupied with amusing the baby, now asked, "If you'll forgive me, Saburo, what has she done to you and your sister that you hate her so much?"

Saburo flicked a glance at her. "You wouldn't understand. And my sister doesn't hate her. I imagine mother has spent every waking hour telling her that she's a bad wife and a bad mother and doesn't keep the house clean enough or cook the right food. That can make even the strongest person break down after a while. And besides there's my brother-in-law." He sighed. "No, it's better she's with me. I don't have a wife and children."

"Then it's settled," said Hanae. "She stays."

Saburo looked at her. "You'll be sorry when she starts in on you."

"Oh, she has already. I don't mind. I smile and thank her for her concern and go about my business. Of course, there's cook." She frowned.

Tora asked, "What about cook?"

"Cook is leaving."

Saburo said, "I told Mother not to meddle, but she will go to the kitchen and criticize. And she's started cooking for me."

"I'll speak to cook." Tora rose.

This was the signal for them all to return to their duties. Tora reached for Hanae again.

11

The Shrine Fair

kitada was unhappy and worried about Tora's tale. The incident had been shocking, especially when carried out by *sohei,* and those members of the Enryaku-ji monastery. He considered the custom of great temples to train some of their younger monks to defend their community against marauding robbers deplorable. Yet while he disliked it intensely, he could understand such a move when the government was apparently unable to control criminal gangs.

What was unforgiveable, however, was the use of soldier monks against another temple. It was this sort of warfare which had led Enryaku-ji and Onjo-ji to strengthen their forces by hiring mercenaries, declaring them lay monks, and providing shelter, food, and pay for them. Both local temples had standing armies of *sohei*, and clearly their mercenaries were criminals who had begun to prey on the local population.

In fact, his own assignment was intended to settle a dangerous disagreement between the two temples in order to avoid another war and bloodshed. Yet his knowledge of the hostilities between presumably peaceful disciples of the Buddha made him increasingly afraid that a mere legal judgment would not prevent such a disaster.

He had been short with Tora, but the situation was too delicate to cloud the issues with charges against the four *sohei*. No doubt these would be rejected anyway, the rapes denied, and the kidnapping explained as the legitimate capture of a run-away peasant.

But even more upsetting had been Tora's manner. Akitada feared that Tora was thinking of doing something foolish.

He pondered the situation most of that night and rose the next morning without having found a solution. For the time being, Tora was safely at home in the arms of his wife. It might remind him that he had responsibilities these days. At least he hoped so. The four *sohei* were another matter. The incident troubled him enough that he sought out the peace of Kosehira's garden in an attempt to settle his mind.

His feet carried him to the *koi* pond, and there he came across Lady Yukiko again. Like last time she was kneeling on the mossy ground, feeding grains of rice to the fish. She wore pale green silk, like the earliest leaves of spring, and the sheen of her long hair made him want to touch it. He stopped and turned to leave, but she had already heard him and was rising to her feet.

Embarrassment caused her to flush. She said softly, "Oh! It's you."

And he said, "Forgive me. I didn't mean to intrude."

For a long moment they just looked at each other. Akitada was aware of a powerful desire to capture her image as she stood there, sun-dappled in the morning light, a perfect image of the world's beauty in spring.

He caught himself eventually, feeling strangely sad that this beauty was no part of him. Not for him such freshness or a new beginning. He was middle-aged, her father's age to be precise, and a father himself. He controlled his heart and said, "And how are Black Dragon and Setting Sun today?"

She smiled and set his heart racing again. "Very well. Come and see, my lord."

The formality of "my lord" put him in his place. He wished she had used his name and yet was glad she did not. He came closer and inspected the *koi*. "I'm afraid I said something to offend you last time," he said. "Will you please forgive me?" He dared a sideways glance and saw the delicious color on her cheeks again.

"It wasn't you. It was my forwardness. I had no right to pry into your life. I'm ashamed."

That moved him, and he reached out a hand. "Never be ashamed of a kindness," he said. "I was flattered. You see, I'm not much used to admiration and it took my words away."

She put her hand in his. The smile returned. "You needn't tell me. It's enough to have met you in person."

Her hand was small and warm. Holding it reminded him of cradling a young bird. He felt a great affection for her, a protective, fatherly affection. "We've met before, you know. You were about six or seven, I think."

She took her hand from his and turned away. "Oh. Did we? I don't recall. I was a mere child then."

The loss of that hand was strangely painful and that realization made him push both of his hands deep into his sleeves. "You were a charming child even then," he said lightly. And then added, "All of you children impressed me as delightful."

"I don't believe you," she said, kneeling again to look at the fish. "My brothers and sisters strike me as pretty wild. My whole family is rather odd, you see. I have wondered why this should be. The best explanation I can come up with is that our parents are happy because my father is happy. We laugh a lot. I'm old enough to have learned that this is a very rare and perhaps improper thing in families."

Here it was again, this wonderful capacity to see past the obvious to gain a deeper understanding. He said, "It is a rare and wonderful thing and one that I envy. But how can someone as young as you know such things?"

She looked up at him. "Do you think me a child? Or is it that I am a woman and therefore should not have much understanding?"

Taken aback, he said, "No, of course not."

She got to her feet to study his face. "I wish . . ." she said in a rush. "I wish you would trust me. I wish you would feel that you could talk to me without thinking me too young or too much a woman."

This made him smile. "My dear Yukiko," he said, "You do have a mirror, don't you? It is impossible to look at you without thinking those things."

She blushed again, and he enjoyed the play of rosy color on that smooth skin. "I do trust you," he said, becoming serious. "Or at least, it's not a matter of trust. You should not worry your pretty head about tales of past adventures by someone my age. And in any case, it wasn't a matter of courage or heroism, as you and perhaps your father think. I had no choice. I was horribly afraid. And if I escaped in the end, it was by luck rather than ingenuity."

She cocked her head. "You might leave it to me to decide."

He gave a snort. "My dear young lady, the truth is these tales would shock and upset you. They are full of blood and death and suffering, so let it be."

"Now you're angry again. I should be angry that you have such a low opinion of me, but I shall wait. Some day you'll tell me your past. I have great patience. Perhaps you'll make me wait until I'm old, so old that you no longer think of me as a woman."

He knew that would never happen. For a moment longer he let himself look at her for the sheer joy of it. Then he said, "I must speak to your father."

She gasped.

"Tora reported an incident at the harbor. It troubles me and I'd like to get your father's view of it."

"Oh." She sounded disappointed. "He's in his room, I think. Will you come back tomorrow?"

"You mean here?" She nodded. He said rather stiffly, "I don't know. We are getting rather busy. But I thank you for a charming conversation."

∞

It was almost as bad as their last parting. He saw the hurt in her eyes and wanted to tell her how very much he had enjoyed her company. But he bit his lip, and she inclined her head and walked away. At least she did not run like before.

Akitada was cast into confusion. What was the matter with him? Was he so starved for female companionship that he was attracted to a mere child? A part of him corrected the "child" immediately. Yukiko had a woman's body under the layers of pretty silks she wore. He had watched her movements, seen the swell of her breasts, the soft curve from hip to slender waist, the slim, tapering thighs and had felt uncomfortably hot under the collar. Even now . . .

He turned abruptly and headed back to his room. A pity Tora was not here. A spirited bout of swords or *bo* would get rid of the irrational and shameful desires he felt for his best friend's daughter. Meanwhile, he had best avoid being alone with her.

This plan did not work out too well after all. Akitada accompanied Kosehira to Otsu headquarters as usual. And as usual, he spent the morning hours working on temple documents. The problem was that Kosehira begged him to accompany his children to a small shrine fair in the city during the afternoon.

The outing had been discussed for a few days and Kosehira himself had planned to look after his brood, but more pressing business had cropped up. The children would arrive by carriage, accompanied by a maid. Both of his older sons had gone off hunting, and so Yukiko was in charge, but Kosehira approached Akitada, saying he would feel better if a man was with the group. All sorts of riffraff frequented fairs.

Of course Akitada agreed. It was little enough, and he enjoyed a fair. Memories intruded again: The O-bon festival and the lost child who could not speak. That year he had lost his own son to smallpox and had been filled with a deep longing for another child. How very long ago it seemed!

He convinced himself that Yukiko would have her hands full restraining the younger children, and they would have no time for private conversation. In truth, he rather looked forward to seeing the children's faces and watching their delight at the antics of the acrobats.

The carriage arrived just before the noon rice. When Akitada met it, Yukiko had already herded her charges out. They were waiting on the veranda of the headquarters building, eager to set out for the fair.

They walked the short distance, the boys close to Akitada, while Yukiko followed with the girls. They resembled other groups, small families of father, mother and children, on their way to an afternoon's entertainment. Akitada had provided himself with several strings of coppers. He intended to enjoy himself and treat the children.

The shrine beckoned with brilliant red *torii*, entrance arches that marked the threshold between the human world and the realm of the god or gods residing there. Akitada was not familiar with this particular divinity but suggested that they pay their respects before plunging into the festivities. And so they filed in under the *torii*, paused to rinse their mouths at a water basin, and then approached the sanctuary, decorated with the customary ropes of rice straw and chains of folded paper. Akitada bowed and clapped his hands to greet the god, and beside him, the boys did the same. A short prayer later, they made room for the girls.

Akitada watched Yukiko's graceful figure. She wore a pale rose-colored gown with an embroidered Chinese jacket over it because the days were still cool. The smaller girls were also in white, rose, and pale green spring colors. They reminded him of the cherry blossoms that were just coming into bloom—perhaps the reason for the traditional colors of spring clothing.

Akitada caught a glimpse of happiness. It was spring again, and beauty and joy were still in his world and in his heart.

The children were not interested in immaterial things. Their joys were firmly vested in food and entertainment. They wished to sample as many treats sold by food vendors as possible. As they joined the crowds passing among the gaily decorated stalls, Akitada began dispensing his coppers. They had not eaten since their morning gruel and fell upon rice buns, grilled fish on wooden sticks, pancakes with octopus centers, fried noodles, roasted chestnuts, and sweet bean pastries with an appetite that was amazing. Akitada laughed, paid, sipped some very good noodle soup himself, then tasted a bite of sticky honey cake offered him by Arimitsu, and peeled some chestnuts for one of the little girls.

In between there were the sights and games. Colorful paper lanterns swayed from the corners of stands, vendors sold kites decorated with fierce dragons and tigers (here Akitada indulged both of Kosehira's sons), amulets, bead necklaces (the little girls took great delight in selecting theirs), carved bears and birds and (interestingly) a large number of Jizo carvings just like the one he had found on Judge Nakano's desk.

All of the youngsters competed in a game that required them to catch small koi in a large wooden tub by using a scoop made from paper. The trick was to be quick because the spoon soon became sodden and drooped. Arimitsu proved to be the only one who succeeded. Generously, he returned the little fish he won to the water.

Now and then costumed dancers passed through the crowd, pausing to put on a show and gathering coppers from the onlookers. A group of young men dressed like the magical *tengu* birds appeared suddenly, darting at children with shrill cries and fleeing only if bombarded with dried beans. And everywhere there was music. Musicians played flutes, zithers, and lutes, as women sang and men recited heroic tales.

It was all wonderful, and Akitada forgot about his troubles when he saw the delight of Kosehira's children.

He thought of his own, feeling guilty that they weren't with him, but they would soon see their own fair, and one that was much bigger than this one. At any rate, the outing was a complete success until Akitada missed the youngest boy. Arimitsu seemed to have disappeared into the crowds during the *tengu* performance. Both Akitada and his brother had seen him when the bird men first appeared. In fact, Akitada had bought both boys small bags of beans to throw at them.

A frantic search ensued. The events of the Masuda affair surfaced again in Akitada's memory. He had visions of the governor's son being kidnapped. There were always evil and greedy people about who thought they could enrich themselves by taking the children of the wealthy. How would he explain to Kosehira that he had failed him in the worst way?

It was Yukiko who kept her head. She said, "The little rascal got interested in something and forgot his promise." They had all promised solemnly to stay close to Akitada and Yukiko or their visit would be cut short and they would be sent home in disgrace.

Akitada was not reassured. "He was just here," he said. "What if someone snatched him?"

"He would have screamed and kicked. Why don't I stay here with the children while you take a look around?"

Sensible Yukiko!

He found Arimitsu quickly. The boy had joined a small crowd of children and adults watching the performance of a puppeteer. In his relief, Akitada gave silent thanks to the gods of the shrine, whoever they were. He was about to seize the child and lecture him about keeping promises, when the puppeteer caught his attention. He was one of those men who walk about with a large box slung around their necks. Inside the box were puppets, and the top of the box was the stage where the puppets performed. This man was good at his craft, and the story the puppets enacted was an exciting tale of betrayal and revenge. The man had reached the point where the hero confronts the villain and they battle it out with their swords.

Arimitsu was spellbound and had not noticed Akitada slipping through the crowd to stand beside him. The tale ended with the death of the villain, speared through the chest by the hero's sword, and the puppeteer put away the dolls and instead brought out a wooden bowl he passed around for donations.

Akitada added a few coppers and said to Arimitsu, "It was a fine performance, but should you not have told us where you were going?"

The boy was startled. "Oh. I thought you knew? I thought you were looking my way when I came here. Wasn't it grand? Wasn't it the best thing you ever saw? And that sword fight was almost as good as watching you and Tora the other morning."

"You were watching?" Akitada was surprised. "We didn't see you."

"Oh, we were peering through the fence."

An awful thought struck Akitada. "Who is we?"

"Arihira and me."

Akitada breathed a little easier.

"And Yukiko came and looked also."

So much for that young woman's manners. Akitada was embarrassed and angry. How dare she spy on him? What next? Would she pop in when he was taking his bath?

The day was spoiled for him. He returned Arimitsu to his siblings and ended the excursion in a bad mood. The children, aware of his irritation, were subdued, and Yukiko shot questioning glances his way that he ignored. When they climbed back into their carriage for the trip home, she confronted him.

"It was very good of you to come with us," she said. "I'm sorry that Arimitsu was disobedient."

He looked at her coldly. "It doesn't matter. He's only a child."

She hesitated for a moment, then said, "Yes," and got in the carriage.

12

Enryaku-ji

The arrival of Saburo's formidable mother had caused considerable trouble. Cook had packed her things and planned to leave the next day. She was outraged at the newcomer's interference in the kitchen and her criticism of her meals. The maid had similar complaints concerning housekeeping chores and objected to Mrs. Kuruda's meddling in Lady Yasuko's attire. The children objected to being told they could not play any noisy games. This extended with special prohibitions to Yasuko, whose participation in the boys' activities had shocked Mrs. Kuruda. Hanae and Ohiro said little, not wanting to offend Saburo, but it was clear that they tried to stay out of his mother's way as much as possible.

The whole household had to be pacified. Tora managed to get cook to postpone her departure until after Akitada's return. The rest of the family promised to be patient. He urged this by suggesting that Mrs.Kuruda would eventually return to her daughter's house. Privately he had no such convictions. Saburo's mother had declared firmly that her daughter and that good-for-nothing animal she had married no longer existed for her. She intended to devote her remaining years to her son. It was clear that she planned to assume control of the wifeless Sugawara household. She claimed her heart went out to Lord Sugawara, left without the support of a loyal spouse, and to those darling children who would need motherly supervision.

When Tora mentioned this to Saburo, he listened with horror and told Tora that he was almost afraid that his mother intended to marry his lordship herself.

This made Tora laugh heartily. But he was preoccupied with his own dilemma. On impulse, he said, "Saburo, I may need your help."

"Of course, Tora. What can I do?"

Tora told him about the *sohei*. He described the scene at Otsu harbor. After an initial spark of interest when Tora described the warrior monks, Saburo's face lengthened. When Tora finished with the abduction of Kinzaburo and the rape of his wife, he said nothing.

Tora was surprised by this. He asked, "Well? You're the expert in all things involving warrior monks and monasteries. We've got to do something."

With a sigh, Saburo said, "What did you have in mind?"

"I'm going to Enryaku-ji to find Kinzaburo. It would help to know something about the place."

"You've never been to Enryaku-ji?"

"No." Tora was beginning to find Saburo's lack of enthusiastic support puzzling. "Come on! Give! I need to know how to get him out."

"If there were a war, would you consider creeping into an enemy camp to abduct their general?"

"You think it's impossible? Pah. I've done harder things."

Saburo looked at him for a long moment. "So have I. That's how I got this." He gestured at his mutilated face.

Tora gaped. "Monks did that to you?"

"*Sohei.* It's not quite the same thing."

Tora did not know what to say. Suddenly his endeavor looked not only difficult but foolhardy. To rescue Kinzaburo, he would have to get into Enryaku-ji. This was simple enough as many pilgrims came and went in the temple grounds daily. The problem was that Kinzaburo most likely would be kept by the *sohei* in an area that was not accessible to ordinary worshippers. Originally he had hoped to bluff his way in somehow, verify where Kinzaburo was kept, and then free him in the dark of the night. But if those cursed monks treated a fellow monk the way they had Saburo, he doubted he would be allowed to live if they caught him. The risk was too great for a family man.

And there was another matter. He was getting too old for this business. Lately he had been plagued by headaches, and his encounter with the *sohei* seemed to have aggravated them. He felt discouraged. Putting his head into his hands, he muttered, "What can I do?"

"If it weren't for my mother, I could come with you. I know the place better than you. We might not be successful, but it would be worth a try."

Tora looked up. "Would you do that? After what they did to you?"

Saburo gave him his crooked smile. "I remember some faces. They come to me at night. I'll never forget."

"Oh. You mean you'd look for those who did this?"

"Of course. That's what I dream about when I'm awake."

"But why can't you leave your mother? She's safe here."

Saburo shook his head. "You don't know her. I dare not do this to my new family."

Tora laughed. "Come on. She's a busybody, but at heart she's kind and she tries to be helpful. What could she possibly do?"

Saburo said darkly, "She's the one who sent me among the *sohei,* and you ask 'what can she do?'"

"Then send her back to your sister."

Saburo turned away. "I can't," he said dully. "They won't have her. They know her too well. Besides, she's my responsibility. It will be best if I leave. She can keep house for me, and I'll find some work to feed us both."

"No. You belong here." Tora paused. "Well, there's nothing to be done then. I'll tell the master. When he hears she's your mother, I'm sure he'll make her welcome."

Saburo's head sank lower. "Yes. But it isn't right."

"You'll stay?"

Saburo nodded. "For a while. But what will you do?"

"I'm having a look at Enryaku-ji. See if I get any ideas. How about some directions?"

Saburo looked at him anxiously. "What do you plan to do?"

"I'd just like to get an idea of the place."

"You'll go back to Otsu first?"

Tora nodded.

"There's a road up the mountain. All roads to Enryaku-ji are good. The main temple is actually surrounded by smaller, outlying temples. But you want to know about the *sohei*. They have their own place in one of the smaller temples. Few visitors ever go there, but it has its own main hall, lecture hall, and several training halls. They call them training halls, but they are really dojos. They teach fighting skills there. The place is tucked away on a steep mountain ridge. You can get to it from the main road. There's a path that climbs the side of the mountain before you reach Enryaku-ji's main gate. The *sohei* are separate from the other monks and come and go this way when they need to visit Otsu. The path leads to a gate, but the gatekeepers there won't admit you. The whole complex is walled and surrounded by watch towers."

"I was afraid of that. Any other way in?"

"Yes. You can get there from the Enryaku-ji grounds. That path is behind the Kaidan-in, the ordination hall. It's well hidden and is for the monks only, and the *sohei* if they're summoned by the abbot or partici-pate in any of the temple observances. If you encounter anyone there, you'll be stopped. And if you're not, you still won't get into their compound."

Tora grinned. "I'll be very careful."

Saburo gave him a hard look. "Promise that you'll come get me before you try anything dangerous."

"I will. Thanks, brother."

∞

When Tora returned to Otsu, he found his master was preoccupied with the governor's family. He was said to be visiting a shrine fair and had left no instructions for Tora. As it was not yet midday, Tora decided he had plenty of time for a visit to the temple.

So he got back on his horse and took the wide road that led from Otsu up the side of Mount Hiei to the huge temple complex that was Enryaku-ji. This time of year and in this weather the road was busy. Most of the pilgrims in their rough white cotton robes and wide straw hats, walked leaning on staffs, their provisions slung in bags over their shoulders. Some of the upper class faithful traveled by horse or in litters. All in all, there was a steady stream going up the mountain and coming back down.

Their spirits were high. For many of them, this was a welcome release from their usual labors and the long winter months inside their houses.

It was, of course, also good for their souls.

Above them rose the green mountain to a blue sky dotted with small clouds. The holy mountain, Mount Hiei, guardian of the capital. Tora believed mountains to be inhabited by ancient gods, but it was Enryaku-ji and other mountain temples that claimed to protect the people below.

The road climbed through forest dotted here and there with cherry trees bursting into bloom. Birds darted through the branches, and small wildflowers bloomed in the grass.

Soon Tora could see the tops of pagodas and some roofs of temple halls rising from the forest. There were many of these and they were widely separated. He began to realize the enormous size of the complex and got the first inkling that his plans might be beyond him. For the time being, he persisted. Closer to his destination, he came across the first roadside vendors. They sold all sorts of foods, amulets, straw sandals, straw hats, and straw coats, umbrellas, rosaries, and other items useful to pilgrims.

As it was long was past midday, Tora stopped for a bowl of noodles at one stand. The food was vegetarian, and any hopes he might have had for a cup of wine vanished. There was water, though, at a token price.

Eventually, he reached the entrance to the main temple—there were apparently many of these, scattered over the mountainside and associated with Enryaku-ji. He turned his horse over to a young monk, made a donation, and walked through the large, roofed Monju-ro gate into the temple grounds.

There was little to distinguish this mountain temple complex from many others. True, the halls and other buildings were in excellent condition, the red lacquered columns, railings, and eaves brilliant in the sun, and the gilding even brighter and very rich. But he found the pagoda unsatisfactory because it had only three levels. On the other hand, the sheer number of buildings stunned and bewildered him. How would he ever find his way around this place?

For a while, he just wandered about like the rest of the visitors. He paused before the Amida hall, thinking it rather small and unimportant looking. The Daiko-do, or great lecture hall, was more impressive. Following the general stream of pilgrims, he passed among many other halls, the Kanjo-do, used for initiations, the Yokokawashu-do, another large building, and the Komponchu-do with its colonnaded gallery. Beyond rose mountains, forests, and craggy rocks toward more halls and pagodas.

The monks' living quarters were tucked away behind the main buildings, and nearby were storage buildings.

Ordinary monks in gray or black or pale robes stood or wandered about, offering to direct visitors and answering their questions, but Tora saw no *sohei*. He decided not to trouble the helpful monks with his own questions.

The sun was setting and he was getting tired before he gave up on seeing all of the huge temple complex and turned back to the main compound. He located the Kaidan-in, a small ordination hall, and found it awkwardly close to the lecture hall where a great number of monks seemed to be stationed. The path Saburo had mentioned skirted the side of the building. It was unmarked, and a monk stood there to make sure none of the visitors would be tempted to explore it. In fact, the more Tora thought about it, security was very good here. The monks he had seen mingling with visitors and pilgrims, offering to direct them, seemed to have been placed there as guards. It gave him a creepy feeling. No doubt, someone had already noted him as neither a sightseer nor a pilgrim. He paused to scan the area casually and caught several monks looking his way.

He had been careless.

They had something to hide!

Tora quickly mingled with the pilgrims, seeking out the heaviest concentration of people and moving with them, joining new groups, but always staying as close as possible to the Kaidan-in. A short time later, he got his chance. Across the way, in front of the pagoda, an outcry went up. Someone had fallen or fainted. Immediately, people started to drift in that direction, and with them went the watchers.

When Tora saw that the monk next to the secret path had joined them, he slipped past the side of the building and jogged away from the crowds and into the woods. He saw no one. The path turned sharply left and then ascended toward the mountain ridge behind the temple complex. After a while, Tora slowed and steadied his breathing. No sense in alerting any other posted watchers. He proceeded more slowly and cautiously, especially when he neared the summit. But again he was quite safe. And then the path took a final turn, and Tora saw a complex of buildings before him. In contrast to the temple below, these were very plain. The wood was unpainted and had darkened from the weather. The roofs of the halls were covered with bark.

Some of the buildings were more than one story tall and had wooden roofs weighted down with rocks like the row houses of the poor and the warehouses of merchants. The whole thing had a utilitarian look about it, but it was walled all around, and the walls rested on rock and had watchtowers, and the gate he saw from where he was looked heavily reinforced.

It was closed.

And it was getting dark and chilly. Soon he would not be able to see much anyway. Regretfully, he turned back. The light faded rapidly, and when the forest closed in on him again, he realized he had been foolish to take this path so late in the day. It was nearly dark under the trees. There were rock outcroppings and loose stones underfoot, and haste was of the essence. Soon he could do little more than descend the steep inclines by slipping, sliding, and catching himself by grasping tree branches. He had given up long since any effort to avoid noise or to listen for it.

That was how it happened.

He was wondering if he was still on the same path or if he had somehow left it to flounder about in the forest on a mountain side that might at any moment propel him into a gorge, when a hand seized his shoulder from behind. Before he could react someone kicked his legs out from under him. He fell heavily, and a large, heavy body fell on top of him.

13

Searching for Tora

On their return from the fair, the children reported gleefully to their father, showing off their kites and beads, and sticky faces and fingers. Kosehira laughed, eyed Akitada and Yukiko with some interest when they remained quiet, and then packed his family off to their home and baths. Akitada he begged to remain a little longer.

They went to Kosehira's study, where Kosehira gestured for Akitada to sit and offered him wine. Akitada accepted, though he would have preferred water. His mouth was uncomfortably dry.

He drank, then asked," What's on your mind, brother?"

Kosehira fidgeted. "I'm very grateful you looked after my family." He gave Akitada another one of his searching glances. "Hmm. I hope the children weren't too much of a nuisance. I know I've spoiled them."

"Not at all. They were delightful. I enjoyed the afternoon very much."

That got him another sharp glance. "Yukiko helped look after them, I hope."

"Oh, yes. I told you, they were no trouble."

"She's old enough to have some sense," Kosehira said. "Mature for her age. Don't you think so?"

"She is charming, Kosehira, and will make some deserving young man very happy." Akitada had become embarrassed during this interrogation and asked, "But wasn't there something else you wanted to discuss?"

"Yes, of course. It's just that I'm very fond of her. Fond of you, too." Kosehira now looked rather red himself and emptied his cup. " As to the other matter . . ." He paused.

Akitada wondered at this "other." It sounded as if both Yukiko and the other matter had been on Kosehira's mind when he brought Akitada back here. He waited.

"Chief Takechi came to see me a short while ago. There's been another death, it seems. He was anxious that you should be told."

Akitada's thoughts flew to the unfortunate couple who had kept house for Judge Nakano. Had there been some sort of quarrel? "What happened?"

"Another old man has died. Takechi says it looks like Nakano's death. Only this one was some poor fellow who earned a few coppers sweeping streets."

"Strange. I'd better have word with him." Akitada rose.

"Tomorrow is soon enough. It's been a long day." Kosehira stretched. "You wouldn't believe the number of petitions I had to read today. On second thought, maybe you would."

"I'll be glad to take some work off your hands while I'm here, Kosehira. You only have to ask."

Kosehira chuckled. "Thanks. It may come to that. But let's go home for today. I want a bath, some wine, and a good meal, and then bed."

That sounded wonderful and Akitada said so.

∞

But it was not an altogether restful evening after all. When they reached Kosehira's house, it became clear that Tora had not returned from the capital. After his initial irritation, Akitada worried. He worried enough to propose that he should get back on his horse and ride home to find out what had happened to Tora.

Kosehira objected. "He's just decided to spend another day and night with that pretty wife of his. You don't need him, so what does it matter?"

"I don't know. He promised to be back this morning." Akitada remembered that Tora had been angry with him when he left, and what he had been angry about. "I don't like this at all. I think he had some wild idea of rescuing a man from the *sohei* on Mount Hiei."

This required explanations which effectively spoiled Kosehira's good mood. "You're sure that he meant to be back in Otsu this morning?"

Akitada nodded. "By midday at the latest. I think he returned, found me gone to the fair, and decided to pay a visit to Enryaku-ji."

Kosehira was instantly relieved. "Oh, that makes sense. He'll be back shortly then. Let's go have that bath."

Akitada was by no means reassured, but he decided not to panic just yet. They had a relaxing bath and excellent hot supper on trays in Kosehira's room with some of Kosehira's good wine.

They talked about the *sohei*, whom Kosehira deplored as much as Akitada. When Akitada shared Tora's story, Kosehira made up his mind to send a message to the abbot, demanding explanations and proof that Kinzaburo was indeed one of the temple's peasants.

He said glumly, "Nothing will come of it, of course. They'll have the proof. But at least they will be warned that I'm keeping an eye on their hired thugs."

"I think I'll send a protest of my own. They did, after all, attack Tora. I'll demand they turn the attacker over to the local police for public brawling."

They smiled at each other, satisfied for the moment.

Refilling their cups, Kosehira returned to a more delicate subject.

"Speaking of your household, brother," Kosehira said, a little diffidently, "how are you managing it? I mean, it must be very difficult with the lovely Tamako gone. I recall, you always insisted that one wife was all you ever wanted. As you saw, I have three kind and cheerful ladies. They take all cares for my children and the household affairs off my shoulders."

Akitada grimaced. "I know. I've been envious of your happy family. I miss Tamako every day. I'm sure the children do, too, though they seem content enough. But the wives of two of my retainers are good women. Especially Hanae, Tora's wife."

"You'll forgive my saying so, brother, but that's hardly the same as a wife. There are other needs." He gave a soft chuckle and raised his cup. "Here's to lovemaking, Akitada. The sages have taught us that a man needs it regularly to keep his body strong and healthy."

Akitada laughed. "I do my best," he said. "Such things are easy enough to arrange. Why do you ask? Do you have someone in mind?"

Kosehira gulped. "Well," he said after a moment, "I could make enquiries if you wish. I haven't had much occasion . . . I'm a family man, brother. Three desirable ladies are enough for me."

Akitada apologized, and they changed the subject.

∞

Tora had not returned by the next morning either, and Kosehira offered to send a servant to Akitada's house. Akitada, by now seriously worried as well as angry with Tora, decided to go himself.

He arrived at home before the midday rice, much to the surprise of Genba who greeted him.

"Is Tora here?" Akitada snapped before Genba could do more than bow and offer a welcome.

"No, sir. Isn't he with you? He left early yesterday."

Before Akitada could say anything else, a strange woman interrupted them. She came from the direction of the kitchen. "Genba," she called out. "I need you to run to the market. That fool of a cook forgot to buy shrimp. You know how much his lordship's children like them. If you ask me, they've been given too many sweets. All they want is moon cakes and sweet dumplings."

"Who's that?" Akitada asked.

"Tora was to explain sir. She's Saburo's mother. Mrs. Kuruda."

"Saburo has a mother?" Foolish question, but somehow the issue of Saburo's family had never come up. Akitada had always assumed that someone as grotesquely scarred as the man he had met in Naniwa must be alone in the world. This oversight angered him further.

The short, round woman, no beauty herself, reached them as he swung himself out of the saddle. She took in his clothes and hat and made him a small bow. "If it's business for his lordship," she informed him, "he's not home. He's a guest of his Excellency, the governor of Omi. "I'm sure I can be of service if you wish to leave a message. Allow me to show you inside."

Normally this would have been amusing. Genba was grinning, but Akitada had no time to be entertained. "I'm Sugawara and this is my home," he snapped. "I'm told you're Saburo's mother. Where is he?"

At this, she made him a better bow. "A great pleasure, my lord. My son has told me much about you. It's been an honor to meet your charming children and look after them. But children need their parents. Alas, poor mites, they've lost their mother. If you don't mind my saying so, you really should spend more time with them, my lord. But business presses. I understand that well enough. My late husband was an official himself. His duties were more important than anything to him. I learned soon enough that as his wife I must be both mother and father to my children. If I do say so myself, I'm very good at it by now. I've enjoyed looking after Lady Yasuko and Master Yoshi. But I'm rattling on. You must be hungry. I'll run and see about some food and wine. Genba, you'd better hurry and get those shrimp."

Akitada was momentarily speechless. Then he said, "Stay, Genba." To Saburo's mother, he added, "You are welcome here as Saburo's mother, but I assure you there is no need for you to manage my household or my children."

She waved that aside with a smile that revealed crooked front teeth. "It's no trouble. I'm used to working hard and I'll go on working if it helps my boy. A mother's care is never done, don't you agree? No, don't answer. I know you're a sensible gentleman. A Chinese sage said you must honor your parents. He knew what he was talking about. His mother slaved and suffered for him. I imagine yours worked and worried for you. Yes, I can see I'm right. Now that I'm here, my Saburo will have his mother's support as long as she draws a breath." She looked over Akitada's shoulder. " Ah, here he comes now. What a clever gentleman you are to have asked Saburo to work for you. The boy is simply brilliant. He has a great future ahead of him. Saburo, here's your master come home when we least expected it. I must see about his dinner." For a moment she looked distracted. "Shrimp would have been nice, but never mind. I'll think of something." With another bob, she was off.

Saburo knelt and touched his forehead to the gravel of the courtyard. "I'm very sorry about this, sir. She suddenly showed up. Please forgive her. She's a very silly woman."

"Get up, Saburo," Akitada said wearily. "She is your mother?"

Saburo stood, head hanging low. "Yes, sir. She has no place to go."

"Then she is welcome here. Where is Tora?"

Saburo looked up, startled. "He didn't get back to you?"

"No."

"I think . . ." Saburo faltered. "I may be wrong. It isn't like Tora not to report back to you, but perhaps he's gone to Enryaku-ji."

"Ah! I half suspected it. But he hasn't come back from there either."

"Yes. It's extremely troubling." Saburo twisted his hands together and glanced over his shoulder in the direction of the kitchen. "I should go look for him, but my mother . . ."

Akitada frowned. "I'm sure your mother is quite safe here. Do you know much about the monks at Enryaku-ji?"

"Yes, sir. I was sent there once."

"I didn't' know. Neither, for that matter, did you mention your mother. Is there anything else I should know?"

Saburo flinched. "Probably. I'm very sorry. I was afraid you would dismiss me again. I can see now that keeping silent made things worse. My mother and I will be gone as soon as Tora is found. I don't like to impose on you and the others. She's a difficult woman. But I think I'd better go look for Tora right away."

"You can make a home for her here," Akitada said rashly. "After we've all had something to eat, I want everyone to come to my study. We'll discuss it then."

Saburo looked uneasy, but he nodded.

∞

Mrs. Kuruda was the first to arrive. After making him a bow, she glanced around. "If you don't mind, my lord, I could do wonders with this room. After a good cleaning, I'll have your things rearranged in a more pleasing manner. It could do with a bit of straightening, too."

His study was neither dirty nor disordered, and he definitely did not want this woman to touch it. He snapped, "Do not touch a thing in this room!"

She opened her mouth to argue, but the others arrived, and the room, though sizable, was hardly large enough to hold them all. The children had come as well and were wide-eyed with curiosity.

Akitada smiled at them and said, "I came looking for Tora and instead find Saburo's mother. Thank you all for making her welcome, both for Saburo's sake and because it's the proper and kind thing to do. Mrs.

Kuruda, you are welcome here. I hope you'll become a part of my household." Seeing Saburo's mother open her mouth to respond, he raised a hand. "No, there's no time now. The others will help you settle in. They have my trust, and I hope you will, too. In my absence, Hanae is in charge of household matters. Genba looks after the house and grounds, and the horses." He saw a look of dismay on her face, but it was just as well to establish her position early. She had sounded as if she planned to give the orders in the future.

With a glance at Hanae, he went on, "Tora did not reach me yesterday. Saburo and I think he ran into some problem on Mount Hiei. Saburo knows the area well and will look for him. I have to return to Otsu."

A troubled silence fell. The children looked upset. In an effort to lift their spirits, Akitada reminded them of the Sanno festival. That brought smiles, and in the end, everyone bowed and left except for Hanae.

She asked, "Is my husband in some kind of trouble? Has he been foolish or disobedient?"

Probably both, Akitada thought, but he shook his head. "He is looking into some business connected with my work. I expect he got side-tracked. Saburo is going to find him."

Hanae bit her lip and gave him a searching look. "Be safe, both of you."

It was difficult to fool women.

∞

On the way to Otsu, Akitada and Saburo exchanged whatever information they had that would help track down Tora. Saburo also spoke briefly of his past and his upbringing. He apologized again for not having shared his background.

Akitada blamed himself. He had treated Saburo from the start with suspicion and told him frankly that he had no respect for "spies" and very little respect for monks. As a result, Saburo had kept his past to himself as much as possible. And since he had cut all ties with his family, he had seen no need to mention them either.

Saburo's mother created a problem Akitada had not desired, but his obligation to his retainers implied that he look after them and their families as if they were his on flesh and blood. Mrs. Kuruda would remain a fixture in his household until she died—or until she decided to return to her daughter's house.

But as they talked, Akitada became increasingly uneasy about letting Saburo search for Tora. In the end, he said, "Saburo, I think it will be better if I go to speak to the abbot and see if I can get them to release Tora."

Saburo glanced at him. "He will deny any knowledge of him, sir."

"Probably, but perhaps I can make him uneasy enough to let him go anyway. I'm in charge of a legal case that's been brought against the temple."

Saburo was silent for a moment. Then he said, "Will they ask you to exchange favors?"

Akitada grimaced. "Probably. It is a hateful thought, but Tora is more important to me than either temple."

"In that case, sir, would it not be better if you had proof that Tora is there?"

"Yes, but we cannot wish for the impossible."

"Let me take a look. I may find something. I know the place very well." He added more softly, "To my regret."

Akitada stared at him aghast. "Are you saying that what happened to you, to your face, happened there? Monks did that? On the holy mountain? They did this in the Buddha's name?"

Saburo looked away. "They were *sohei*. The warrior monks are mostly lay people. And they are no better than criminals. Many of them were criminals at one time. All of them are very tough fighters. I was never a fighter, just a spy. They needed to find out who had sent me."

"Dear gods! Under no circumstances will you return to that place. You should have told me."

Saburo shook his head. "I've learned my lesson and will be more careful this time. Besides, I feel responsible. I shouldn't have let Tora go by himself."

"No. I won't allow it."

Saburo said nothing. They rode silently side by side, both thinking about the problem.

Finally Saburo said, "I have an idea, sir. And it's perfectly safe."

"Yes?"

"I expect Tora rode up the mountain. He must have left his horse somewhere. If it's in the temple's visitor stables, we will know that he is still there."

Akitada reigned in his horse. "Yes, of course. You propose to check the stables and come back to Otsu?"

"Yes, sir."

"And you'll do nothing else?"

"I promise."

"Very well. Report to provincial headquarters."

They parted company on the outskirts of Otsu, Saburo to take a road up the mountain to the temple, and Akitada to ride into town.

∞

After looking in on Kosehira to report on Tora's likely whereabouts, Akitada went to see Chief Takechi.

Takechi greeted him eagerly. "Thank you for coming, sir. Frankly, this is quite beyond me. Kimura says it's the same thing all over again. A bump on the back of the head that wouldn't kill a child, and then the same signs of suffocation."

"The spots on the whites of the eyes?"

"Yes." Takechi ran a hand over his face in a distracted manner. "I suppose it's murder. Unless some sort of new disease is going around."

"Who is the victim?"

"An old fellow by the name of Tokuno. A street sweeper."

"Where is the body?"

"Back in the jail. Kimura's finished with it. It will soon be released for the funeral."

"Shall we take a look?"

Takechi made a face. "If you insist. I must warn you. Kimura's cut him up pretty badly."

Akitada smiled briefly. "I think I can bear the sight. Lead the way."

When they reached the room where Akitada had viewed Judge Nakano's body, Kimura was still there. He stood frowning down at the corpse of an old man whose age-ravaged body had been further damaged by the cuts made by the coroner. Most of these had been sewn back up somewhat carelessly, but the body nevertheless presented a shocking sight. Akitada had seen men disemboweled, trampled by horses, and beheaded. All of these methods of killing humans had involved a lot of blood. This corpse was quite pale and bloodless and far more shocking.

Kimura bowed.

Akitada said, "The same as Nakano's case?"

Kimura nodded. "I still don't believe it. It must be murder. The only way it could have happened is that the murderer stuffed something in the man's mouth and then held his nose."

"Ah." Akitada nodded. "It could have happened that way. Any proof?"

"No."

"No bruising around the mouth and nose?"

"Not really. But if the victim was unconscious, it would not take much force. They were both old men."

"What about that bruise on Nakano's head. Did you find the same thing here?"

"Yes, sir. Though it's nothing I could be sure about."

Takechi cleared his throat. "There was one thing though, sir." They both looked at him. Takechi reached into his sleeve and handed Akitada the small carved figure of Jizo. "This was lying on top of him when he was found."

14

Death of a Sweeper

The small figure looked identical to the one they had found in Judge Nakano's study and to all the other little figures sold at the shrine fair. Akitada felt a small shiver run down his back and glanced at Takechi. "Surely," he said, "this is extraordinary."

Takechi nodded. "If it's murder, sir, it would seem that both men were killed by the same person."

"What do we know about the dead man?"

"Not much. Tokuno lived alone, earning a few coppers by sweeping the roads and carrying away refuse and night soil. The night soil he sold to farmers. He owned nothing but the clothes on his back and a decrepit handcart."

"An outcast?"

"No. Just a poor old man."

"Still, someone who had nothing in common with the judge." Akitada turned the small figure in his hand. Takechi's murders were becoming more puzzling by the moment.

The chief said, "Exactly. It makes no sense. Perhaps a madman is at work."

Akitada nodded slowly. "Such things have happened. And the fact that he left behind this very odd token of his visit may prove that he isn't in his right mind."

The coroner had listened with raised brows. "May I have a look, sir?" he asked.

Akitada passed over the carving.

Doctor Kimura said, "It's a Jizo. They sell those at all the fairs. There must be hundreds about. Travelers and pilgrims buy them for protection."

Akitada nodded. "Yes. I saw them for sale at a shrine fair. But why leave such a thing behind after a murder?"

Kimura frowned. "Perhaps it's a message."

The chief was unconvinced. "A message for whom? It's not as if either old man had a large family."

Akitada said, "And what does it mean? Why would a killer want us to know that it was his work."

"Well, if he's mad, he doesn't need a reason," the coroner offered.

Akitada frowned. "I don't think he's mad in that sense. You said, people buy these for protection if they are on a journey? Perhaps he is a pilgrim."

Kimura said, "Women might do so because they've lost a child at birth. Jizo protects the children who had no chance to follow the Buddha. In fact, he helps all those suffering in hell."

Takechi scratched his head. "That covers a lot of ground."

Kimura asked, "Have there been other cases like this here or elsewhere?"

The chief and Akitada exchanged a glance. Takechi said, "Heaven forbid. I haven't heard of any. Are you suggesting that this person travels about killing people?"

"I don't know," Kimura said with a smile. "I'm just the coroner."

Takechi gave him a look and said again, "It makes no sense. What does he get out of it?"

Silence fell. They stood looking down at the pitiful thing on the mat. The first flies were gathering. Akitada hoped that the corpse had given up its story completely, for they could not keep him around much longer.

Takechi had the same thought. "I suppose we'd better release him for burial if you're done, doctor."

"I'm done."

As they left the jail building, Akitada said, "I'd like to talk to the man's neighbors. Do you mind? I have a very unpleasant feeling about this."

Takechi did not mind. They walked through town and into the modest neighborhood where Tokuno had lived. Takechi stopped in front of small house that looked as though it needed a few repairs. The roof was missing boards and the door hung crookedly in its opening.

"The neighbor says the door had been like this for years," Takechi said." The killer didn't force it."

"The sweeper lived in a house? Did he rent this place?"

"No. It belonged to him. I know it looks in bad shape, but he got too old to take care of things."

"Still, a sweeper usually doesn't own a house."

Takechi nodded. "This one was poor enough in spite of it," he said, looking up at the house.

Next door, a woman came out to peer at them. She shaded her eyes against the sun, then approached, bowing. "I'm Mrs. Kagemasa. Can I be of service?"

Akitada thought her well-spoken and polite and smiled at her. "We are here because your neighbor has died," he said. "I'm Lord Sugawara and this is Chief Takechi."

She bowed again. "I recognized the chief. Is something wrong with Tokuno's death? The constables didn't say."

Takechi said, "He may have been murdered. Were you home the night he died?"

"Oh, no," she murmured. "Murdered! Oh, the poor man. These days, what with all the fairs, there's so much riffraff about. We were home but asleep. We heard nothing. I blamed myself for not looking in on him the day before. I thought he got sick. He was an old man after all."

It sounded much like the comments about the judge. He, too, was thought to have died of old age. Akitada asked, "Being a neighbor, you probably knew

Tokuno for a long time. Has he always been this poor and lived alone here?"

"Oh, no. Tokuno used to work at the tribunal. He was a jailer. He had a family, but they all died, even his son. His son had an accident ten years ago. He fell off a boat and drowned. After that Tokuno wasn't the same man anymore."

Takechi and Akitada looked at each other. "When did he stop working at the jail?" Takechi asked.

"Oh, years ago. It must be nearly twenty years now."

"Before my time," Takechi said to Akitada.

"How did he manage to support himself all those years?" Akitada asked the woman.

"At first the son was still alive. He was a fisherman. After he drowned, Tokuno became a porter for a while until the work got too heavy for him. He was getting to the point where he couldn't do much anymore. The neighbors would sometimes bring him food. But his health was so bad we thought we'd have to ask the monks to take him in."

"Onjo-ji monks?" Takechi asked.

She nodded. "They'll look after poor old people. Besides, he still had the house to pay for his keep."

Akitada suppressed a snort. No doubt, houses paid off handsomely. The temple could sell or rent them, and the old people by that time did not have long to live.

They thanked the woman and went into Tokuno's house. It revealed not only careless housekeeping, since there was no woman to look after it, but also great poverty. There was little food in the dirty kitchen area, and that was mostly cheap millet and a few wilted leaves of vegetables that had probably been given away by a market woman at the end of the day. Tokuno's clothes were mere rags, but among them they found something interesting. Hanging from one of the hooks that held clothes were also a leather whip and a rusty chain and manacles. The whip was old and stained, and Akitada shuddered at the thought that they had once bitten deeply into prisoners' backs and legs.

He pointed them out to Takechi who merely nodded. "He was proud of his former job, I guess."

"He was the sort of brute who enjoyed hurting people, I think."

"That, too. Very common among jailers."

"Not such a nice man, then. And we know that Nakano was no saint either. Perhaps the killer had a reason to kill these two."

Takechi paused in his rummaging in an old trunk and looked at Akitada. "An old grudge?" he asked uncertainly. "I don't know. Most people who end up in court or jail wouldn't dare raise a hand against those in charge."

"I hope things have become better in Otsu."

This met with silence, and Akitada flushed. "Sorry. Of course, they have. I wasn't thinking. I know neither you nor the governor would employ men like these two."

Takechi smiled. "Never mind. I get angry myself when I think about the way things used to be done."

They were soon finished and had not found anything helpful. Takechi said, "I'll have my constables talk to all the neighbors in case someone saw something, but I have no great hopes. Mrs. Kagemasa next door will have talked to them already. Now that she knows it was murder, she'll be making the rounds again. Shall we go back?"

"Yes. I'm concerned about one of my men. I think he went looking for that porter the *sohei* abducted. He hasn't come back. If he isn't back by now, I'll have to see the abbot about the situation."

Takechi was curious, and Akitada told him what Tora had said.

The chief said angrily, "If we get proof of illegal arrests, maybe we can round up some of those brutes and put an end to that sort of thing. I've heard such stories before, but we could never prove anything."

∞

Tora had not returned.

Akitada sought out Kosehira. His friend was more optimistic about Tora's presumed capture by Enryaku-ji's *sohei*.

"One thing," he said, "They can't keep him. He's your man. Those brutes didn't know that when they attacked him. We'll get him back."

"I hope we're not too late." Akitada was beginning to get a sick feeling about the whole affair. The new murder in Otsu had not helped. He suppressed his fears quickly and told Kosehira about Chief Takechi's find, the figurine of Jizo found with both bodies, and their suspicion that someone was murdering old men for some perverted reason of his own.

Kosehira was shocked by the idea. "Oh, come," he said, clearly trying to regain his good humor, "two old men don't prove anything. Old men die. You said yourself that the coroner wasn't sure it was murder. And those carved Jizos are all over the place."

He had a point. But all the same . . .

"I wonder," Akitada said, "could we check if there have been any other cases either here or elsewhere. Can you find out?"

"For the province, yes. Maybe even for the capital. But this is a big country. And how many police officers would have taken the notice Takechi and you did?"

"I know, but you could try? And could we check back to Tokuno's service as a jailer here in the tribunal?"

"Probably. Our archives are in good shape. Very well, Akitada. I'll do my best."

Akitada took his leave to spend some time with the officials working with the temple documents. They had made progress, but so far the verdict seemed to be that both temples had engaged in dubious practices against each other.

Akitada praised their work, made some suggestions, and left.

To his relief, Saburo was waiting for him. "Well?" Akitada asked.

"His horse is still in the main stable. The monk in charge claimed it belonged to them. I recognized it and told him if they didn't release it, I'd have the provincial guard there. He just bowed and said I must do as I wished."

Akitada said angrily, "They aren't afraid of us. Well, we shall see about that." He glanced outside. It was getting late and soon would be dark. "Another night for Tora, I'm afraid. But early tomorrow I shall pay a visit to the abbot. Thank you, Saburo. You did well."

15

Abbot Gyomei

The next day broke dark and wet. A strong wind from the lake drove sheets of rain across Otsu, and it was impossible to see the temple on Hiei. The mountain range crouched like a black monster above Otsu.

Akitada ate his rice gruel and then dressed in his second best robe. No point in ruining his best one in this rain. Then he and Saburo climbed into the saddle, covered with straw rain coats, shoe covers, and wide hats. Kosehira had ordered a contingent of the provincial guard for their retinue. They wore their ordinary armor and tried to put on stern faces.

While the straw raincoat protected Akitada from the worst of the wind, it was a nuisance keeping his floppy hat on. Eventually he removed it and rode bareheaded.

Anger and worry made him keep up a good pace, and they reached the main gate of the temple by mid-morning. The rain had changed into a fine, watery spray that obscured details as if veils had been drawn across the entire mountain. All around them, this wet fog shrouded trees, roofs, and galleries. Except for one solitary monk they had passed on the road, they were the only visitors. This, too, made the temple grounds feel like another world, some place not altogether human and somehow threatening to trespassers.

Akitada bit his lip. Nonsense, he thought. It was threatening enough without becoming supernatural. The monks had snatched Tora who, more than likely, had trespassed where he was not wanted.

Two young monks detached themselves from the shelter of the great gate and ran toward them.

"Welcome to Enryaku-ji!" they chorused. One carried an oiled paper umbrella which he now opened. Smiling up at Akitada, he said, "Allow me to guide you, sir. Soncho here will take your horse and show your people the way."

Akitada looked down at him. "I'm Sugawara Akitada and have come to speak to the Grand Abbot later. At the moment, I wish to inspect your stables."

They looked at each other in consternation. "The stables?" asked the first monk after a moment. "Your lordship wishes to see the stables?"

"You heard me," Akitada snapped. "Lead the way."

They both came with them to a lesser gate and another, smaller, compound. There were service buildings here: kitchens, stables, and overnight accommodations for pilgrims. At the stables, Akitada and Saburo dismounted and went inside. The stables were large but in this weather, there were few horses stabled. Tora's mount was not among them. The monks had followed and were now in conversation with some stable hands.

Looking nervous, Saburo said in a low voice, "They moved it. I must have attracted their notice when I asked questions about it."

"You're safe with me," Akitada said. "They can't do anything to you. But stay with the others and wait."

He was very angry, and next spoke brusquely to the monk who had greeted him. "I've seen what I came to see. Now take me to Gyomei."

The monk was apologetic "I regret, but the Seal of the Law is not available. Will the Master of the Law do?"

With an effort, Akitada recalled his visitor at the tribunal. "Prior Kanshin? Yes. I'll speak to him. My men will wait here."

He was taken into the temple grounds. The place was eerie in its emptiness. The fog hung over the entire compound, obscuring the world and muffling sounds except for their steps in the gravel and the dripping of rainwater from the eaves. Akitada shuddered. He doubted he would be able to find his way out of this strange place. Suddenly he wished he had taken his retinue along. Or at least Saburo.

They reached a small hall that seemed to back against the forest behind it. The monk walked up the steps to a veranda and opened a door, standing aside for Akitada to enter. Akitada stepped into a plain room with a dais along one wall and a few cushions placed along its length. Behind him the door closed.

He swung around and saw that he was alone. The irrational thought that they had taken him prisoner also crossed his mind. He went back and tried the door. It opened onto the foggy world outside. He closed it again, feeling foolish.

"Master of the Law, Seal of the Law," he muttered under his breath. "Silly titles. We'd all be better off if Buddha had never come to our islands."

But that, too, was silly. He started pacing. Where was Tora? How dare they take him and steal his horse? He'd see about that.

The skirt of his silk robe slapped against his legs and he became aware that it was soaked. In fact, his collar was wet also, as was his hair. So much for straw raincoats and hats. He dabbed at his head and remembered the court hat in his sleeve. Tying it back on without a mirror irritated him further.

Why this long wait? His rank and current position demanded a good deal more respect than this. How long should he wait before sending for the men of the provincial guard and making a search of the monastery for the elusive Gyomei?

Eventually, he went to the dais and perched on its edge. His thought went to Kosehira who must have had a most frustrating administration, given Enryaku-ji and

Onjo-ji encroached on his territory. From Kosehira, his thoughts went to his daughter. He found he could not be angry at Yukiko. Perhaps his anger had been mostly with himself for desiring her. He had simply transferred it, blaming her bad manners for his own discomfiture. Why could he not treat her like the charming child she was, a lovable child, to be sure, but not beddable.

But again he felt the warmth of desire rise to his face and was ashamed.

Into this mood walked an extraordinary character. A door behind him had opened noiselessly, and Akitada became aware of the presence only from a slight wheezing sound. He started up and turned.

A short and slender old monk in a plain, somewhat ratty, black robe had shuffled in and stopped a few feet away. He was bent with age, but bright black eyes peered up at Akitada.

Having been caught in dubious and worldly fantasies, Akitada was not at his best. "Umm," he said," who are you?"

The old monk smiled. "Lord Sugawara? I'm Gyomei. Forgive the long wait. I was in my hermitage up the mountain a ways, and at my age the journey down was slow. Terrible weather we're having."

Akitada now saw that the hem of Gyomei's robe was wetter and muddier than his own and that his bare feet in sandals were mud-caked. Something about this man made him bow quite deeply.

"Your Reverence? Forgive me. I did not intend to put you to so much hardship."

Gyomei came closer. He smiled and pointed to the dais. "It was nothing. Please be seated."

They sat side by side, and Akitada searched for a way to say what he was there for. Gyomei waited, still smiling at him.

Akitada cleared his throat and plunged. "Your Reverence must be aware of our work trying to clear up the misunderstandings between Enryaku-ji and Onjo-ji?"

Gyomei smiled and nodded.

"Umm, we are making progress, but that is not why I came today."

Again the abbot nodded.

"I plan to give myself the pleasure to visit your beautiful temple another time when the weather is better." He added a small chuckle and knew he was making a terrible job of this. What was it about this man that put him so ill at ease?

Gyomei finally took pity on his floundering. "One of the monks said it is about a missing horse, but I must have misunderstood."

"A horse? No. Or rather the horse does seem to have disappeared also. No, Tora, my senior retainer, came here two days ago and hasn't returned."

Gyomei raised bushy white eyebrows. "You must be fond of him to have come looking for him in person."

Akitada was becoming angry again. He said coldly, "I look after all of my people, but Tora has been with me longest. In any case, his horse was seen in your stables, and this means Tora never left. I'd like him turned over to me."

Gyomei looked at him for a long time. Then he nodded. "If he is here or in any of our branch temples, he will be returned to you. I know nothing of this. Allow me!" The abbot rose and padded to the door he had come through. Putting his head out, he said something in a low voice. There was an answer, and he said something else.

Then he returned to Akitada and sat back down. "There will be some refreshments. I apologize for your reception."

Akitada, irritated and worried again, said, "No matter. I didn't come to eat."

Silence fell.

Gyomei produced a rosary and started to pray silently.

When the door opened again, two young monks entered, one bearing a stack of towels, and the other a tray with flasks, cups, and bowls.

Gyomei handed Akitada a towel and took one himself. He carefully dried his shaven head and face and dabbed at his robe. "Dreadful weather," he said again, then smiled. "I must make an effort to meditate on accepting things the way they are."

Akitada made a perfunctory job of drying his head. There was not much he could do, even after removing his hat again. His hair was carefully tied into a neat top knot. The advantages of shaving it off became apparent, and the thought brought back his irritation. "Have you told your people to get Tora?"

Gyomei carefully folded his towel and returned it to the waiting monk. "I have. They don't seem to know anything. May I ask what brought him here?"

"He was looking for a peasant arrested by your *sohei*. From what he told me, the peasant was a free man. They also raped the man's wife."

Gyomei stared at him. "Our *sohei* did this? There must be some mistake."

"No mistake. Tora is a very careful observer and doesn't make such accusations lightly."

"But perhaps the soldiers belonged to another temple?"

"No. And your Reverence forgets that Tora's horse was here until recently, proving that he came to Enryaku-ji and never left. I must insist that you release him immediately. After that we can discuss the situation of the peasant."

Another silence fell while Gyomei seemed to ponder this. After a while he said, "This is a very large mountain and we have many monks."

Akitada said nothing. He waited stonily and without touching the food and drink.

With a sigh, Gyomei rose again. Before he could give new orders, the door opened and Kanshin, the prior, hurried in accompanied by the same two senior monks who had called upon Akitada. They spoke briefly and softly with the abbot, then all of them came to Akitada.

Kanshin and his companions put their hands together and inclined their heads. Akitada did not return the greeting or get to his feet.

"We regret deeply," said Kanshin, "that your retain-er seems to have become lost on our mountain. "We will immediately send out searchers and pray that noth-ing has happened to him."

An icy fear gripped Akitada at those words. So this was the way they meant to play their game? Whatever they had done to Tora would be explained by a fall off a cliff. And that meant that their victim would not be able to deny it. Akitada would sit here, waiting, until they thought the time right to produce the mangled body.

He jumped to his feet. "I insist on joining the search party. And we'd better start wherever your *sohei* are quartered."

Kanshin recoiled a foot or so and turned a panic-stricken face to the abbot. Gyomei said, "The weather is really dreadful, Sugawara. Why not let my monks do the job? They are young and have given up the pleas-ures of life."

This angered Akitada further. How dare this monk suggest he was nothing but a pampered nobleman who did not like to get his head wet. He said harshly, "You can have little notion to what length I'll go to get my retainer back alive." He hoped his tone carried the threat that was implied. To his satisfaction, Gyomei blinked. He suddenly looked uneasy.

Rising to his feet, he said, "We shall do as you ask. Please be careful. The path up the mountain is steep and treacherous in places, especially in the rain. I still think you must be wrong. None of our people would dare capture a retainer of one of the noble guests of our esteemed governor. Prior Kanshin will organize the search. If you will forgive me, I must return to my solitude now."

Kanshin was nothing if not efficient. Very quickly, a group of capable-looking monks had gathered. Two other senior monks joined Kanshin, and they started their journey up the mountain. Akitada had been supplied with another straw coat and hat but refused the straw boots as too unreliable for mountain climbing. He had rarely undertaken a more unpleasant journey.

The wet mists still hung over the mountain and obscured the path ahead where trees and rock outcroppings appeared as if seen through layers of gray gauze, producing a sensation of traveling into a huge spider web.

Or into nothingness, a more appropriate concept for a Buddhist institution—which did little to reassure Akitada of a successful outcome to this journey into the unknown.

When they finally reached the secluded valley and the small compound which had been assigned to Enryaku-ji's *sohei*, Akitada was struck by two things. Clearly the temple and monastery proper liked to keep their distance from the warrior monks, and their existence was treated in an ominously secretive fashion.

He strode ahead to join Kanshin, noting with satisfaction that the prior looked as sodden as Akitada felt. "I take it this place is reserved for *sohei*? How many do you keep?"

Kanshin hesitated. Then he said, "The precise number escapes me. We also offer temporary residence to traveling warriors here. And a few young people come for training."

Akitada compressed his lips. This answer covered any number of possibilities. The temple might well be gathering an army, bringing in outsiders to augment the ranks of its people. Given the fact that the mountain temple could be defended far more easily than Onjo-ji in the city below, this was troubling.

One of the monks had gone ahead to announce them, and the gates opened. They filed in, a long line of wet monks with a bedraggled court noble in their midst.

The courtyard and the buildings were not very different from other temple complexes, but the occupants here wore armor or ordinary clothes. Several wore the white cowls draped over their heads and lower part of their faces. A few were bare-headed, and of these some had shaved their heads, while others had long hair and beards. Clearly, these so-called monks had adopted the spiritual path only in so far as it suited them.

More disturbing was the fact that quite a few looked like thugs and hired killers.

However, since their party was led by senior monks of Enriyaku-ji, they were received readily enough, and the senior monks and Akitada were led to one of the halls where an older warrior received them. Akitada took him for the commandant. He had shaved his head and wore better armor than the ones Akitada had seen outside.

Prior Kanshin made the introductions and explained their errand.

The commandant—his name was Seison— eyed Akitada with interest. He seemed to weigh his options, but then said readily enough, "It is true that we found a trespasser two nights ago. Since he refused to identify himself or his purpose, we have kept him locked up until such a time when we can ascertain those things." He gave Akitada a small smile. "We are by way of being the guardians of the temple. It seemed safest to make certain the man had no ill intentions before freeing him. Of course, he may not be the man you are seeking."

"That's easily ascertained," Akitada said, feeling somewhat relieved. "Bring him here."

The commandant gave an order, and after a short wait, two heavily-armed men brought in a chained Tora. He had added a bloodied lip to the black eye which had turned an ugly yellowish purple.

The expression on his face when he saw the wet and mud-stained Akitada was relief mixed with embarrassment. His mouth opened and closed, and he hung his head, muttering, "Sorry, sir." His guards grinned.

"He's a tough one, General," one of them said. "Tried everything to escape."

Tora glared at him, then lowered his eyes to the man's arm. It was bare, and Akitada saw the tattoo of a circle inside a triangle. He looked at Tora and saw him nod. "Is that the man you saw, Tora?"

"Yes, sir."

With an angry frown, Akitada turned to the prior. "Yes, this is Lieutenant Sashima. Release him immediately."

Kanshin gestured, and Tora's guards reluctantly began to undo the chains. Tora rubbed his wrists and
said, "Thank you, sir. These men fell upon me two days
ago as I was enjoying a walk near the temple. I had no
way of getting a message to you."

The prior raised a hand. "You did not identify yourself. If you had, this would not have happened. Your
behavior, we were told, was suspicious, and you were
found in a restricted area after dark."

"I got lost. And it wasn't quite dark yet." Tora glowered. "As for why I didn't identify myself, your people
jumped me. I took them for a gang of highway robbers."

There was some muttering from the *sohei* at this.
Akitada ignored it and said, "Indeed, it seems very
strange that peaceful monks should arrest harmless visitors to their temple and then rough them up. And why
have restricted areas? I think the lieutenant had good
reason to suspect criminal intent."

Kanshin fidgeted. "Well," he said, "it appears to
have been a misunderstanding. Your lordship must be
aware that Enryaku-ji faces constant threats from our
enemies. We are forced to protect ourselves."

Akitada ignored this. Stepping to Tora, he asked,
"Are you all right?"

Tora moved his shoulders as if checking for damage, then nodded. "I seem to be in one piece, sir. No
thanks to these thugs."

Akitada turned back to Kanshin. "You will return
Lieutenant Sashima's armor and sword, as well as his
horse. Then I want the chains on that man." He point-

ed at the *sohei* with the tattoo. "He's being sought by the Otsu police in connection with crimes against citizens. There are others, but this man has been recognized."

Kanshin blanched. "Impossible. I cannot permit it."

"You cannot refuse an order from an imperial investigator, Prior. Such an action would have an impact on the present investigation into the charges brought against Enryaku-ji."

"But the charges were brought by us against Onjo-ji."

Akitada smiled coldly. "It works both ways, Prior."

Kanshin cringed, then nodded. "Very well. If the man is indeed found guilty, we will not stand in your way."

"Then let's go home!"

16

Spring Rain

The return journey was, if anything, more miserable than their earlier ascent to Enryaku-ji. They had Tora back, but the continuous rain became more aggravating now that this worry was gone. The horses slipped on wet rocks and mud so that the riders had to pay close attention. Their clothes, already wet, were becoming more so and chafing their necks. Thus, there was no conversation until Akitada, Tora, and Saburo reached Kosehira's villa and released their escort for the remainder of the trip down into Otsu and to the tribunal.

As they dismounted in the villa's courtyard and handed their horses to a groom, Akitada said, "Let's see if we cannot get a bath."

They could and met again in the villa's roomy tub to soak away the miseries of the day, or in Tora's case, of several days.

Tora was sore but relieved. "I think I'll sleep here tonight," he said, slipping lower in the hot water.

His bruised face made Akitada reconsider the lecture he had planned. "Did anything useful come out of your adventure?" he asked sourly.

"They blind-folded me and kept me locked up close. I thought that was strange, but maybe they meant to convert me."

"Nonsense. You were recognized." Akitada glared at him. "Your going there was a hare-brained idea."

"Yes, sir." Tora tried to look ashamed. "And I never saw Kinzaburo either."

Saburo said, "But we have one of the *sohei*. We can make him talk. I bet we'll learn all about Kinzaburo and a lot of other facts useful to his lordship."

Saburo was right. If the *sohei* would in fact confess. Akitada had some doubts about this. He said, "I don't approve of beating confessions out of prisoners."

At this point, they were interrupted. The door flew open and Kosehira bounced in.

"Ha, ha!" he cried, all smiles. "I just heard. There you are, Tora. Back with us, safe and sound." He took another look and added, "Poor fellow. Were they very rough?"

Tora sketched a bow. "Not at all. It's nothing, sir. Thank you for helping and sorry to give you so much trouble."

"Never mind that" Kosehira approached to peer at them more closely, then dipped a finger in the water. "Ha!" he said, "room for one more, I think," and started taking off his clothes.

Saburo whispered to Akitada, "I think I'd better say good night, sir."

Kosehira's hearing was excellent. "Don't you dare, Saburo," he said, stepping out of his full trousers and casting them carelessly on the pile of silk robes he had just removed. He was portly and performed his ablutions without embarrassment while carrying on the conversation. "Did you find that fellow you were looking for, Tora?"

"No, sir." Tora was smiling. Unlike Saburo, he was enjoying the prospect of sharing a bath with one of the great nobles in the land. He sobered. "They kept me locked up. I saw nothing. I figure they've got lots of secrets to protect."

"No doubt," muttered Kosehira, casting a leg over the side of the tub and plunging in, sending hot water over the side and its three occupants. "Ahhh, hmmm!" he sighed, closing his eyes. "That's better."

For a while they enjoyed the warmth silently. Akitada recalled his fear that Lady Yukiko would someday surprise him in his bath and quickly banished the thought again.

"So," said Kosehira and looked at Tora, "it was all for nothing?"

"Afraid so, sir."

"Not quite," said Akitada. "I arrested one of the *sohei* involved in the attack on Kinzaburo and his family. He's safely in the tribunal jail by now."

Kosehira's eyes widened. "Did you, now? How did you manage that?"

"Tora pointed out his tattoo. Tomorrow, we'll transfer him to the Otsu jail and confront him with witnesses. He won't be terrorizing women and children again."

"He's a stupid bastard," said Tora, cheerful again. "Couldn't resist being the one to bring me out in chains."

"I can't believe they let you take him." Kosehira was dumfounded. "He can claim sanctuary on temple land."

Akitada smiled. "I told them I have extraordinary powers while I'm looking into this matter of temple improprieties."

"And do you?"

"No. At least I don't think so. It was the best I could do at the moment. If we had left without him, we'd never have seen him again."

Kosehira burst out laughing. "I don't believe it. You stood right there before the abbot and took one of his men?"

"It was the prior Kanshin. The monk who paid me a visit earlier. The abbot did not seem interested in getting involved."

"Ah. I've only met old Gyomei once. Yes, he either pretends to be above all this wrangling or he really has no idea what is going on." Kosehira had become serious again. "I don't have to tell you how difficult things have been with Enryaku-ji and Onjo-ji squabbling like bad little boys while they are grabbing land right and left. I've been told many times that I have no power to administer my own province. It seems most of it is owned by the temples."

This was the first time Kosehira had voiced a complaint. Akitada looked at his friend with new eyes. He wanted to know more about his life but could not ask with Tora and Saburo present, so he only said, "I hope I haven't caused trouble for you. Tora thinks the man will talk when confronted by local witnesses."

Tora nodded. "Those tough-looking bastards with tattoos always end up being cowards," he said bitterly.

"Well then, tell me everything that happened," Kosehira said.

They complied, taking turns. At one point, Kosehira was shocked to hear that the monks had taken Tora's horse.

"Can't have monks stealing horses," he muttered.

Saburo, who had been fairly quiet, said, "They do so already and have been doing it for years. They claim shipments of horses for the temple even though they come from private estates and are intended for the market in the capital."

Kosehira looked astonished. "You know this for a fact?"

Akitada said, "Saburo was once one of them. Or rather, he was a *sohei* who spent some interesting time on Mount Hiei."

Kosehira's eyes widened again. "Really? Is that . . . I mean did they . . .?" His eyes were searching Saburo's face.

Saburo looked away. "Yes, sir."

"Dear gods!" Kosehira fell silent. After a while, he got out of the bath. "I think I have enough to occupy my mind for a while," he said, sounding dejected.

Akitada joined him. "I'm sorry, Kosehira," he said softly. "I did not mean to spoil your well-deserved relaxation."

"No, no," said Kosehira, wrapping a cotton gown around his paunch. "Will you join us for dinner?"

"Thank you. That's very kind of your ladies."

Kosehira smiled. "It's among his family that a man finds true happiness, Akitada. Remember that."

∞

It was still raining steadily later when Akitada made his way along the covered gallery toward the pavilion of Kosehira's ladies. The garden lay in a green haze, the leaves glistening and the blooms on the azaleas drooping with moisture. A warm scent of wet earth, moss, and growing things came from the ground and, as he passed an azalea growing close to the gallery, its heady scent filled the moist air with an almost intoxicating power. He stopped to breathe more deeply and was filled with a great longing for Tamako.

Her scent had been orange blossoms, but he recalled her vividly in their own spring garden, bending over a flowering azalea to breathe in its fragrance. Kosehira had been right. His true happiness had been then, with her and the children in their garden. And he had lost it.

"Akitada?"

He returned from his dream of happier times and saw that Yukiko had come from the pavilion, perhaps to fetch him or to greet him. She had paused a little distance away, looking like a spring flower herself in her pink robe.

"I'm sorry, Lady Yukiko," he said, taking a guilty pleasure in seeing her pretty face, that graceful figure in pale rosy silks. Had not his wife favored this color? She had been quite different from this charming girl. Tamako had worn her clothes with a quiet grace; Yuki-ko had the quick movements of a young deer. Emotion suddenly constricted his throat.

But Yukiko came toward him slowly, almost shyly. "I'm the one who is sorry. I interrupted your thoughts. You looked happy."

"A delightful interruption. Am I late for dinner?"

"No. I came out to smell the rain. The garden always smells quite wonderful at this time." She chuckled softly. "Do you smell it, too? The azaleas. I love the scent. It's always especially intense in a slow rain."

"I had the same thought a moment ago. Your garden is beautiful in all kinds of weather."

"You will always be welcome here."

It was a strange thing to say. He was a guest, a temporary visitor who must leave, perhaps never to return. "Thank you." He looked out over the garden once more, and she came to stand beside him.

"You are lonely, I think," she said softly. "I know all about loneliness."

He was startled and upset by her comment. "How can you be lonely here amidst your family. I would think you would never wish to leave them."

She looked up at him, her eyes sad. "One can be lonely in a crowd. I love my family, but I feel they have their own lives, that I am somehow apart." She turned away. "And adrift."

She said this last in a voice filled with such sorrow that Akitada reached out to put his hand on her shoulder. She made a small sound, turned toward him, and came into his arms, laying her head against his chest.

Akitada's thoughts were in turmoil. What had happened to her to cause such sadness? How could he make things better? And then: what was he doing, standing here, holding Kosehira's daughter in his arms? Someone might come at any moment. Yet he drew her a little closer. The top of her head almost reached his eyes. Her hair gleamed a beautiful bluish black, and he could see part of her neck, just below a dainty ear. It was a neck he wanted to kiss so very much that he felt his hands trembling with the effort not to do so.

All around them, the rain fell with a soft music of its own, and the scent of spring flowers and warm, moist earth filled the air. At that moment, Akitada knew he was lost.

Somehow they parted, neither speaking, and walked slowly toward the pavilion.

Akitada did not know how he managed to get through the cheerful family meal on this occasion. He ate automatically, answered absent-mindedly, and tried not to look at Yukiko. He failed miserably. A few times their eyes met and both looked away quickly.

He lay awake for a long time that night, torn by longing and ashamed. Somewhere among the muddle of thoughts and dreams and fears, he wondered what she would do if he asked her father for her.

It was conceivable that she would accept. She had spoken of her admiration for him. Mistaken though she was about his past, it might be enough for her to agree to marry a man who could be her father.

But he could not, would not do that to her. He would never ruin a young woman's future simply because he had fallen in love with her. She deserved better than an elderly and low-ranking official without prospects, but with a family and a past. Kosehira's oldest daughter could become an imperial consort, and if not that, the wife of a prince of the blood or a chancellor.

No, he could not do that to her. Especially not when he loved her.

And that meant his life here in Otsu, in Kosehira's household, had become unbearable.

17

Raid on the Tribunal

Akitada was woken by one of Kosehira's servants. When he felt the gentle touch on his shoulder, he turned toward it, thinking in his half-awake state that it was Yukiko. Perhaps . . . Yukiko in his bed . . . ready to come into his arms. He muttered something.

"Wake up, sir! There's news from the tribunal."

It was night, and he had some excuse for his confusion. Blinking, Akitada sat up. "What?" he asked. What happened?"

"There's been an attack on the tribunal, sir. His Excellency said to get you up. He's leaving for town now."

"An attack?" Akitada scrambled up. The servant, a dimly seen figure by the light of the single oil lamp he must have brought and set down near the door, held out his trousers for him.

"Yes. On the tribunal. In the middle of the night. There are many dead."

Akitada asked no more questions. With the man's help, he threw on his clothes, stepped into his boots, and ran outside.

"In the courtyard, sir," the servant shouted after him. "They're waiting for you."

It was still dark outside. Impossible to tell the time. The rain had stopped, but there was a thick cloud cover. The courtyard was lit by torches. By their light, Akitada saw some eight mounted men and a group of others on foot.

Kosehira called out to him, "Hurry! We have your horse."

He saw that Tora, also mounted, held the rein. Saburo was with him. Akitada swung himself in the saddle and asked, "What happened? Somebody attacked the tribunal?"

Kosehira said, "*Sohei,*" and Akitada realized the magnitude of the mistake he had made.

"Dear heaven," he said. "I'm sorry, Kosehira. I should have thought they'd try to get him out."

Kosehira said gruffly, "You informed me. It was up to me to warn the tribunal. Let's hope it isn't too bad. They drove them off."

Akitada guiltily recalled his self-satisfaction in announcing his arrest of the tattooed *sohei*. Kosehira had been delighted by the tale. It struck him for the first time that Kosehira's faith in him was not only greatly exaggerated, but positively dangerous. But he said nothing. There was nothing to say and no time.

The gates to the tribunal opened, and armed guards clustered around them. In the courtyard, torches lit the scene, adding to the sense of disaster. The soldiers parted to let the governor and his people through.

Inside they found a scene of chaos. Blood spattered the gravel, and several bodies lay about as soldiers hurried to stand at attention. On the veranda of the main building clustered servants and clerks who had been stationed in the tribunal overnight.

The captain of the provincial guard met Kosehira and saluted. "There were about twenty of them, Excellency," he said. "They forced their way in, claiming they were under orders to pick up the prisoner. Because they were from Enryaku-ji, the gate guards admitted them. They got all the way to the jail where Sergeant Okura met them and refused to release the prisoner. That's when they drew their weapons."

Kosehira'a eyes searched the courtyard. "How many hurt?"

"Two of ours are dead, sir. Sergeant Okura is severely wounded. He doesn't look good. Fifteen wounded. Five of theirs are dead. They took their wounded."

Sickened by what had happened here, Akitada dismounted.

Tora's voice cut across the sober exchange between Kosehira and the captain. "Where's Okura, Captain?"

The captain gestured toward the barracks, and Tora rode over, dismounted, and went inside. Akitada walked from body to body, forcing himself to look at what he had caused. In some cases, it was difficult to tell if the dead were *sohei* or guards. Only two wore the white cowl on their heads. The rest had the same armor as all soldiers and had not shaved their heads or facial hair. In a few cases, Akitada noted that their weapons were *naginata*, the halberds preferred over the sword by many *sohei*. Given that they had had no warning, the tribunal guards must have fought like tigers.

Kosehira joined him. "These men don't look like monks," he said.

"They don't all take vows. And besides, Enryaku-ji may well have added mercenaries to its own army."

Kosehira shook his head. "Terrible."

Akitada straightened up from peering at the face of a very young soldier who had bled to death when halberds had severed his leg. "One of yours?" he asked.

Kosehira nodded. "I think so. He's so young. What will his parents do?"

The elderly depended on their children to support them. Akitada had no idea how aged or needy this family might be, but the loss of even one promising son and his income would be a blow. He sighed. "I am to blame, and I will speak to the parents of the men you lost when your people tell me more about them."

"Nonsense. You are not to blame. When provincial guards sign on for duty, they expect to risk their lives protecting the tribunal and those in it."

"Nevertheless I must express my condolences. Apparently, the brutes got the prisoner."

"A pity. Okura was a very brave man, and so were the others."

"Yes, Tora likes Okura very much. Let's go see the wounded."

More dismal sights met their eyes there, but at least the men who lay side by side in one of the barracks rooms had been tended, and their wounds had been bandaged. Sergeant Okura was the most seriously hurt, having received two sword wounds and a slash from a halberd. Tora was kneeling by his side. On the other side crouched a young doctor Akitada recognized. He was pleased to see they had sent for Dr. Kimura.

Kosehira bent over the wounded man, "My dear sergeant," he said, "how are you feeling?"

Okuro tried to smile and made a halfhearted attempt to sit up and bow but was firmly pressed back down by Kimura. "I'm all right," Okura said, his voice croaking a little at the pain his movement had caused. "I'm sorry we lost the bastard."

"Nothing to apologize for." Tora said. "Nothing, when you resisted a force of some twenty men or more? It's a miracle you're alive. They'd better promote you for what you did last night."

Akitada cleared his throat, but Kosehira nodded. "Well said, Tora. But first Lieutenant Okura must get well. Doctor, a word?"

Kimura rose to his feet and walked away a little distance, leaving his patient with Tora. Akitada and

Kosehira joined him. Kosehira asked, "How is he really?"

"He lost a lot of blood and two of the wounds are deep. The third, to his shoulder, is minor since his armor protected him. The deeper wounds will become poisoned, I expect, and he'll suffer a fever, but with great diligence to the dressings and to containing the fever, he should survive. If the leg wound worsens, he may lose his leg."

Kosehira sighed and said, "Dreadful! I count on you, doctor. He's a good man."

"I'll do my best, Excellency."

Kosehira glanced around the room. "And the others?"

"The others should do well enough." Kimura paused. "Judging by the bodies of your enemies outside, they must *all* be good men."

Kosehira smiled. "Yes. They are! They are all very good men! How lucky I am!"

Akitada did not see much luck in the event, but he said nothing. He felt depressed and discouraged.

∞

A strange thing happened that day. When he returned to his room at Kosehira's villa many hours later, he saw that the servants had tidied it, rolled up his bedding and taken away his wet clothes. But on his desk lay something new, a letter folded many times around a flowering branch. The blooms were azaleas, but sadly crushed and wilted.

He picked it up. The letter had been crumpled as if someone had trodden on it. His stomach lurched when he realized it was from Yukiko.

How had it got here? Had she brought it while he was gone?

No, surely not. She would not have left such a thing in open sight for the servants to find. No, she must have brought it during the night and pushed it under the door, and neither he nor the servant who had come to wake him had noticed it. In the dark, they had stepped on it, and later a servant had found it and placed it on the desk.

Slowly, fearfully, he untied the letter and unfolded it. It was a poem.

"The drops of pattering rain did not wet my sleeves;
It was my loneliness . . . and yours."

He swallowed hard, then raised the paper to his lips. Dear heaven, what was he to do? He could not answer, must not acknowledge this. He must not do anything to make things worse.

The pain of that restraint would be with him from now on, and every day would remind him how close she was, how easy it would be to go to her.

Her words told him she was lonely . . . no, that she was lonely for him. In vain, he tried to comprehend the astonishing fact that she loved him.

What could so young a girl know of love? Love brought with it pain, the fear of loss. He had lost the son he had loved more than his life and nearly gone mad with the grief. And then he had lost Tamako and had wanted to die. He knew the price of love.

He refolded the letter carefully and inserted it in the thin notebook he carried with him. It would be safer to destroy it, but that he could not do.

∞

Over the coming days, his despair did not exactly lift, but it moderated somewhat. The attack on the provincial headquarters by a large group of Enryaku-ji *sohei* had a number of major repercussions that were mostly desirable. At any rate, they kept both Akitada and Kosehira far too busy to spend much time at home.

Item: Both Kosehira and Akitada dispatched reports to the emperor. These resulted in numerous visits from senior officials to the governor as well as to Abbot Gyomei of Enryaku-ji.

Item: Abbot Gyomei for once left his mountain and visited Kosehira and Akitada to deliver his personal regrets. He told them that neither the attackers nor the prisoner had returned to the temple.

Item: Bands of *sohei* and other warriors left the mountain temple and departed to other provinces.

Item: As a result, a similar exodus took place from Onjo-ji, presumably because it no longer felt the need for an army to defend itself against Enryaku-ji's troops.

Item: After due investigation, the court issued several strongly-worded proclamations against the raising of troops by temples or shrines.

This last item had merely symbolic significance; private estates could still hire men to protect themselves. In fact, the largest landowners maintained standing armies. And since many of the estates existed under the protection of temples in order to avoid taxes, it was merely a matter of calling up support when needed.

But there was no sign of the escaped *sohei.*

Still, Kosehira regained his sunny mood and congratulated Akitada on having struck a major blow against that pesky Enryaku-ji. It helped that the wounded tribunal guards made excellent progress. Even Lieutenant Okura was out of danger. This greatly pleased Tora who had spent most of his time by his bedside.

Throughout this time, more delegations from Enryaku-ji arrived, often led by the prior himself. Their intention was to declare their peacefulness and their complete support for the emperor and his representative, the governor. They also renewed apologies to Akitada, making him a present of a very fine horse. Akitada refused the gift, which struck him as close to being a bribe.

In this manner, nearly two weeks passed. During the entire time, both Akitada and Kosehira were so busy that they only spent the nights at the villa. Akitada slept the sleep of the exhausted and was relieved that his dreams did not involve Lady Yukiko. He saw her a few times from a distance. Once or twice she was standing on the veranda as they arrived or departed. He avoided the garden for fear of surprising her there.

Only one other thing troubled Akitada from time to time. He worried that, for all his bravado and cheerfulness, Tora had suffered some lingering physical damage. His movements had become slower and there were times when he grimaced at some exertion, such as getting on his horse or rising up from the floor. After nearly a week, he and Tora took up their sword practice again, but Tora seemed listless uncomfortable. They practiced behind the kitchen building where no one saw them except the cook and his staff.

After their second bout since Tora's stay on the mountain, Akitada asked, "Are you sure you are feeling all right? Should you be checked out by Kimura?"

"I'm fine, sir," Tora said, turning away. "Forget it. I'm just getting old and useless."

Sorry that he had spoken, Akitada said, "Nonsense," and did not mention it again. But he sent Tora home for a while to look after things and rest.

He saw Takechi several times. The prisoner had been identified by temple authorities as Kojo and said to be an ex-soldier who had taken vows. On the governor's orders, wanted posters were put up all over Otsu and along the highways east and west. So far there had been no results.

Among the gestures of apology extended by Enryaku-ji was also the promise to help in the conviction of the criminal *sohei* and mercenaries. The temple wished to disassociate itself completely from the incident. A delegation of monks paid a visit to Kosehira to inform him that Kojo had been officially dismissed and would be unwelcome on Enryaku-ji if he should seek assistance there.

Kinzaburo had been returned to his small farm. Reunited with his family, he still faced a legal battle for his freedom. The noble lord who held sway over Kinzaburo's farm had turned over his authority to the temple to avoid taxes. Kinzaburo's small portion of land had somehow become part of the great estate.

But on the whole, Tora's adventure with the *sohei* had ended well.

Chief Takechi said as much to Akitada, adding, "I wish I could report progress for the two murders. However, a strange story's just come to my ears."

Akitada, who had not given Takechi's murders much attention, said, "Really? Something to do with the judge?"

"Not the judge. Or the jailer for that matter. No, it's about that Jizo figurine. Something happened in the Echi district east of here. They had two unexplained, and so far unsolved, deaths. Two elderly peasants, best friends, were found dead within days of each other. They interrogated the families but found no motive, though in the first case, which was clearly a murder, they briefly arrested the man's daughter-in-law. In the end they couldn't prove anything. But when they were searching the area where it happened—the old-timer was drunk and on his way home when someone struck him from behind—they found one of those carvings among the weeds beside the road."

Akitada sat up and stared at the chief. "You don't say? The same carving? The same sort of figurine as the one in the judge's room and on the body of the jailer? And both men were old, you say?"

Takechi nodded. "Yes, it's very strange."

A silence fell as Akitada tried to understand how a cheap and common little thing like the Jizo carving could suddenly appear near the bodies of murdered men in distant locales.

Takechi scratched his head. "It could be a coincidence. Those Jizo figures are common enough along the great highway. Many travelers buy them. And besides, it may have been lying there for days before the murder."

"I don't like this, Takechi," Akitada said. "We have to look into it. When were those two men killed?"

Takechi reached for a document. "More than a month ago. The peasant called Wakiya died on the night between the twelfth and thirteenth day of the second month, his friend Juro three days later, on the evening of the fifteenth day. Mind you, they found no Jizo with the second man. And his death may have been an accident. He was drunk and fell into a gorge."

"For purpose of discussion, let's include him. The judge died . . . let's see, that was this month, wasn't it?"

"Yes. On the second day. And Tokuno died on the fifth day of this month."

Another silence fell. Finally Takechi asked, "What are you thinking?"

"It seems inconceivable, but it looks as if someone is going around killing elderly men and leaving small Jizo carvings near their bodies."

"But why?"

"If we knew that, we'd know how long it has been happening and how many more will die. It may be significant that they are all old and all men."

Takechi shook his head. "But to kill people just because they are old? That's terrible."

"Yes. And if it is their age that makes him kill them, it will go on. This person won't be satisfied with the deaths of the four men we know about. Since you have only just heard about the two peasants, there could have been other deaths. Perhaps they remained unsolved, or worse, an innocent person was convicted."

"We must find out, but where to begin?"

"The connection between Nakano and the jailer is weak. Now we have two more deaths that may be linked to each other but don't connect to the ones here. The best solution would be if there were a connection because then we might know why they were killed and by whom."

"The two from Okuni were ordinary peasants, sir. They've lived in the village all their lives. What could link them to Otsu and a judge?

Akitada got up. "I suppose for the answer we must go to that village and find out, don't you think?"

18

Poems

Neither Akitada nor Takechi could drop everything to travel to a small village called Okuni at a time when both were extremely busy. They merely agreed that they would have to go as soon as a chance offered.

Takechi returned to his regular duties, and Akitada immersed himself in the paperwork for Onjo-ji and Enryaku-ji.

One morning Akitada found another poem. It had also been slipped it under his door, but he found it before the servants could.

It was from Yukiko and the contents were upsetting enough.

"In the garden, the cuckoo called, but when I looked, I only saw the moon," she had written, then added, "Why have you grown distant?"

He sighed in exasperation. What was he to do? Speaking to her would merely worsen things. Besides, he did not really trust himself. He could not write her. Exchanging love letters with his friend's daughter under his own roof was reprehensible. For the first time, he considered taking flight and returning to the capital. In the end, he did nothing, knowing it was cowardly.

Kosehira had kept his promise of having his staff search the archives for cases handled by Judge Nakano during his years of service. These documents arrived in Akitada's room at the tribunal the day after his conversation with Takechi. He regarded the number of boxes resting on his desk with a frown, then sighed and started on the first one.

By midday, he had only covered half of Nakano's trials. If anything of note was in those documents, it suggested that Nakano was an indifferent judge who frequently ignored witnesses produced by the defendant and rushed to judgment without much regard to due process. But the cases were old, the defendants who had been found guilty were either patently guilty or most likely long since dead. From the dubious cases, Akitada made a small list of names. This included one where a woman was charged with drowning her newborn child. She confessed readily enough, saying that she and her husband were too poor to feed another child. A sad case, especially since her sentence of a public lashing was so brutal that it was fatal. Still, he made a note of it because it might account for the Jizo. The little god protected children who had died before hearing of Buddha.

The other cases concerned men who might have claimed mitigating circumstances, particularly where death was the result of a brawl. There was a lot of fighting in a harbor town.

He stopped at noon and decided to invite Takechi to a bowl of noodle soup. It would give them a chance to discuss the murders.

Takechi was at police headquarters, looking distracted as he sifted through the day's new paperwork. He accepted the invitation eagerly, and they walked the short distance to the large and popular restaurant.

When they had given the waiter their order, Takechi asked, "Have you had any news of Kojo since the raid?"

"No. By all accounts, he's an ugly customer. He took his fury out on his guards at the tribunal. I'm almost sorry that we no longer have the same customs Tokuno enjoyed."

Takechi grinned. "Me, too. Too bad we don't have a confession."

"What about the witnesses? They can identify him, can't they?"

Takechi nodded. "Yes, but without the four men, we don't have enough to go to trial. Still, the governor will be glad to be rid of the fellow. Those *sohei* make dangerous enemies."

The waiter returned with two large bowls of noodles and smaller bowls of pickled radish. The noodles were in an appetizing broth, and several large slices of fish rested on top. They began to eat. The soup was delicious.

Takechi lowered his half-empty bowl first. "If they catch Kojo or the others, we'll have to bring Kinzaburo back for the trial. The aged neighbor woman got a good look at Kojo. She was positive he was the ringleader of the four who abducted Kinzaburo. She was pretty sure he was also with the three that returned to take their turns raping his wife. Unfortunately, the wife will not testify. She's frightened and ashamed."

"Given what a brute he is, it's amazingly courageous of the neighbor," Akitada said, setting down his empty bowl.

"Yes. I wish they were all like that. Mind you, she was filled with a righteous anger. I got the feeling she was more upset about the rapes than about the abduction."

Akitada pondered this. Surely rape wasn't as bad as murder or a severe beating. Women got raped all the time because some men had a notion that the woman's resistance was merely a token sign of propriety and that the woman in the end enjoyed it as much as the man. He knew this was not always true. Some women really were forced—and surely Kinzaburo's wife was one of them—against their will. But did they receive any lasting damage?

He voiced the thought to Takechi who considered the idea before saying, "A wife would fear that her husband will reject her after another man has misused her."

"Perhaps, but surely then the blame falls on the husband. That is, if she was in fact a helpless victim."

"Yes, but there's a problem. What if he doesn't believe her?"

Akitada sighed. "Well, in this case at least we know she's innocent and those men behaved like animals."

"Worse. I don't believe animals engage in group rape."

They had finished their soup and exchanged a glance. "Another?" Akitada suggested.

Takechi nodded. "It *is* very good." He asked, "Did you find out anything about the judge and the jailer?"

"I've been going through Nakano's cases all morning. There was little that stood out." Akitada told him about the sentences he recalled as being harsher or more undeserved than the rest.

Takechi shook his head at the child-drowning. "I know the family," he said. "A sad story. She had five children in six years and her husband beat her regularly. He drank and gambled. After her death, he took in a number of loose women. Beat them, too, but they had the good sense to leave him. He died in a brawl, I believe. To everyone's amazement, the children turned out well. Hard-working, all of them. The girls married good husbands, and the boys have trades they made a success of. You never know, do you?"

Akitada shook his head. "Any chance one of the children would avenge their mother?"

"I'd say none."

"Well, I'll keep looking. So far there's nothing on Tokuno but the fact that their years of service must have overlapped."

"Yes. But what does that mean? Judges and jailers never meet. The judge hears the case and pronounces sentence, and the jailer looks after the prisoners before and after the trial, at least until they are sent into exile."

"That poor woman who drowned her child. She died after a brutal sentence of whipping. Could Tokuno have swung the whip?"

"Maybe, but usually there's a special man for the public punishments."

They had finished their second bowls of soup more glumly than the first. Takechi was the first to find his smile again. "Thank you for this excellent meal. I hope you'll allow me to reciprocate soon?"

"Certainly. I enjoyed this very much. Perhaps I'll have a more useful report next time."

As they parted in front of police headquarters, Akitada thought again how much he liked Takechi. Their backgrounds were too different to allow the sort of friendship that existed between him and Kosehira, but if things had been otherwise, Akitada would have liked to count Takechi among his close friends.

∞

At sundown, Akitada finished with the documents relating to Judge Nakano. He had added a few more names to his list of suspicious cases, but nothing struck him as promising. With a sigh, he went to see if Kosehira was ready to leave.

At home, another poem awaited him:

"That scent of sandalwood on your sleeve; it is with me still. But I lie awake and only the moon lights my room."

It was a seductive verse, and it's invitation was clear. He grew warm at the thought of Yukiko, half asleep in her bedding, longing for him. Biting his lip with frustration, he crumpled up the letter. What did she expect? That he would slip into her room under cover of darkness to make love to her? Yes, he thought, that was precisely what she suggested.

He spent a very disturbed night, worried that she might take the initiative and come to him instead.

∞

In the morning, an excited Kosehira greeted him. He was waving a letter in the air.

"Look at this!" he cried. "It took me by surprise."

Akitada approached warily. Letters had become dangerous in his recent experience. But Kosehira was smiling.

"It couldn't be better!" he said "And I didn't have to wrangle an invitation. Here! Read!"

Akitada took the letter. Scanning it quickly, he saw that it was from Nakahara Nariyuki. He vaguely knew him as a prominent nobleman who was in the service of the retired emperor. The letter was an invitation to a pheasant hunt for Kosehira and Akitada. Puzzled by Kosehira's delight, he handed the missive back, saying, "Very kind of him, but I don't hunt. Still, I suppose I must accept. Where is his estate?"

"Oh, Nakahara lives here in Otsu. Has for years. His house is on the small side since he spends most of his time at His Retired Majesty's palace. As that is a short distance from Otsu, it's a feasible journey back and forth, but it means he doesn't entertain much. His staff is too small." Kosehira chortled. "If you ask me, he's a bit of a miser. Looks like he solved the problem of welcoming you by getting Taira Sukemichi to invite us to a hunt."

Akitada frowned. "I see. But that makes us Taira's guests, not Nakahara's. I should be able to get out of it."

Kosehira laughed again. "You don't understand how these things work, brother. Taira owes Nakahara a lot of favors. I think it was Nakahara who got his father the post of overseeing the imperial pheasant reserve. Now Nakahara is a regular guest at every hunt. And you cannot offend Nakahara. He's much too important in politics in the capital. Don't look so dejected. You'll like it. It's spring, the country around there is beautiful, and there is a surprise."

Akitada was afraid to ask. "What have you cooked up, Kosehira?"

"Taira's lands include Okuni. Now what do you say?"

"Okuni?" It took Akitada a moment to remember. "You mean the village where the two old men were killed?"

"The very one."

"Oh." Akitada considered. They would leave Otsu, and that was indeed fortuitous at the moment. And there was the promise of investigating the puzzle of the Jizo figures. Yes, it would be just as well to remove himself from the lovely Yukiko before he lost his mind completely. He smiled at his friend. "Very well, if you have a mind to go, I look forward to it. But Kosehira, keep in mind that I don't like killing animals for sport and haven't handled a bow in a decade or more."

"As to the bow, you won't need it. They use falcons. A very refined form of hunting that emperors engage in." He smiled broadly. "We'll make a nobleman of you yet."

They laughed.

Suddenly Akitada felt lighthearted again. Kosehira always had this effect on him.

∞

But the next morning brought another poem. He heard the letter slide under his door.

She had written, "The storms of spring have scattered the blossoms, and my heart has grown wintry cold." This time she had added, "I must see you before you leave!" and had underlined the "must."

He felt a sudden fear that she might do something rash unless he talked to her. Tucking the note away, he opened the shutters to look out.

The stars were still out though the night sky paled in the east. They were to make an early start, and any moment a servant would come to wake Akitada. No doubt Kosehira and his family were also stirring. It was an impossible time for a meeting.

Yet Akitada dressed quickly and went out into the dark garden. It was still filled with scent of late azaleas and other flowers. In the dim light under the trees he walked carefully. She was waiting at the koi pond as he had guessed and looked up at his step.

"Who is it?" she asked softly.

"Akitada," he said in an equally low voice. "This isn't wise, Lady Yukiko. We may be seen."

"I don't care." She came quickly to him. "I had to see you before you go," she said. "There was no other way since you would not come to me."

He flinched. He could not see her face clearly, but thought she looked pale and tense. Perhaps this mood was preferable to the passionate declarations of love, but it suggested that he had caused her pain. He felt a wave of tenderness. He did not want to hurt her.

"Forgive me," he said gently. "It has pained me greatly to treat you this way. I have been a coward."

She said nothing to this but lowered her eyes.

"I'm not worthy of your fondness, Yukiko. You must not think of me any longer. Not in this way. I . . . I cannot be what you wish."

She made an impatient sound and turned away. He felt like a brute.

"Yukiko," he pleaded, "you have honored me beyond anything a poor fellow like me deserves. But I am your father's age. In fact, we call each other 'brother.' You must see that I can be no more than an uncle to you and his other children."

She still said nothing. There was a strange stiffness to her slender back. He wanted to go to her and hold her, but this time he would not do so.

He said uncertainly, "It hurts me very much to see you like this."

She turned then, and he saw in the dim light that she had been crying. "No," she said, dabbing impatiently at her face with one of her sleeves, "It's not your fault. I'm ashamed. I have been foolish and must ask your pardon for behaving like a silly, love-struck girl. You see, I'd been encouraged to think you might . . . no, I won't blame others." She covered her face with her hands, then looked up again. Her eyes were swimming in tears. "What you must think of me! I'm not at all this way as a rule. I'm quite sensible. I never write poems to men, not even in my thoughts."

He said helplessly, "They are lovely poems. I shall treasure them."

She raised her chin a little. "I made a mistake. You see, I thought—mistakenly—that you liked me. That you were just shy, or reluctant to approach me because I am my father's daughter. I know better now. Please forgive me for having troubled you."

"There's nothing to forgive." He wanted to tell her that she had filled his heart with joy and love again, but that was impossible. In the end, he simply added, "I must go. They will be looking for me. Good bye, Lady Yukiko."

As he turned away, he felt sick with the pain of this parting.

19

Falconry

Kosehira was puzzled by Akitada's mood on the long ride to the imperial pheasant reserve and kept trying to cheer him up. He pointed out that the weather was clear, the rice paddies already green with new rice, and ahead lay some fine entertainment. After several miles of silence or mono-syllabic comments, he asked, "Is anything the matter, brother? You seem very glum. Is it the hunting still that troubles you?"

Akitada returned to the present and forced himself to smile at Kosehira. "Nothing is wrong, brother," he lied, then offered, "I'm a little preoccupied with those Jizo murders. If someone is going around killing people, he must be stopped quickly. Unfortunately, I don't know where to begin to look for him. If the two murders at Okuni turn out to have been the work of the same killer, we have a very serious problem. I'm sorry if I'm bad company. I shall try to do better."

"Granted this seems to be a puzzling case, but you could let the police worry about it for a while." Seeing Akitada's face, he laughed. "Never mind. I do appreciate your concern and you'll get your chance. Tonight, however, I'm afraid you'll have to be nice to your hosts and partake of the welcome dinner they will have arranged for us."

Akitada, a little ashamed that he had been unappreciative of Kosehira's efforts to entertain him, said, "Perhaps you might tell me a little about them and their passion for falcons so I won't make a fool of myself tonight."

Kosehira complied eagerly.

"As I told you, Nakahara serves the retired emperor, the father of His current Majesty. His passion for the falcon hunt goes back to his youth when he attended His Majesty Sanjo on such occasions. He recommended Taira Sukenori for the position of supervisor of the imperial pheasant reserve, a nice little assignment that brings in both a salary and hunting privileges." Kosehira chuckled. "You'd be surprised how many people owe favors to each other and to people above them. Nakahara is able to offer us a special entertainment because Taira owes him this favor."

"And do we owe Nakahara now?"

"No. Don't worry. We are simply receiving a courtesy."

"I'm relieved."

"Taira Sukenori has died, but his son Sukemichi now holds the post. More favors were called in."

Akitada sighed. "I'll never learn this game. My sister is the one who takes an interest in such things."

Kosehira laughed. "You don't need to learn it, but it's good to know those things. It makes it easier to deal with people. And once you get past their commitments, you may find them entertaining creatures after all."

"I hope so. I'm trying to convince myself that familiarity with pheasant reserves and hunting with hawks may come in handy one of these days."

They were traveling with two of Kosehira's servants who followed behind. Tora had begged off to spend time at home with Hanae. Akitada had been glad. Since his stay on the mountain, Tora had seemed gloomy and distracted. Akitada hoped his family would cheer him up.

He had his own wounds to lick. The parting from Yukiko had been awkward for both of them, but she had carried it off rather better than he. Her apology, delivered in the face of his avoidance of her, had been admirably brave. Where he had taken the coward's way out, she had faced him. Akitada had never thought of himself as an unfeeling cad where women were concerned, but that was precisely what he had become. He had made her cry, and that was unforgiveable.

Shaking off these unpleasant memories, he made an effort to chat with Kosehira and to take an interest in the sights on the way.

Being on horseback again was pleasant for a change. The road was the Nakasendo, a wide and busy stretch of highway which passed along Lake Biwa and connected to the Tokaido, the great Eastern Highway. He caught broad views of the great lake, blue under sunny skies and dotted here and there with the sails of fishing boats. Now and then larger ships passed on their way to Otsu or back to Hikone. To his left stretched fields toward wooded hills, and up ahead the Suzuka Mountains were blue in the distance. There was a good deal of traffic, both by foot and on horseback. Occasional ox-drawn wagons caused brief slow-downs. But the people were entertaining and interesting and gradually Akitada's depression lifted.

Toward sunset, they arrived tired and dusty at their destination in the foothills of the Suzuka Mountains. The Taira manor was a large walled compound and, being near the highway, used to offering shelter to important travelers. In this case, they were expected, and servants rushed to take their horses and to announce them.

Their host greeted them on the wide veranda of the main house. Taira Sukemichi was their age, in his early forties, a handsome man with a small mustache and a ready smile. Apparently he led an active life, for he was lean of body and brown from being out in the sun. He was also affable, greeting them with expressions of joy at seeing Kosehira again and at making the acquaintance of the "famous" Akitada.

Akitada, who hated flattery and knew he was anything but famous, shrank into himself and was at a loss for words. No matter. Kosehira and Sukemichi carried on a lively conversation. Akitada deduced that Nakahara was expected shortly and a fine dinner awaited them. Beyond this, the talk was of hunting and events in Otsu. Akitada listened, putting in an answer now and then about the *sohei* affair.

After a brief tour of the house, Sukemichi took them to a special room where he kept his birds. Akitada had expected these to stay in the stables, but apparently such creatures were highly prized and shared the main house with its owner.

Two servants were specifically assigned to care for the ten falcons. The *takajo*, or master falconer, greeted them and took them around. Along one wall of the room elaborate bamboo perches held the hawks which were displayed somewhat in the manner of fine horses in some wealthy men's stables, each bird occupying its own perch, tethered by silken cords with tassel in many colors. Noble birds indeed!

Akitada eyed them askance. Not only did he dislike their fierce stares and the way they ruffled their feathers when he approached, but he thought displaying wild birds in this manner and at such expense (given their special room, their silk ropes, and their personal keepers) was wasteful; and frivolous.

Sukemichi clearly did not share this view. He introduced each bird by name, giving its ancestry and value, and describing its performances enthusiastically. His father, he said, had also kept falcons and used them for hunting pheasants for the imperial table. He had frequently entertained important guests, though he had never been able to play host to an emperor.

"My father almost managed it once," Sukemichi said, "but then there was a murder here, and the investigation dragged on. In the end, the court canceled."

Akitada's ears sharpened. "A murder?" he asked.

Sukemichi looked a little embarrassed. "I wasn't here at the time. I was still a student at the university."

Kosehira made polite noises and asked a few questions about falconry, but Akitada did not bother. They were handsome birds in spite of their dangerous manner, but he hoped he would not be expected to carry one of them to the hunt scheduled for the next day.

Nakahara joined them soon after. He appeared to be in his sixties, was fat, pale-skinned, and had a mustache and goatee. After greeting Sukemichi and Kosehira effusively, he turned to Akitada. "What a great pleasure, Sugawara," he said, smiling. "I have looked forward to this with great anticipation. Are you still solving murder cases? I recall the whole capital was abuzz when you unmasked that insane painter who had been carving up his victims."

Akitada did not like to be reminded of that case. He had nearly lost his life when he went after the man who had abducted his little son Yori. He shuddered in retrospect and said, "Thank you, but my involvement was personal. The praise should go to the police who ultimately saved countless lives."

They parted company to retreat to their rooms and prepare for the festive dinner planned for that evening. Akitada feared more conversation about his past and began to feel resentful toward Kosehira for involving him in this visit. Nevertheless, he dressed with care before making his appearance in the room designated for the dinner. The others were already there, wearing their fine robes and chatting about the next day's hunt.

"It's late in the season," explained Sukemichi. "Hunting with hawks is mostly done in winter, but I thought it might be a pleasant entertainment for my friends, and as it happens we need to send some pheasants to the palace."

They were served roasted pheasant for their dinner, along with excellent fish from Lake Biwa and fresh vegetables. Sukemichi's wine was also superior, and Akitada mellowed considerably. Besides, the conversation concerned the pheasant reserve and Sukemichi's passion for hawks.

"My father taught me," he said. "He was a superb falconer. He also hunted with bow and arrow out of falcon season. For both types of hunting we have men go through the scrub land with sticks to scare out the birds. After that, they can be hunted either with bow and arrow or with hawks." He eyed his guests. "I have good horses. If you gentlemen would like to try your hand at hunting with bow and arrow, we can arrange this also."

Akitada said firmly, "Not on my account. I haven't shot an arrow in many years."

Kosehira laughed. "We'll settle for watching the falcons do the work. How do you train them?"

"Oh, my *takajo* does that. Though I buy most of my birds already trained. A trained bird will take down its prey and return to its master's hand where it is given a treat for good work. The dogs fetch the kill."

The pheasant meat was tasty, and Akitada thought the hunt might prove interesting after all. Not much seemed to be required of him besides his presence and praise. He asked, "So this practice has been going on here since long before your time?"

Sukemichi glanced across at Nakahara. "My father was the first in our family. It was an imperial appointment. After his death, the office passed to me. At first, my father had some trouble establishing himself among the locals. There were factions that supported another man, and they tried everything to blacken my father's character. Fortunately, he prevailed against his detractors."

The conversation turned to the proper preparation of pheasant. Akitada listened with half an ear. He thought the comment about Sukemichi's father and his troubles interesting. Information about the local people might throw a light on the murders of the two old men. When there was a lull in the chatter, he said, "Perhaps you can tell me something about the village Okuni. It's nearby, I think. What are the people like?"

Sukemichi looked surprised. "Oh, it's just a small place. Insignificant. Mostly rice farmers live there, and a few of our retainers and staff. It's pleasant enough, but up in the hills. The terrain is too awkward for hunting, but people aren't allowed to live on the reserve, so they built their houses there and carved out some rice paddies. The older people work the farms, while their children work for me or for the reserve. Why are you interested?"

"I heard they had two unexplained deaths recently. The victims died within days of each other. Both were old men on their way home after drinking."

Sukemichi nodded. "Yes, it's true. One was murdered. The other fell down the mountain because he was drunk. Drinking is a problem among some of the locals. But I'm surprised that you take an interest in peasants." He paused and frowned. "Come to think of it, I believe both used to work for my father and were given land when they left his service. The one who was murdered had also been drinking. Peasants tend to get carried away by festivals and cheap wine, and violence isn't unheard of under those circumstances. I doubt that the deaths merit your attention."

Kosehira chuckled. "Akitada takes an interest in all kinds of cases. And I promise you, if he starts poking around, he finds out the most shocking things."

The two other men smiled politely, but it seemed clear that they thought Akitada an eccentric and expected little excitement from the death of two old peasants.

The meal ended in the customary manner, with more wine consumed on the veranda where they had a fine view of the moonlit landscape stretching into the distance under a starry sky.

Later, when Akitada and Kosehira walked to the room they shared in the guest pavilion, Kosehira said, "You know, that business about Sukemichi's father having had some troubles after his appointment reminded me that someone accused him of having murdered a guest. It was just ill will. They caught the killer."

Akitada raised his brows. "You don't say? What happened?"

"I don't recall. But it was all very unpleasant until the *betto* confessed. It seems the guest had become too familiar with his daughter. It was shocking behavior by the guest, of course."

Akitada winced. It was an ugly tale and nothing to do with him. He had quite properly avoided an entanglement with Kosehira's daughter.

But the image of Yukiko haunted him that night.

20

The Hunt

As they were dressing in their hunting clothes the following morning, Kosehira observed, "You know, this business about favors owed and commitments bringing about mutual advantages, reminds me that there are better bonds, such as friendship and ties by marriage. You and I, we shall always rely on each other, I hope."

Akitada looked up from tying his trousers. "Well said. I'm very fond of you, Kosehira. That will never change. You have always supported me, even when doing so was very unpopular. But more than that, your cheerfulness lifts my dark spirits amazingly. Thank you, brother."

Kosehira looked embarrassed. "Not at all, brother. And didn't you come to my aid when I was accused of high treason?"

Akitada laughed. "Let's just say we try to look out for each other, which is as it should be."

"Yes," said Kosehira and reached for his boots. "And that will always be true even without family ties."

Akitada pondered this exchange all day, returning to it again and again. There had been something about Kosehira's remarks that had not been entirely casual. Why had Kosehira raised the subject of their friendship? They had never needed to mention it before.

The hunt was a much smaller version of the elaborate imperial celebrations memorable in the past. The current emperor was not interested in falconry, but his predecessors had enjoyed it and often participated themselves.

It was before dawn when the light was pale silver and wisps of fog lay over the dew-heavy fields of new grass. Sukemichi and his guests rode, Sukemichi with a bow slung over his shoulder. The falconers and dog handlers walked, carrying or leading their animals.

The air was particularly fresh and fragrant with green, growing things at this time of day. The hazy mountains, themselves draped in layers of white mists, rose against a faintly pearlescent morning sky, their crests already ringed with the gold of the rising sun. The sun would clear away the mists, and they would have another fine spring day.

Neither Akitada nor Kosehira had accepted the offer of a falcon. They said they preferred to watch.

Sukemichi planned to use his favorite, a white hawk called "Snow Dragon," while Nakahara had chosen a gray that was known for his aerial acrobatics and had the name "Storm Wing." The *takajo* carried a third hawk that was a little smaller than the other two.

"Ah," said Sukemichi, "the beaters are in place." He pointed across the plain of young grasses toward a belt of shrubs and small trees. Akitada saw nothing. They dismounted and Sukemichi and Nakahara each took one of the falcons.

"Let's start," Nakahara said. A shrill whistle sounded. Akitada saw some movement among the distant trees. A moment later, a pheasant flew up and Nakahara cried, "Get him!" tossing his falcon into the air. The bird caught itself and darted away, rising on powerful wings to intercept the pheasant which had stayed close to the ground. In a moment it was over. The hawk went in for the kill and both birds disappeared in the grasses. The whistle sounded again, and the hawk reappeared, without its prey, to return obediently to Nakahara's gloved hand, where he was fed a reward from a pouch Nakahara wore attached to his belt. One of the dogs, released, dashed off and returned a moment later with the dead pheasant

Before anyone could comment, more pheasants flew up, and both Sukemichi and the *takajo* released their birds. The white falcon was a beautiful sight as it rose into a blue sky and the rising sun caught it in flight, turning its wings to gold.

The hunt was a great success. They bagged sixteen pheasants and returned, accompanied by their attendants carrying the pheasants tied to poles. The beaters and falcon handlers sang, the dogs pranced, and their masters smiled contentedly.

A formal ceremony followed. Ten of the pheasants, suitably decorated with crimson ribbons and green branches, were dispatched to the retired emperor. A handsome Taira retainer carried them, dangling from his shoulder as he sat astride his horse.

Later a celebratory meal and plenty of *sake* awaited the hunters.

It was during this meal, served on the wide rear veranda of Sukemichi's house, that Nakahara turned to Kosehira and said, "Is it true what I hear, Governor? You are about to give your daughter in marriage to the eldest son of the chancellor?"

Akitada's eyes flew to Kosehira's face. Kosehira caught his glance, flushed, and looked away. "You're premature, Nakahara," he said. "The possibility has been mentioned, but you know how those things go. The chancellor and I are both considering our options. It's true that the young people know and like each other, being second cousins and spending time together as children, but no decision has been made. As for me, I confess I'm fond of Yukiko and shall not force her into a marriage she dislikes."

"Very wise," said Sukemichi, "though young people rarely know what's best for them. I recall being madly in love with our *betto*'s daughter when I was eighteen. My father wouldn't have it, of course. Later, she came to serve in our house and I enjoyed her without the obligations of marriage. My father was a wise man." He chuckled and raised his cup! "To our children's happiness!"

They drank.

The wine, very fine *sake*, tasted like bitter medicine on Akitada's tongue. The news was a painful cure for his foolish love. Yukiko, favorite daughter of Fujiwara Kosehira, was meant to be the wife of a future chancellor.

He hardly knew how he got though the rest of the meal. He drank too much and, when called upon, recited some very bad poetry on hunting. It did not matter. Everyone else was also drunk.

Somehow he and Kosehira got back to their room and fell asleep.

Akitada awoke at sunrise to Kosehira's snoring. His head felt like a hive full of angry bees. He staggered up and went outside, suppressing the urge to vomit and instead drank a lot of cold water from the well. A servant came to ask if he needed anything, but Akitada waved him off.

When the memory of Yukiko's marriage to the chancellor's son surfaced from the muddle of his brain, he felt like getting drunk all over again. Instead he took a walk in Sukemichi's garden, which was not nearly as beautiful as Kosehira's and did not have a *koi* pond. It served to sober him, however, and in the end he went inside again to get dressed.

∞

The headman in Okuni village was called Masaie. He turned out to be quite young for this position of trust.

As is customary in small villages, he was also a tax collector and farmer, working his father's land.

He knelt and bowed deeply to Akitada.

"Please get up, Masaie," Akitada said. "My name is Sugawara Akitada. I'm a guest of Lord Taira and came to ask you a few questions." He looked around the small room which held little beyond a stand for paperwork. "Where do you put the people you arrest?" he asked curiously.

"There aren't many arrests," the headman said getting to his feet. "It's drinking and fighting mostly, and we just take them home to their family. They pay a fine the next day."

"Well, I heard a strange story in Otsu recently. You've had two murders here."

The headman scratched his head. "One murder, your Honor. An old man. Wakiya. The other fell to his death. I really didn't have anything to do with it. The prefect sent his own men down to investigate."

"Are you certain the second man fell?"

"Certain? No, but he was at the bottom of the gorge. I suppose he could've been pushed. But who would push an old man down the mountain? He was drunk. It's more likely he fell. May I ask why your Honor is asking these questions?"

"In Otsu two other old men died. These two were knocked down and then suffocated."

Masaie frowned. "Old men die. Some are even killed. Otsu is nothing to do with us."

"That remains to be seen. I understand you found a small carving near the first victim?"

"Yes, a small figure of Jizo. They're selling them at all the fairs. Wakiya didn't buy it, but the road is well traveled, and anybody coming back from the fair could've dropped it. The prefect's office didn't think it had anything to do with the murder, but we reported it when someone from the governor's office asked."

"I see. Hmm. The same little figurines were also found with the Otsu victims."

The headman's eyes widened. "The same? Are you sure, your Honor?" He flushed. " Begging your pardon."

Akitada smiled. "I know. It seems strange. And I'm not sure, no. As you say, they are common, and Otsu also had its share of fairs. It's spring after all. But it did seem puzzling."

"There's a lot of drinking going on during those spring fairs. The dead men in Otsu, had they also been celebrating?"

"No. One was a judge. He died in his home. The other was a street sweeper. He also died at home. Both were knocked out and suffocated. The judge's death looked natural at first, but Otsu has a good coroner. He found sign of suffocation."

"Even so, begging your pardon, your Honor, I don't see the connection between old Wakiya and your two victims."

"Only that there was a Jizo with each body. It seems likely the murderer left them. And that murderer may be going about killing old people."

A silence fell, then the headman said, "If it's true, it's terrible. What can I do?"

"Anything you can tell me about Wakiya and Juro may help."

Masaie scratched his head. "Well, Wakiya was almost eighty and Juro seventy-five. Both were born and raised here. They were farmers, though they used to work for the Taira family until they got too old for it. Both liked to drink, though Wakiya was worse. Or at least his daughter-in-law claimed he was. She didn't get along with the old man. I thought maybe she did it when we found him with his head bashed in. He was close to the house, and she has a bad temper. In the end it came to nothing, but some people still think she did it."

Akitada, recalling the two in Otsu had been a brutal jailer and a corrupt judge, asked, "Were Wakiya and Juro well liked in the village?"

"Not really, but we honor the old." He paused and chuckled. "Well, we tolerate them *because* they're old, if you know what I mean."

Akitada nodded. "What did they do that irritated people?"

"Wakiya quarreled with his neighbors, and Juro tried to cheat at dice. He was always caught. It wasn't bad enough to make people want to kill them."

"No. What about when they were younger?"

"That was before my time. Hiromasa may know. He was headman before my father."

Akitada had hoped for a connection between the four old men. "Did they ever visit Otsu?"

Masaie looked surprised. "Probably. Everybody does. People visit the great temples and have a good time."

"Yes, of course. Would either or both have been involved in a crime?"

"Lord Taira wouldn't have employed them if they had broken the law. He gave them both a small piece of land for a farm when they left his service."

"It's not unusual to settle some land on aging servants," Akitada commented.

"Well, it was for Lord Taira. He wasn't known for his kindness around here."

"I see. Well, I suppose I'll have to settle for what you told me. Thank you, Masaie. Now I'd better have a talk with Hiromasa before I go back to Otsu."

The headman took him to Hiromasa's house. They found a whitebeard feeding his chickens. He turned out to be hard of hearing and spoke the local dialect so strongly that Masaie had to translate.

"This is Lord Sugawara," Masaie shouted in the old man's ear. Hiromasa turned his head and nodded to Akitada. Masaie shouted, "He's come about Wakiya and Juro. Wants to know all about them."

The old man grinned toothlessly, and said quite clearly, "They're dead."

Akitada nodded. "Do you know who would kill them?"

Masaie had to repeat this, and the old man started to speak at length and unintelligibly. Masaie kept nodding, interjecting questions from time to time: "What happened then?" "Why?" "Are you sure?"

Akitada waited impatiently.

In the end, Masaie nodded and turned to Akitada. "Interesting story, sir. He says they were lazy good-for-nothings but their *karma* was good. One day old Lord Sukenori gave them both some land and dismissed them from his service. It was a great good fortune for them. Wakiya was from a poor family and Juro had no home at all. Both started farming but, being lazy, they were always in trouble at tax time. Lord Sukenori forgave them their debts, but people disliked them for it." Masaie paused. "But I don't see anybody killing them now after twenty years."

"No, that's true enough. Ask him if he suspects anyone."

Masaie shouted "Who would kill them?"

The old man made a face and spread his hands in the universal gesture of not knowing the answer. Then he said something and cackled.

Masaie translated. "He says the Taira will be glad to get their land back."

Akitada sighed inwardly. Sukemichi might have got two parcels of rice land back, but he owned so much that this would hardly constitute a motive for killing two old peasants.

21

Taira Sukemichi

The problem with the four deaths was that they made no sense. All the men had in common were their gender and age. Could the killer simply be mad and kill old men randomly? It was unlikely, but try as he might, Akitada came up with no answer, and the memory of Yukiko intruded again.

The news that she would marry the chancellor's son cast him into an insufferable gloom. He should have expected it. Kosehira's cousins were men of power and influence, and such men arranged marriages amongst each other. He knew little of this particular scion of the ruling family but pictured him as a spoiled and haughty brat who was probably involved in affairs with court ladies. They all thought of themselves as Prince Genji.

Even if Yukiko would become this young man's senior wife—something that was by no means certain when there were princesses of the blood available—Akitada thought she would be made profoundly unhappy in such a marriage. Her spirit and intelligence would be crushed as one among many wives and concubines of a powerful man.

But perhaps her fate would not be much better elsewhere.

He thought of his own marriage. While he had not kept other wives or mistresses, he had not always been an attentive husband. Well, in truth, he had rarely been attentive to Tamako, though it was usually work that had kept him away. But he and Tamako had shared their lives, had talked about their worries, had grieved together the deaths of loved ones, and in between they had found time to laugh. Tamako had always been the most important person in his life. Yukiko deserved as much.

But he could not marry her. Nothing had changed. He was still too old, too poor, too stodgy, and too dull. And now, knowing of Kosehira's plans, he certainly could not ask his friend for her. Kosehira would turn him down, and that would end their friendship. And if he felt constrained to agree to the match, Akitada would forever live with the knowledge.

The ghosts of his past haunted him as he returned to the Taira manor. Most disturbing were certain memories he had of himself as a husband and father. He did not much like that other Akitada and pitied Tamako.

He also pitied his children, and to a lesser degree the loyal men and women who served him.

Kosehira met him like this upon his return. Seeing his face, he asked, "What's wrong? What has happened now?"

Akitada looked at his friend sadly. "Why do you like me, Kosehira? I don't deserve it. I've been thinking about my marriage. I've not been a good husband and father."

"Nonsense. You're the best husband I know, which is why I— " Kosehira broke off. "What brought this on?"

And suddenly Akitada could not help himself. He burst out, "This talk about Yukiko's marriage to the chancellor's son. Kosehira, surely she deserves better. He'll ignore her for his mistresses."

Kosehira gaped at him, then said, "Nothing is firm. The matter has merely been mentioned. Why do you care so much?"

Akitada flushed. "No reason. It just occurred to me how hard a woman's life is. She has no choice in the matter of a husband."

"You don't know my daughter very well. And you don't know me very well, either. Yukiko has been consulted. She will not be forced into a marriage against her will."

"Oh!" Akitada sighed. "Sorry. I still struggle sometimes with my memories. Please forgive me."

"There's nothing to forgive. We are friends. It pleases me that you care for my child." Kosehira smiled. "If you're done with your investigation, perhaps we should head home?"

"I've done as much as I could. The heavens know what is going on. I certainly don't."

∞

After they took their leave of their hosts and started the journey homeward, Akitada's mood lifted somewhat. He even took some interest in another fair in the next town they passed through. This one was at a fox shrine and honored the *kami* of rice growing. Here, too, the small Jizos were for sale. Their sight sent shivers down Akitada's back in spite of the general merry-making.

They reached Kosehira's villa after sunset, tired and hungry. After a bath, they ate, though neither paid a great deal of attention to the food, and then parted to seek their beds.

Akitada was up early the next day. He dressed quickly and walked into the garden, his heart beating fast in anticipation. But there was no one at the *koi* pond. He stood for a little while, watching as the fish rose to the surface in hope of food. They shared his disappointment, then sank once more to the bottom and Akitada left.

He had no idea what he would have said to her. He had merely hoped to see her. A fool at forty is a true fool. He shook his head and wished Tora were here and they could practice with their swords.

Later at the tribunal, he tried to distract himself with work. The excursion to the pheasant reserve meant that stacks of documents had piled up at his desk. He worked till midday, then left to see Chief Takechi.

Takechi greeted him eagerly. "Ready for some more noodle soup, sir?"

"I had hoped you'd remember your offer."

At the noodle restaurant, Takechi asked, "Well? Did you find out anything useful?"

Akitada shared the information about Wakiya and Juro.

Takechi said, "I still don't see a connection. Do you?"

Akitada said, "No, but I'm convinced there is something. If only I could grasp it. I had hoped you would."

Takechi looked pleased by this. Their soup arrived and they ate for a while in silence. When they had finished, Takechi sat back and smacked is lips. "Good food is a great blessing. I hope I never lose the taste for it."

Akitada laughed and gestured to the waiter for refills. "I suppose," he said, "it is something that will still be left to us in old age."

"That and our memories."

Akitada knew all about memories, but at that moment, he had again the feeling that he was close to some fact they had overlooked. "All four," he said "were old and not far apart in age. Perhaps something happened to them in the past., something that involved all of them. We should concentrate on some event in the past."

Takechi looked doubtful. "What event?"

"I don't know. Wakiya and Juro could have come to Otsu on a pilgrimage. The headman in Okuni said it was likely. Suppose they met the judge?"

"And the jailer? You think they committed a crime?"

Akitada sighed. "It's not likely, or they would have known in Okuni. It must be something else."

The waiter arrived with more soup and they ate, more slowly this time and thoughtfully. But in the end, the bowls were empty and neither had come up with an answer. Takechi paid and they strolled back to his office, where one of the constables came running to tell them there was an urgent message.

They hurried inside, and Takechi opened a letter from the tribunal. A second letter was inside. It was addressed to Akitada. Takechi scanned his note while Akitada was still unfolding his letter.

"Taira Sukemichi's been killed," Takechi said.

Akitada read and nodded. "I must get back to the tribunal. It's hard to accept. I just saw the man yesterday when we left him. What can have happened?"

∞

Kosehira received him with a similar comment, adding, "We must go back right away. Do you mind?"

"Of course not. What does your message say?"

"It's from the prefect in Echi. He was sent for by Sukemichi's family. At least they didn't take the law into their own hands. Sukemichi was found in his garden, bludgeoned to death." Kosehira paused. "Nakahara had just left. For some reason, they suspect him, and the prefect wants him brought back. I don't believe it for a moment. Short, fat, middle-aged Nakahara bludgeoning a strong young man like Sukemichi? It's ridiculous."

"I would agree. What about his family or one of the servants?"

"Much more likely. Besides, a robber could've got in and, being caught by Sukemichi, decided to kill him. Anyway, you'll find out who did it. I'll come along to introduce you to the prefect."

Akitada did not share such confidence. "That's a bit high-handed.," he said with a smile. "I thought you invited me for a rest from my stressful life in the capital."

Kosehira had the grace to look guilty. "I'm truly sorry, Akitada. I couldn't know this would happen. Do you mind very much?"

"Not at all, brother. I was teasing you."

"Well, you've already involved yourself in local crime. This is a much more important case."

Akitada's smile faded. "They're all important," he said soberly.

Kosehira nodded. "Yes, of course. I only meant that this one will create problems if we don't find the perpetrator. The Taira family is likely to make trouble."

"I see your point. Well, I'm at your disposal. Should we speak to Nakahara first? He must be back by now?"

∞

Nakahara's house on the outskirts of Otsu was indeed modest, but it was surrounded by a large garden. They were admitted by an elderly servant who reminded Akitada of Seimei. Nakahara came quickly, looking surprised. "What a pleasure! But you look serious. Is anything amiss?"

Kosehira said bluntly, "Yes. Sukemichi's been found murdered."

"Wha—?" Nakahara gulped.

Akitada thought his shock was genuine. "Let's sit down," he suggested. "We are going back but wondered if you could tell us anything. You left after us."

"I know nothing," gasped Nakahara, gesturing to some cushions. "Nothing at all. He was alive and quite well this morning. I left very early. What could have happened?

They seated themselves. Kosehira asked, "You parted on good terms?"

"What do you mean? Of course we parted on good terms. I thanked him for the entertainment and left with my servant. It was before sunrise. He was still in his bed clothes. We talked on the rear veranda outside his room. It was perfectly amicable." Nakahara paused. "Surely you cannot suspect me?"

"Apparently the local authorities do. Because you left very early." Kosehira said.

Nakahara glowered. "Of course I left early. It's a long trip home. As you should know well enough."

Akitada decided to smooth over the tension. "I think the governor is merely trying to find out if you were the last person to see Lord Sukemichi alive and under what circumstances."

"I have no idea. I assume he went back inside to get dressed. You'll have to ask his servants." Nakahara was not so easily reassured . "How dare they say such things!"

"Were you aware of any problems Sukemichi might have had? Some family discord? An argument the evening before?"

"Guests generally aren't involved in family affairs," Nakahara pointed out.

Akitada thought of his own position in Kosehira's home. He had become involved. Putting his feelings for Yukiko firmly from his mind, he persisted, "You were a frequent guest, I think. Was there anything out of the ordinary that you recall?"

Nakahara shook his head, then said, "I heard the dogs bark during the night, but that was probably just some animal."

When they ended their visit, Kosehira tried to apologize, but Nakahara remained very stiff and resentful. "I trust you'll keep me informed?" he said. "My relationship with Sukemichi was excellent, regardless of what you may think."

"Ouch," said Kosehira as they got back on their horses. "I didn't do myself any good there."

Akitada said, "He'll calm down," but thought privately that Kosehira was probably not going to be much help questioning Sukemichi's family.

After another hard ride, they reached the Taira manor and found the local prefect, a middle-aged man called Ishimoda, already in charge. Ishimoda, who had been appointed by Kosehira, came to greet them and did his best to provide information to his superior.

This got a little tedious since Ishimoda made it a point to put himself forward as a brilliant investigator.

"Having been notified of the death," he said, "I immediately dropped everything to rush over here, knowing that a man of Lord Taira's importance—what a great loss to the nation!—deserved the best we had to offer.

Alas, picture my shock and sadness when I was led to his body—such a handsome man at the height of his powers—and saw the bloody end some vicious criminals had brought him to." He paused briefly to dab at his eyes with a tissue.

Akitada took the opportunity to ask, "Where was the body?"

"Oh. Didn't I say. I'm still distraught. My apologies."

"Just answer," Kosehira said wearily.

"Ah, yes. He was in the garden. A beautiful garden, very fitting."

"Fitting in what way?" asked Akitada.

The prefect looked blank. "Why, because of his fine taste, of course."

"Do we know why he was in the garden? Did he have a particular purpose for being there?"

"Oh. Of course, as it was quite beautiful . . ." Seeing both Akitada and Kosehira glaring at him, he fell silent.

Akitada suppressed a sigh. "We are trying to find out if he met someone there."

"Oh. I see. Well, he was still in his bed clothes, so I wouldn't think so. That is, other than Lord Nakahara, of course. Did his lordship come with you?"

"No. There was no need. He left Sukemichi alive outside his room." Akitada added, "The fact that the body was in the garden might suggest that he was meeting a member of his family or a servant."

The prefect looked shocked. "You cannot possibly suspect his family, sir."

Kosehira said firmly, "Of course we can. We can suspect everyone until we have the killer."

Ishimoda blinked. "Yes, I see, sir. I'm very sorry. But I don't know why he was in the garden. Perhaps he saw something or someone?"

Kosehira nodded. "That is quite possible. If he saw a stranger for example, he might have gone to investigate."

The prefect brightened. "That must be it then."

Akitada asked, "Did the servants have anything to report? Did anyone hear anything, for example?"

"No, sir."

Akitada sighed. "Take us to the body, Prefect."

They had brought Taira Sukemichi into the reception room of the manor. There he rested on the dais, dressed in what appeared to be his best court costume, his hair arranged and topped with a court hat. It was impossible to see any injury.

Akitada glanced at those present. Sukemichi's family and household knelt below the dais. They wore the pale hemp mourning robes, and Sukemichi's three wives were heavily veiled. The mourners had stopped their wailing at their entrance and watched as Kosehira and Akitada approached the body, bowed, and stood looking at it.

There was a small stain on the new *tatami* mat Sukemichi's head rested on. It suggested that the fatal wound had been to the back of the head and was still oozing a little. Sukemichi's face was peaceful.

Akitada regretted his death. Sukemichi had been a generous host and if perhaps a little too enamored of falconry, had not been unlikeable. Yet someone had hated him enough to kill him. Or perhaps it had indeed been a robber, surprised by the unlucky Sukemichi.

After a suitable time, the prefect, Kosehira, and Akitada bowed again, then turned and bowed to the family. After that they left the room.

Outside, Akitada said to the prefect, "It will be necessary to speak to the family. Would you please let them know?"

∞

Only Sukemichi's senior wife and his eldest son received them. They were in a smaller room behind the hall where the body lay, and the chanting of the monks could be heard clearly through the wall. It cast a special gloom over the interview.

They expressed their condolences to Lady Taira, and his young heir, a fourteen-year-old, who looked confused. Having become Lord Taira so abruptly and being expected to direct the fortunes of his family was clearly beyond him. His mother, who sat to his side and slightly behind him, was no help at all. She never lifted her veil and seemed to wait for them to leave.

An uncomfortable silence fell after they had all said their piece and the new Lord Taira had bowed each time. Kosehira cleared his throat and addressed the boy. "Regrettably, the prefect has some questions concerning what happened. It is a bad time, but I'm certain you will wish your father's murderer caught as soon as possible."

The youngster nodded. "Yes. But I know nothing and neither does my mother."

Lady Taira confirmed this. "My husband's death is a great shock. We are quite unable to grasp it, let alone give you any information. I speak for all of us."

"Forgive me," said Akitada, "but did Lord Sukemichi spend the night alone?"

Lady Taira gasped, and her son blushed to the roots of his hair. He shot a glance at his mother and said, "I believe so."

"And was it his custom to walk in the garden after rising in the morning?"

The boy raised his chin and asked, "Why are you asking these questions? Are you not looking for the robber who killed my father?"

Akitada took pity on him. "Of course, but we need to find anyone who may have seen or heard something. Besides, if we can establish that your father customarily walked in the garden, the killer may have known this and lain in wait, you see."

The boy's eyes widened. "You mean someone planned to kill him?"

"It's possible."

"Oh. Sometimes he would go into the garden, I think. Maybe his servant would know." The new lord subsided into misery again.

They said a few soothing words and departed. Outside, Kosehira said to Akitada, "I guess the wife didn't spend the night in Sukemichi's bed."

"No, but someone else may have. She had a strong reaction to my question. And the son was clearly embarrassed. We'd better check with the servants."

Ishimoda offered timidly, "Must we ask such questions? It seems unnecessary and is clearly offensive to her ladyship."

Akitada eyed him with a raised brow. "We must, Prefect. After a murder there is no privacy left. All the family secrets are inspected."

Kosehira said nothing, but he looked unhappy. Akitada got an inkling of how most people felt about his own methods, indeed, about his meddling in murder cases. He steeled himself against his doubts. Not only was it right to pay this debt to the murdered man, but leaving his murderers free was surely an offense against the gods.

22

Family Secrets

There was a rather strange scene in the court-yard when they emerged. One of the servants, a middle-aged male, was headed toward the gate, pulling a well-dressed young woman by her arm. She was sobbing loudly. His grip on her arm was certainly not gentle, and he gave her an occasional jerk forward to make her walk faster.

Kosehira said, "I wonder what that's all about?" Leaning over the railing, he shouted to the servant, "You there! Come here, and bring the girl with you!"

The man stopped to look back. Giving the woman a push toward the gate, he started toward them. The prefect called out to his men, who seized the young woman and brought her back. The two stood at the bottom of the stairs, looking frightened.

"Well," said Kosehira, "let's find out why he was in such a hurry to take this young woman away."

They walked down to the pair. The young woman was very pretty, even with her eyes swollen from weeping and her nose red. Akitada noted that her clothes were good silk, not the cotton or ramie he would have expected of a servant. She also wore her hair long. He thought he knew what had been happening and why she looked so frightened and distraught.

Kosehira perhaps also guessed, for he spoke quite gently to her. "My dear," he said, "don't be frightened. Nobody will punish you. Just answer our questions, and if you are truthful, I'll see what can be done for you. Who are you and what are you doing here?"

She sniffed, bowed, and said, "This person is called Mineko. I'm one of the maids. Her ladyship told Kato to take me away."

Kosehira looked at the servant. "And you are Kato?"

The man bowed and said, "Yes. I serve his lordship as major domo. I was showing this girl the way out. On orders of her ladyship."

The girl hung her head.

"It seems to me," said Akitada, "that this is a strange time to deal with unsatisfactory servants when your master has just died."

Kosehira said, "I agree."

The majordomo compressed his lips. "No doubt her ladyship had her reasons."

The girl fell to her knees. "Please help me. I don't know where to go. I was born in this house."

Kosehira and Akitada exchanged a glance. Kosehira asked the major domo, "By any chance, was this young woman favored by Lord Sukemichi?"

The servant said nothing, but Mineko cried eagerly, "His lordship was very kind to me. He would never send me away like this." Tears welled up again and she pressed a hand to her stomach.

Akitada thought he recognized the gesture. "Are you with child?" he asked her. "His lordship's child?"

Ishimoda gasped audibly.

She flushed a deep crimson. "Oh, no! Never. His lordship was like a father to me."

The majordomo sneered, "If she's with child, it's because she's been lying with the stable hands."

She burst into protestations, and Kosehira said firmly, "Stop this. Mineko will stay here with the other maids until the matter is cleared up. And you, Kato, will do well to remember that you may be given twenty lashes if you've been lying."

Kato paled and bowed.

When they had left, Kosehira said to Akitada, "If she was Sukemichi's mistress, it would give his wife a motive, surely?"

"Perhaps. If she felt very strongly about her husband's affairs." Akitada turned to the prefect. "Show us where the body was found, and on the way perhaps you'd better tell us what your coroner said."

If the prefect was surprised that Akitada asked the questions, he did not say so. He told them that the fatal wound had been to the back of the head and that Lord

Sukemichi's skull had been broken to pieces so that some of his brains had escaped.

"A very powerful blow to the head then?"

"Several blows, sir. The first probably felled him. Then the killer hit him again and again to make sure he was dead."

Kosehira muttered, "That's a lot of hate."

"Or fear," said Akitada. "Fear of being discovered, if he was a robber. In a panic, a man can become both strong and vicious."

"That's true, but what about a woman?"

"Less likely, but Lady Taira is in her thirties and looked tall."

They had arrived in a part of the garden some distance from the house. The prefect pointed to an area of disturbed moss and earth beside a path of stepping stones. A darker spot in the moss showed where Sukemichi's head had lain and bled. His feet had been near the path.

"So he was walking along and the killer came up behind him," said Akitada. "I suppose it's just possible that an intruder, afraid of being caught, circled behind Sukemichi to strike him down. But it's more likely that the killer was hiding and somehow lured Sukemichi to this place. Have your men searched the area?"

"No, sir. We didn't wish to disturb the family."

Akitada frowned at him. "There has been a murder. It's more important that everything be done to find the killer."

Ishimoda glanced at Kosehira and said, "Yes, sir. Allow me to arrange for a search. What are the men to look for?"

"Did the coroner offer any suggestion s about the weapon the killer used?"

"Not really. He said it could've been anything. A piece of wood or a branch or a staff."

Akitada sighed. "Let's have a look for it, shall we? A piece of silver for the man who finds it."

The prefect bowed and left to organize the search. Kosehira was going to turn back also, but Akitada stopped him. "Just a moment. I bet the constables didn't bother to search around the body." He peered closely at the ground, then walked a few steps either way along the path that Sukemichi had walked in the last few moments of his life, looking this way and that among the shrubs, ferns, and mossy stones on either side of the path.

He found it just about an arm's throw from where Sukemichi had fallen. The small figurine rested in a tuft of uncurling ferns. Akitada bent closer, hardly daring to breathe.

It could not be.

Sukemichi was much younger than the others: a mere forty years to their late sixties and seventies. And he was a ranking nobleman within his own domain.

But if a robber could have entered here, then the Jizo killer could have done the same.

Akitada straightened and called to Kosehira. The prefect had also returned and joined them.

Kosehira peered. "Dear me! It's another one!" He picked it up to show the prefect.

Ishimoda chuckled. "It's nothing. Just a cheap toy. It probably belongs to one of the children. We found it beside the body and tossed it aside."

"It's not a toy," said Akitada, taking the Jizo and turning it in his hands. "The killer left this. It's like the one that was found with the peasant Wakiya. You will have to send one of your men back down into the gorge where they found the other peasant. I think he'll find another Jizo down there."

The prefect gaped at him as if he had lost his mind.

Kosehira said, "Yes, I think you'd better, Prefect. Lord Sugawara thinks someone is killing people and leaving those things behind."

"But that sounds mad." The prefect looked confused.

"He may be." Akitada held up the Jizo. "But if you find a Jizo in the gorge, we will be sure that the same man killed at least five people."

Before the prefect could say anything else, one of the constables returned at a run. He waved a broken length of wood. "It was outside the wall," he gasped. "I climbed up to get a better look, and there it was on the other side, caught in the crook of a branch. He must have thrown it over the wall."

"Good man!" Akitada took the piece of wood. It was part of an ordinary walking staff, the kind people used on long journeys, sturdy but not as thick as the fighting staffs he and Tora had used. He looked at it carefully. One end had splintered off. The other was the part that touched the ground, and it bore traces of blood and a few black hairs. The killer had broken his weapon when he had killed Sukemichi and thrown the useless pieces away. "Yes," he told the constable, "you have found the weapon that killed Lord Sukemichi. Or part of it. The rest must be in the same area." He gave the grinning constable the promised piece of silver and sent him off to search for the other piece.

∞

Later they began the questioning of the servants, the house servants first, and the stable hands and gardeners afterward.

Sukemichi's personal attendant, a stiff, middle-aged man, froze further when asked about his master's sleeping arrangements. Reluctantly, he told them that his master had had an occasional female servant in his room, but had slept alone on the night before his death. As for his relations with his wives, he had been accustomed to visiting them in their quarters. He could not identify Sukemichi's bed partners.

The prefect looked uncomfortable, but Kosehira only waited until the servant had gone before saying, "I suppose if he's taken to sleeping with that maid, his wives would not have been pleased. What if the Jizo really is a coincidence?"

Akitada frowned. "It took great strength to kill Sukemichi. I don't think it was the work of a woman, though she could have ordered or hired a man to kill her husband. If he came from outside, it was either fortuitous for him that Sukemichi wandered about the garden alone, or he lay in wait for him. I don't think this is a domestic quarrel. From what we have seen in the other cases, I would guess he came from the outside."

"Oh," said Ishimoda. "I see now that it makes sense to think it was this killer. I confess it's a relief. Much better than involving the family."

Kosehira gave him a pitying look. "He could have acted for someone in the family," he said.

Akitada agreed, but he suspected strongly that this killer had his own motive. They continued their questioning without coming up with useful information. There was some agreement that the dogs had barked during the night, but evidently all the gates had been locked. Sukemichi had insisted on security because of his falcons. None of the people currently working inside the compound were recently employed, and none had the sort of freedom that would have allowed him to visit Otsu to carry out the other murders.

And there was still no clear motive.

The maid Mineko had nothing to offer except more tears and the fact that she had done nothing to deserve being dismissed.

One curious fact emerged when they were talking to the oldest servant in the compound. He was nearly seventy, a stable hand, and gave his name as Tosuke. Impressed by the old man's sturdy appearance, Akitada asked him if he had any plans to retire as Wakiya and Juro had done.

"Oh, them!" Tosuke said with a sneer. "Lazy bastards both."

Someone else had called them lazy. It seemed curious that Sukemichi's father should have rewarded laziness with a gift of land. An idea began to form in Akitada's mind. He said, "I take it you remember the time when Lord Sukemichi's father was alive and they worked here?"

"I may be old but my memory's good," Tosuke snapped. "Maybe better than yours."

Tosuke clearly took advantage of the fact that old people were allowed to say things that would get younger ones in trouble. With a smile, Akitada asked, "What do you remember about them?"

"Them or the old lord?"

"Either, if you don't mind."

"I don't mind as long as you make plain what you mean."

Akitada almost apologized. "Very well. Were you surprised when Lord Sukenori gave them both a piece of land of their own?"

"No."

"But it seems unlikely that he would reward laziness."

The old man said darkly, "Not if it suits him."

"Ah. So why did it suit him in their case?"

"How should I know? I wasn't there."

"You weren't there when?"

The old man snapped, "I can't be everywhere. Only the *kami* can do that."

Akitada detected a steely glint in the old eyes and got a premonition that he was not going to get any more information. He tried anyway.

"I take it that something happened involving Wakiya and Juro. You weren't there at the time, but you have a notion that they performed some service for which Lord Sukemichi gave them their land. Am I right?"

The old man cocked his head. "Have it your way. I wasn't there, but I know they were lazy bastards."

With an inward sigh, Akitada gave up. When the old man had gone, he said to Kosehira, "I wish we had the time to delve more deeply into the story of Sukemichi's father's surprising generosity, but I'm afraid it will take too much time and may well be irrelevant."

23

The Pact

Saburo was aware that something was wrong with Tora. He had realized it quickly after they had brought him back from the mountain. Once or twice, he had tried to ask him what had happened, but Tora had shaken his head and said, "Nothing."

Tora's glum mood had deepened greatly after the raid on the tribunal. At first, Saburo thought this was due to Sergeant Okura's condition, but the sergeant had improved and Tora had not. His return to the capital and his wife and son had done little to lift his mood.

Not that Saburo did not have his own troubles. There was his mother for example. Only this morning, she had informed Hanae that it was high time she had another child. Pretty Hanae had burst into tears.

Saburo had told his mother, "I don't want you to say hurtful things to my friends. You've made Hanae cry. Why did you do that?"

His mother had scoffed, "Women are a good deal tougher than you think. We are made to bear children. You should be glad I bore you. But I get little thanks from you or from your sister. I've slaved away my best years so you should have everything, and look at you! You went away never to return, and your sister threw me out of her house. But do I cry? No. I came from her to you to offer my help and support, because that is what mothers do."

Saburo wished fervently she had not come. He had to watch her constantly lest she make more trouble. Cook would have walked out several times already if Saburo had not bribed her with pieces of silver from his savings.

As for his leaving her, it had been she who had given him to the monks who had made him a spy and sent him among their enemies.

He touched his scarred face. These days, he felt little beyond a scruffy growth of beard and greasy makeup to cover the worst. But those wounds had gone deep. And his visit to Enryakuji had brought back the horrors of that torture and given him nightmares again. And now he also worried about Tora's moodiness. He had seemed all right when they brought him back, but Saburo knew some wounds go below the surface. And the fact that Tora would not talk about his stay even to him, suggested that something had left permanent scars beyond the bruises to his face and the wounds to his wrists.

The incident between his mother and Hanae convinced him to make another attempt to find out what was going on with Tora. He found him outside his small house, just sitting there on the steps to the veranda and staring down at his hands.

"There you are," Saburo said in a tone of false cheer. "I came to apologize for my mother once again. I'm afraid she upset Hanae."

Tora looked up. "It doesn't take much these days," he said listlessly. "Don't worry. It's not your mother. It's me."

Well, it was an opening.

Saburo sat down next to Tora. "So, what's up with you then?"

Tora sighed. "Everything. I'm no good to anyone anymore."

Saburo raised his brows. "What makes you think so?"

"It's nothing to do with you."

So he had been shut out again. Saburo thought a moment, then said, "I think it has everything to do with me."

Tora raised his head. "Don't be silly. How could my problems have anything to do with you? I tell you, it's not your mother."

"All right. I'm glad about that anyway. She's a great trial to me."

Tora's lip twitched.

Encouraged, Saburo forged on. "I think it has something to do with what happened on the mountain."

Tora turned away and started to get up.

Right, thought Saburo. That's it. I thought so. He said, "Sit down, brother. I feel responsible for letting you go into that place when I knew better. If I tell you what happened to me, will you talk about what happened to you?"

Tora turned his head away. "Nothing happened to me."

Saburo heaved a sigh. "I know it's hard to talk about. I've kept it in for five years. But at some point it wants out, or it eats you from the inside. As if you'd swallowed a snake and it was chewing up your insides."

Tora snorted. "You've got a way with words. You may have swallowed a snake, but I didn't. Nothing's eating me."

"Will you listen? I've never talked about this to anyone."

Tora nodded, but it was clear that he had no intention of sharing secrets.

"I was thirteen when my mother decided I should become a monk. It was obvious by then that I was short and scrawny and would never be much good in the army. She sent me to Nara. The monks there were good to me. They taught me how to read and write, how to keep accounts, and all the most important prayers. At first they sent me out to ask for food and money. I was still a child and looked so hungry and pitiful that people were always generous. But then I got older and was not quite so scrawny anymore. It was at that time that they noticed my only skill. I could climb just about anything and used to run along the monastery roofs like a cat, jumping from one building to the next. That's when they decided to send me to Mount Koya to be trained by the *sohei* there. Only I wasn't trained as a soldier monk. I was trained as a spy. I was very good at spying."

"We've known that you were a monk and a spy," Tora said dismissively. "The master didn't like it."

"No. I can see his point, and I don't have much else to offer. As it is, I'm much older now and out of practice, so I'm not what I once was. But I haven't told you what ended my career."

"You got caught and carved up," Tora supplied.

"Yes. That was later. Five years later. By then I'd made a reputation for myself. One day, my temple decided to send me to Onjo-ji. The two abbots were friends, you see, and Onjo-ji was having some problems with Mount Hiei. They wanted to know how many warriors Enryakuji had hired. There'd been rumors that they'd built a separate monastery on the mountain to accommodate their army. Onjo-ji's abbot was afraid and wanted proof so he could petition the emperor to intercede."

Saburo had Tora's attention now. "And you went up there and found them?"

Saburo grimaced. "Yes. I got what Onjo-ji wanted, but I decided it wasn't good enough, that I could get more by getting inside. I did get inside one night and climbed around the buildings without learning much. So I went back again and again. Once I almost got caught when a guard heard me jump down from a roof. I got away. The next night I found the hall where they had their meetings. I overheard plenty. They were planning to provoke a fight with the Onjo-ji monks and then attack the temple and burn it down."

"How can monks behave like that?"

"Well, there are monks, and then there are *sohei*. The monks squabble amongst each other about doctrine, honors, and land, just like nobles. And just like nobles, they keep soldiers. The soldiers think like soldiers. They plan to attack."

Tora said bitterly, "Most soldiers are honorable. Those bastards had no honor."

"True. In a regular army they wouldn't tolerate such men, but monasteries tend to be pretty gullible. They believe the men that come to them wanting to be monks. And they protect them from the police. To get back to my disaster: I was lying on one of the great beams above them and picking up all this interesting information when a cat got curious about what I was doing there. I tried to shoo it away with my hand, but the cat clawed me. It was an uneven contest. The cat hissed, they looked up, and I tried to flee. The cat was in my way, and in my hurry I slipped and fell right into the middle of their council of war."

Tora's eyes were wide. "What did you do?"

"Nothing to do. They had me, and they wanted to know who sent me." Saburo grimaced again.

"You didn't tell them?"

"Not right away. I had some foolish notion of protecting Onjo-ji, my temple by then. After a while, I didn't care about Onjo-ji, but I was afraid that they would kill me as soon as they knew, and I wasn't going to give them the satisfaction too quickly."

"That was very brave of you!"

"No, it was stupid. I talked in the end. I talked plenty. I made up stories. I was the biggest coward you ever saw. Pain will do that to a man."

"I still think you were brave. But they didn't carve me up. I think they were afraid. Somehow they knew I was connected to the tribunal. Someone came in and told them not to mark me up. That's when they tried other things."

"What things?"

Tora turned away. "I don't want to talk about it."

"Oh." Saburo said nothing for a while, then, "Yes, they did that to me, too."

Tora turned his head, "You didn't mind?"

"Not like the knives, but I did mind, yes."

Tora sat silently, digesting this. After a while he said, "I think I could've taken the knives. They made me feel like I was nothing, like I could be used and thrown away. They tied me down over a rice bale, and one of them straddled my neck." Tora clenched his fists. "I fought. Oh, how I fought!" He held out his lacerated wrists for Saburo to see. "It was no good. They pulled down my pants and I kicked them, but they laughed and made jokes. That's when their general heard the noise and came in. They left me alone after that. But I'd lost my honor by then."

Saburo sighed. "Well, they haven't changed. I was pretty sure they were the same bastards. What do you want to do about it?"

"What can I do? They are gone by now. All I've done was to let a tiger loose in the market place. I've failed my master, I've failed poor Kinzaburo and his wife, and I've failed Hanae. I'm no good to anyone anymore."

"The people who love you know better. You have a family that depends on you. Me, I'm alone. Nobody cares what happens to me. But you've got a wife. Don't let those bastards win."

Tora jumped up, white-faced. "I shouldn't have told you." He went inside and slammed the door shut behind him.

Saburo sat a little longer. When he heard raised voices inside, he got up and left.

∞

Later that day, Tora came to him, looking very uneasy. "Forgive me, brother," he said quite humbly. "I didn't mean to speak to you that way."

Saburo smiled and nodded. "I understand. Don't worry about it."

He expected Tora to turn away again, but he did not. Instead he stood there, looking around and up at the sky while clenching and unclenching his big hands.

"I have to go into town to pay off some merchants," Saburo said after a while. "How about walking with me? The cherry trees are blooming along the canals."

Tora nodded. "Why not?"

At first neither said very much beyond a comment or two on the weather and on the cherry trees. The scene along the canal was a happy one. Children played on the banks and a few young women washed clothes. The trees were covered with blossoms, white turning to pink, but the first petals were already falling. They paused on one of the arched bridges and leaned on the wooden railing to watch the scene below.

Saburo said, "Cherry blossoms always make me sad these days. I courted Shokichi under the cherry trees. It seems like an age ago." He heaved a sigh.

"So?" asked Tora.

"It's hard, being alone."

"There are plenty of women."

"It's not the same."

They fell silent again. Then Tora said, "You noticed we're having troubles, Hanae and me."

"I heard."

"It's my fault. I'm no good to her anymore. I try, but I can't."

Saburo pursed his lips. "I'm sorry, brother. I expect it'll pass."

"No!" Tora grasped his arm and shook it. " I'm no good to anyone. I'm useless. I couldn't even give the master his exercise in Otsu. He sent me home because he has no more use for me. But I'm no use to anyone here either."

It was on Saburo's tongue to point out that Tora had fixed the leaking roof once again and also patched the outer wall, that he had played with the children, and carried wood for the cook. Instead he detached his arm and said quietly, "You are still the same man. They could not change that."

Tora shook his head. "How could you go on living after what they did to you? A man cannot live with himself after that. The shame, it's unbearable."

"Oh," said Saburo, keeping his voice matter-of-fact. "They were cruel bastards all right, but I'd been a monk for years. I got used to sex between men in a monastery. It's nothing."

Tora thought about this, then said, "It wasn't that they tried that. It was being helpless. And I'm still helpless. I've never wanted to kill anyone as much as I want to kill those bastards. Never! I think sometimes that I'll go mad if I don't kill them."

"I see," said Saburo heavily. "Yes, I dream of that almost every day and most nights."

Tora was not listening. "The worst bastard got away. Kojo! I'll never find him again."

"Perhaps we will," Saburo said. "We could try at least."

Tora looked at him. "Did you say 'we'?"

Saburo nodded. "Yes. It may be time for both of us to lay the ghosts and kill some devils."

"He could be anywhere by now."

"He's on the mountain."

"You think he went back? But the monks wouldn't take him back. They said so."

Saburo gave Tora a pitying look. "Mount Hiei is large. There are many temples there. Kojo had friends."

"Would you come with me?"

"Would you disobey the master again?"

Another, longer, silence fell. Then Tora nodded.

24

More Secrets

The morning after a long and futile day trying to get information from Sukemichi's servants, the prefect's constables arrested a vagrant not far from the manor. Before either Akitada or Kosehira could interfere, they had a confession. The man, who was very poor and not in his right mind, admitted readily that he had climbed the wall of the Taira manor and killed its owner.

The prefect was elated to have closed the case so quickly and conveniently. Sukemichi's widow was pleased and momentarily forgot her grief-stricken demeanor. The young lord shared the general relief.

"I don't like it," Akitada told Kosehira as they prepared to return to Otsu.

"Well, he may have done it. He looked strong enough."

"There is no proof."

Kosehira finished putting on his boots and said, "There is a confession. A confession outweighs proof."

"He did not seem a very sensible sort of person to me," Akitada persisted. "It sounded as though he was actually proud of what he confessed to."

"Ordinary people can be quite simple, Akitada," Kosehira pointed out. "Not everyone has studied law at the university and is aware of legal matters. He enjoyed the attention. I expect he'll change his attitude."

"Perhaps, but I still don't like it. And I'm troubled by the Jizo. I don't think that was a coincidence."

"Yes, that was a little strange. But you said yourself that Sukemichi wasn't like the others. He was a ranking nobleman and much younger."

Akitada nodded unhappily. "It's none of my business, but you might tell the prefect not to rush the case to trial."

Kosehira said, "I cannot ask the man to do that. He deals with matters in his district."

"Yes, only the man they arrested—I didn't believe him. I think he's just a foolish creature who will agree to anything you tell him."

At this point there was an interruption. A servant came to announce that the Okuni headman was outside and wished to speak to Akitada. Hoping against hope for something to support his conviction that all five murders had been committed by the same man and that Sukemichi had not been killed by a demented vagrant, Akitada rushed out into the courtyard.

The sturdy figure of Masaie stood waiting. He was looking about him with a lively interest. When he saw Akitada coming down the steps toward him, a broad smile lit his face.

"A very good morning to you, my lord," he said with a deep bow. "They tell me you're leaving us?"

"Yes. The governor and I both have work waiting in Otsu. We'll leave matters in the prefect's hands. What brings you?"

"Two things, sir. You'll be pleased to hear that one of our people went down into the gorge to look for another Jizo. And you were right, sir. It was there all the time."

"Excellent work, Masaie." Akitada found a piece of silver in his sash and passed it over. "With my thanks to the brave young man who climbed down."

The grin was back. "Thank you, sir. He'll be glad of it. His wife's expecting."

"What was the other matter?"

"Well, I'm asking for advice, sir. There's a young woman who walked into the village yesterday, crying her eyes out. It seems Lord Sukemichi's first lady had her thrown out. The girl swears she's done nothing wrong. Sir, she was born in this house and has no family left. A young woman like that isn't safe on the roads. All sorts of people pass through looking to make money at the fairs. Thieves and highwaymen, most of them."

So the maid had been dismissed after all. Akitada's heart hardened toward Sukemichi's widow. Whatever the relationship between her husband and this maid had been, she owed their servants more consideration, especially when they had grown up in the household. Her action had been unnecessarily cruel. He said regretfully, "Masaie, I cannot help you or her. This is a family matter and none of my business."

The headman nodded. "I understand, sir." He bowed and left.

∞

They had nearly reached the highway to Otsu, when Akitada stopped Kosehira.

"Forgive me, brother," he said. "I want to go back to Okuni. Something bothers me about that dismissed maid. You go ahead. I'll try to catch up, or else get there a little later."

Kosehira was disappointed. "I meant to show you the water channels of Azuchi. It's on our way and quite famous as a hiding place for wanted criminals. Why the interest in the maid anyway? So Sukemichi slept with one of his servants. There's nothing remarkable about that."

Akitada agreed it was not remarkable in most noble houses, though neither he nor Kosehira (he hoped) engaged in such behavior. "It's not that but the fact that she has been dismissed so suddenly. There is a reason, I suspect, and I'd like to know it. The family already has too many secrets for my taste."

Kosehira looked astonished. "You think the girl murdered him? Or that his lady suspects her?"

"Probably not. Jealousy alone doesn't quite explain it."

"Hmm. Well, go back then. Be sure you let me know what you learn."

∞

Akitada sought out Masaie in Okuni and asked to speak to the dismissed maid.

"She's staying with a farmer up the road," he said. "Working for her food and lodging." He shook his head. "It's the best we could do. Mostly women like her end up selling themselves to passing travelers. That would be a pity, I think. I hope you can help her, sir."

Akitada said, "I'm very sorry about what happened to her, but I cannot promise that Lady Taira will allow her to return. I only want to find out what happened in case it has some significance for Lord Taira's murder."

Masaie, apparently also intrigued by the mystery of the girl's dismissal, accompanied Akitada to a small farm in a grove of pines. All around, the fields had been cleared and crisscrossed by small ditches. The ditches carried water to the rice fields, already mostly planted.

They found the farmer gone to mend one of his ditches, but the farmer's wife, a hard-faced, middle-aged woman, was home. She looked from Masaie to Akitada and knelt, bowing her head.

"Kohime, is Mineko around?" Masaie asked. "His lordship here wants to ask her some questions about the murder at the big house."

The woman's eyes grew round and she covered her mouth in astonishment as she stood up. "Did she kill her master?" she asked. "If she killed him, take her away and lock her up. You shouldn't have brought her. She might slit our throats while we sleep."

Akitada said quickly, "She did not kill Lord Sukemichi. I want to speak to her because she may know something."

The woman relaxed. "Oh," she said, somewhat sullenly. "The girl's in the back, washing clothes. She's not a very good worker. Spoiled with her fine clothes and smooth hands." She looked at Masaie accusingly.

"Be patient. She'll learn," he said with a grimace. "She's only eighteen."

They walked around the house and found the girl on her knees in the dirt, scrubbing some wet garments on a stone. A big wooden tub stood beside her. Gone was her silk gown. She wore an old gray striped shirt and the sort of pants peasant women wore in the fields. Her hair was cut shorter and tied back with a rag, and she was barefoot, wet, and dirty. But when she turned and looked up at them, Akitada saw that she was still very pretty in spite of the red, swollen eyes.

She dropped the shirt she had been scrubbing and jumped up. "Have you come to take me back?" she asked Masaie eagerly. "Oh, please say I may go back."

Masaie shook his head. "No. I'm very sorry, Mineko. This is Lord Sugawara who was helping to find Lord Sukemichi's murderer. He has some questions to ask you."

Tears of disappointment welled up again. Looking down at the ground, she said listlessly, "I'll answer."

She was young, a year younger than Yukiko. Akitada felt quite sorry for her and felt again a strong dislike to Sukemichi's wife. He spoke gently. "I'm very sorry that you had to leave. May I ask why you were dismissed?"

She rubbed her wet hands against her pants and sniffled. "I don't know why. It was sudden. They wouldn't tell me." She raised watery eyes to his. "I have done nothing. I was at my lessons when the majordomo came and took me away and pushed me out into the street, saying I was never to come back on orders of her ladyship."

From this startling account, Akitada picked one word. "You were at your lessons? What lessons?"

"Lord Sukemichi had me taught by his children's tutor. I'm studying the classics and practicing poetry. I mean, I was." She wiped away more tears.

This was astounding. It was unheard of that a nobleman would bother to educate a maid even if he enjoyed her in bed. And surely such preferential treatment would have aggravated his wife's resentment. Clearly, it had been a painful shock for this girl to leave all that behind to wash clothes in a peasant's yard. He asked, "Did you love Lord Sukemichi?"

She nodded. "He was very good to me. When I was a child, he used to carry me around on his shoulders. And now he's gone and I am nothing." She looked at her work-reddened hands and shuddered.

Akitada exchanged a glance with Masaie, then asked her, "Could you be with child by his lordship?"

She stared at him, turning first white and then red. Forgetting her position, she shouted, "That's a horrible lie! He was like my father. I would never . . . I used to think of him as my father. He would never have done such a thing. Never! You dishonor his memory!"

Akitada felt contrite. "Forgive me. I was trying to understand his wife's anger at you. Do you truly have no family? What about your real father and mother?"

"I don't have a father. My mother came to work at the Taira manor in the old lord's time. She died when I was still small."

Akitada turned to Masaie. "It should be possible to find the mother's family. I have to return to Otsu, but I think you might talk to people here and at the estate. Someone may remember where her mother came from. There might be relatives."

Masaie nodded. "I have asked some questions and will ask some more, but I'm afraid there's nobody. Her mother was a slave, bought by Lord Sukemichi's father."

The girl listened with bowed head and murmured, "Thank you, sir," then turned away to continue her work. Akitada had rarely seen a more poignant gesture of hopeless acceptance of a dire fate. He did not know what to say. He had no right to give her assurances of a better life when he could not promise such a thing. But the sight of her figure bent over her chore haunted him all the way back to Otsu.

∞

In Otsu, work had piled up. They were nearing the completion of their assignment. He was expected to assemble the facts and documents his clerks had gathered and arrive at a legal argument that would settle the continuous litigation between the two temples once and for all.

Over the next two days, he had barely time to eat and sleep, and he slept very little, because at night the ghosts of his failures came to haunt him.

Yukiko, whose love he had rejected;

The weeping maid in Okuni, who had no one in the whole wide world and would surely come to harm;

The dead—Judge Nakano, the sweeper Tokuno, the two peasants Wakiya and Juro, and now also Taira Sukemichi—whose murders remained unsolved;

And the poor fool who had confessed to the Taira murder and would pay the price.

He had failed them all, and all he had left was his duty as an imperial official. And there he had little faith that a decision about the cases would change anything about the war being carried on between the different Buddhist factions and temples. Meanwhile, the dead found no peace and the living, who deserved his help, suffered. Yes, even Yukiko who would marry a man she did not love and who most likely would not love her.

Before dawn on the third day, as he lay awake once again counting up his failures and searching for ways to solve at least one of the problems, he suddenly remembered a conversation with Kosehira. Kosehira had spoken of Sukemichi's father and mentioned that he had almost missed out on his appointment to the imperial reserve because someone had accused him of having murdered someone. It had all come to nothing, to mere malicious gossip, when the real killer had confessed. The tale was old and probably meant nothing. It must have happened decades ago. But he had nothing else, and he and Takechi had wondered about some old case that might somehow have involved both the judge and the jailer. He had similarly wondered about the connection with the two old peasants in Okuni. It seemed a little far-fetched, but at this point the old murder was the only event that might connect the new murders in Okuni and Otsu. Yes, and it could also link Sukemichi's death to the others.

Filled with new energy, he jumped out of bed and got dressed. He must wake Kosehira and ask him more questions about this old murder. But when he opened the shutters to the veranda, he saw that it was still dark. Dawn was barely breaking. The sky had turned a silvery gray, but the trees and roofs of Kosehira's villa stood like black outlines against the shimmering light. Kosehira would still be fast asleep.

Akitada debated the matter for a moment, then decided to go sit on the veranda outside Kosehira's room to wait for him to get up. Stepping down to a garden path that led from his pavilion to the main house, he found the darkness not quite so impenetrable after all. The first birds were making small, sleepy noises in the branches overhead, and Akitada could feel the cool dew through his slippers as he walked across the moss.

He had almost reached the main house when it occurred to him that he could not very well sit outside his friend's sleeping quarters. It would be too embarrassing if Kosehira had invited one of his wives to sleep with him. It was not likely, since husbands generally sought out their wives in their own rooms, but such things could happen. He slowed his steps in indecision, then turned around and retraced his way to where another path led to the overlook. He would go there and watch the sun rise over Lake Biwa.

To his dismay, he found he was not the only one who had come to see the sunrise. She was there already, a slender figure with her back to him. He could not retreat without making a sound, and she would surely hate to see him flee like coward. He cleared his throat.

She turned. He could not see her face because the light was behind her. His heart was beating in his throat and he barely managed a whisper: "Forgive me. I didn't know anyone would be here so early. Shall I go away?"

"No, of course not. I was just about to leave myself." She sounded tense.

He did not believe her. "I came to see the sun rise and expect you did, too. Could we watch together?"

She hesitated, then stepped aside to make room for him. "If you wish."

He came to stand beside her at the railing. She was quite close; he could smell her scent but was afraid to look at her.

The view was lovely, much more beautiful than in the daytime, he thought. The colors were softer. All those greens and blues and browns of land, mountains, and city had a silvery sheen—mist perhaps?—and the sky, a much brighter, iridescent silver, was reflected by the lake's surface as if in a mirror. A thin line of gold had appeared along the ridge of the eastern mountains.

There would not be much time. In a little while, the sun would appear, and they would part. He finally turned his head to look at her.

She had come directly from her bed. A blue silk gown was loosely draped around her. It had caught her long hair, still slightly disordered from sleep, underneath, and one heavy strand half covered her cheek. She held the blue silk together with her hands at the waist, and he guessed that she only wore her thin undergown beneath. She was totally desirable, but only a husband should be allowed to see her like this. The blood pounded behind his temples, and he clenched his hands to keep them from touching her.

In his agitation, he burst out, "I hear you are to marry the chancellor's son."

She stared at him. "Did my father tell you?"

"No. Is it a secret?"

"It was meant to be. Who told you?"

"Lord Nakahara. I assumed it was common knowledge in the capital."

She covered her face with her hands, and the blue gown fell open. He had been right. She was in her bedclothes. A part of him reminded him of the impropriety of his being there, but he could not leave.

"Is it not true, then?" he asked, half hopefully.

She lowered her hands. "He is my cousin. We grew up together. Our parents talked about how well suited we were for each other. I think the idea has been raised again. My father has asked me about it."

"And will you marry him?"

She turned her face away. "I suppose so."

THE OLD MEN OF OMI

Neither had noticed the sun come up, but at that moment, Yukiko was bathed in gold: a golden daughter promised to the heir of the most powerful man in the land.

He found nothing to say. Wishes of good fortune and happiness would have been a lie. After a painfully long silence, he said, rather hoarsely, "You are very beautiful, Yukiko. I shall always remember you this way."

Then he bowed and left.

25

The Old Man on the Mountain

The day after Tora and Saburo came to their decision to hunt down Kojo and as many of his cohorts as possible, Saburo claimed that he needed to visit the Sugawara farm to look into some problems with their bookkeeping. He departed on horseback early in the morning.

Tora knew he had gone into the Hiei Mountains and worried himself nearly sick. He did not want Saburo's life on his conscience; he feared Akitada's fury when he discovered their disobedience and dismissed Saburo again; and he felt guilty because the knowledge of his previous, ill-considered adventure rested heavily upon him.

Even while he knew he should rise above his mistake and bear his humiliation at the hands of the *sohei* as fair punishment, he could not rest. If Kojo were killed or rearrested, then the bastard would at least be punished, the dead could rest more easily, and the injured could take some satisfaction from it. He had a duty to himself and to others.

Still, there was Saburo. He claimed to be acting on his own behalf, but he had not made any effort before, and his torture on the mountain was by now many years old.

In the end, he tried to concentrate on what he must do. It was important that no one find out about their plan or they would be stopped. They would leave after dark, and Tora hoped their venture would be finished the same night. He fidgeted and paced restlessly, until Hanae was in the main house and Yuki was with the master's children at their lessons. Then he hurried to secrete his half armor, sword, short sword, and boots under some straw in the stable. After that he could do little but wait.

Saburo did not return by nightfall, but Hanae confronted him.

"What are you up to?" she demanded.

He tried to look innocent. "Nothing, my love. You look very charming when you put your hands on your hips like that and raise your pretty chin."

"Don't lie to me. I'm your wife and I know you're up to something. First you come home all beaten up and sit around looking miserable, and then you're suddenly different, nervous like a cat in heat. For days, I haven't been able to get a word out of you and you barely looked at your son when he showed you proudly what the schoolmaster had written on his essay. You've been neither a husband nor a father!"

Her words wounded him; she confirmed what he had thought to himself: he was no good to them any longer. He tried a smile and failed. With a sigh, he said, "I'm sorry, love," hanging his head and hoping she would not probe further. To his relief, she came, stood on her tiptoes, and put her arms around his neck.

"Oh, Tora, I didn't mean it. We love you. Don't look like that. Tell me what's wrong. We'll find a way."

He was so deeply moved by her words and her embrace that he almost burst out with the whole story, but he had promised Saburo who feared for his job. So he took his wife in his arms, lifting her slight body, and nuzzling her neck. "I love you, too. More than anything, both of you. It hurts me to have you doubt me." Good! Counter complaints might distract her.

Not so.

Hanae released herself. "So what's wrong, husband?" she demanded again.

He sighed. It would have to be lies. He didn't like lies. Hanae had a way of seeing through them. Perhaps a half truth might work. "It's just that I'm such a failure," he muttered. "I let them capture me, and the master saw how useless I was and sent me home."

"Oh." She was taken aback. "But that's silly. You couldn't help it, and you're wrong about the master."

What did women know about male pride?

Tora nodded. "I just realized it myself. I'll be all right. And where's Yuki? I'll take him into town and buy him a new kite to show how proud I am of him."

Hanae brightened. "Oh, he'll like that. And there's a nice breeze. Maybe you can find an open space and fly it? You'll both enjoy that."

And so Tora and his son spent the afternoon together, shopping for the most gorgeous dragon kite and then flying it on the shore of the Kamo River. It was most enjoyable and Tora decided that he would spend more time with Yuki, who was growing up so fast and was already taller than his dainty mother—and much smarter than his father.

But he did not forget about Saburo and what lay ahead in the immediate future.

∞

Night came and with it rain. Saburo had not returned. Tora kept watching the gate anxiously. Eventually, he joined his family for their evening rice, but he kept an ear out for any sounds of Saburo. Before they went to bed, he made one more round to look for him, claiming that he was checking that all was secure for the night. Alone in bed with Hanae, who was more than usually affectionate, he thought of their plan and somehow found that he needed to make love to her before it was too late. Afterward he held her until she was asleep. But he lay awake and fearful, listening to the rain.

He did not know how much later he finally heard a soft rustle outside their room. Then there was a "ssst", and he almost laughed out loud with relief. Slipping carefully from under their shared quilt, he scooped up the pile of his clothing which he had left conveniently close to their bedding, and tiptoed to the shuttered door. This he eased open carefully and soundlessly. He was about to step outside, when Hanae murmured, "Be careful!"

He paused in shock, then said, "I will, because I love you."

Outside, huddled under a dripping roof, Saburo waited.

"How did it go?" Tora asked softly as they hurried toward the stable.

"All right."

"You picked up a trail?"

"Yes."

A strange peace filled Tora's heart. Somehow, overnight, he had found his courage again. Hanae trusted him; his son loved him; and he was about to get his honor back.

They lit a lamp in the stable and Tora put on his clothes. "Tell me," he said.

"There's an old man. He knows where they are."

Tora noticed how wet and tired Saburo looked. "Are you good to go?" he asked anxiously.

"Yes. Just don't wear me out with talking."

"You want to rest a little? Maybe eat something?"

"Don't be silly. Do you want everybody to know?"

Tora said nothing. Hanae knew something was up, but he hoped she would keep the secret. He dug out his boots and half armor, finished putting them on, and shoved his swords through his belt. "Let's go," he said.

They slipped out through the small gate, thankful that there no longer was a dog to wake, and walked to the nearest livery stable where they rented two horses from a sleepy groom. Then they were on the road into the mountains.

The rain had let up a little. Tora looked up at the sky, but it was still heavily overcast. He sniffed the air. "Smells like more rain," he called out to Saburo.

"What?"

"Rain! Are you asleep?" Tora felt instantly guilty for the jibe. Saburo had been in the mountains for more than a day and a night now without any sleep.

Saburo said nothing.

"Sorry, brother. Should we rest?"

"Later. When we're in position."

Tora was curious what "in position" meant but left Saburo alone to doze as they rode.

When they passed through forest, they could see nothing and had to rely on their horses to find the way. The road had narrowed and climbed. The road surface was loose rubble, wet from rain, and the horses slipped now and then. The moisture in the air intensified. Tora wondered how soon the rain would start again and how they could fight in the dark and on slippery ground. Perhaps they could surprise the *sohei* inside some temple building. He hated to ride into a bloody confrontation knowing nothing about what awaited them.

When they emerged from the forest, he could see that they had travelled quite a distance up Mount Hiei and called out again, "Wait, brother! Where are we? And where are we going?"

Saburo reined in his horse and waited for Tora to catch up. "Just another half hour and then we'll go down into a valley. It's on the back of the mountain from the temple side. They're hiding there in an abandoned hut."

"That's good. We can jump them inside. I hate to fight in the rain." Tora held out his hand to catch the first drops. "How many are there?"

"About five or six. One's wounded."

"That means he was in the attack on the tribunal."

"Yes."

Tora grinned. Saburo was a mere shadow in the darkness. "We'll make short work of them, brother."

Saburo said nothing. He urged his horse forward again, and they continued their climb to a ridge that loomed in solid darkness against a charcoal sky with roiling clouds. The rain fell steadily now.

Sometime later they reached the ridge and started downward. The trees had thinned and Tora realized that their path had deteriorated to a mere track. The horses struggled more going downward, and after a while Tora said, "We should walk, I think."

Saburo stopped and they dismounted. Ahead lay more woods. Tora realized they were headed for a mountain valley with a lone dwelling. The rain let up a little, and he studied the clouds overhead. "What time is it, do you think?"

Saburo snorted. "No idea. Too many clouds. Must be close to dawn."

"We won't get back before daylight then?"

"No. Did you expect to?"

"They'll wonder."

"We'll worry about that later."

They continued in silence until they reached the wooden building in the valley. It was simple, covered with thatch, and nearly black with age and the wetness of the rain. They were no longer in darkness but in a gray twilight.

Saburo rode up to the door, dismounted, and tied his horse to the railing of the steps.

Tora saw this with surprise. Surely the *sohei* couldn't be inside.

Saburo climbed the steps and knocked at the door that hung crookedly from rusty hinges.

Tora dismounted also, his hand on his sword hilt just in case.

But when the door opened, a very old man appeared on the threshold. He had long white hair and a long white beard and wore a heavy, ragged brown robe over grayish white underclothes that were unidentifiable but all cut off at about knee height. His bare legs were thin and dark from the sun.

A hermit, Tora decided with a smile of relief and tied up his horse.

The hermit peered closely at Saburo and said in a cracked voice, "It's you again, is it?"

"Yes, grandfather, and I've brought my friend as I promised. This is Tora. Tora, this is Master Cricket. "

Tora joined Saburo. Placing his hands together, he bowed. "Good morning, venerable master. I hope we didn't wake you."

The old man took a step closer and brought his face toward Tora's. "Hmm," he said, "one of you has good manners. Come inside."

The inside of the hut—it was hardly more than that, having only two small rooms—was dark, but the old man, who must be nearly blind, went unerringly to a small shelf which held an oil lamp, struck a flint, and lit it. "I don't need it," he said. "But you two still have eyes that see. Sit down. There's some water if you're thirsty."

They declined politely. Soaked by the rain, they had no wish for more water, though hot wine would have been welcome.

Saburo explained, "Master Cricket has lived here all his life. Even though his sight is weak, he knows the whole mountain like the back of his hand."

The old hermit snorted. "He thinks I was born here, a child of the mountain pine and the *kami* of Oyamakuhi."

Tora laughed. "Saburo has faith in your wisdom and so do I." He was not sure why they had come to this old man and waited for Saburo to clarify the matter.

Saburo did not oblige. Instead he asked the hermit, "Are they still there?"

"One left last night. He's back. Carried a sack."

Saburo nodded. Silence fell. Then Saburo said, "It's two against five. We may not get them all. Can you hide somewhere or maybe go away for a day or so?"

Tora began to grasp what was going on. "Where exactly are they?" he asked.

They ignored him. The old man simply said, "I've never left this place and I won't do so now."

"They'll know it was you who gave them away. They're brutal."

"No."

"Very well. Thank you, Master Cricket. Let's go, Tora."

Outside, day had broken at the mountain top. The clouds were parting and the rising sun touched it with fire. To Tora, it looked truly like what it was: a holy mountain. He touched the amulet around his neck and muttered a prayer. The valley still lay in a blue shadow, its forest wreathed in mist.

"You might keep me informed," Tora complained. "I'd like to know what I'm getting into. I take it we are to kill all five?"

Saburo nodded. "Kill or disable so they cannot harm the old man. He's a saint. I'll not have him on my conscience."

"You have no sword. Am I to do all the work? And you never answered my question. Where are they?"

"Holed up in a hut used by wood gatherers. It's farther on in the valley."

"Hmm. The old man is blind. Can you trust what he says he saw? How do you know it's them? How do you know there are only five?"

"You'll find out soon enough. Let's go!" Saburo untied his horse and climbed on.

Tora controlled himself. His headache was back and put him in bad mood. And truth to tell, he no longer was so sure of himself. He did not want to die, not when Hanae and Yuki were waiting for him. He did not want to do that to them. Or to the master. He sighed and mounted his horse, hoping the god of the mountain was with him this day.

After following the road through more forest for about a mile, Saburo dismounted. "We leave the horses here and walk," he said, his voice tense.

Tora, his head pounding, was resentful. Why had Saburo not kept him informed? He might have found their hideout, but that did not give him the right to run this show.

After they had led their horses some way into the forest where they were hidden from the track, they tied them to trees.

"What next?" Tora growled. "Or am I to wait for a surprise?"

Saburo shot him a glance. "What? Oh. Sorry. My mind was on how best to handle this."

Outraged, Tora snapped, "You might have consulted me. Maybe you want to do this alone?"

"Tora, calm down. I was about to tell you."

Tora glowered, but he listened. Saburo, having learned from Master Cricket that some *sohei* were living in a wood gatherer's hut, had reconnoitered and verified that they were the men they wanted. Kojo had been sitting outside, drinking *sake.*

"There are five? One wounded?" asked Tora.

"Yes. Not badly wounded."

"Armed?"

"Yes."

"What do you propose?"

Saburo told him and after some reflection, Tora gave his approval. They started walking.

26

The *Betto* Hatta

Akitada found Kosehira not only awake but on his veranda, stretching and peering up at the rapidly changing sky. Already the soft rosy colors of the sunrise were fading to mere brightness, and the sky was turning blue.

Akitada was only partly aware of this. His heart and mind were still filled with the golden image of Yukiko, standing there by the railing, telling him that she would marry her cousin. His idea about the Jizo killer faded in significance, and when Kosehira greeted him with a cheerful, "Akitada! What brings you so early?" he found little enthusiasm in explaining his theory.

Kosehira stared at him. "That old murder? You think an old murder is behind this? I don't see how this could be. Not only was this—what?—at least twenty years ago, but the case was cleared up and the killer confessed. Are you suggesting that he somehow survived and returned to avenge himself?"

Akitada said stubbornly, "I've had a feeling all along that something happened long ago and that it involved the judge and the jailer. I just did not know how the two old peasants from Okuni fit in. Then Sukemichi, their overlord, was also killed and his father was involved in a notorious murder case. In a murder case, mind you, where he was the suspect. What more do you want?"

Kosehira sighed. "I suppose it's the archives then. There should be documents covering any murder case important enough to involve a Taira."

∞

The archives, however, were the place where Akitada's team had been working industriously on the legal documents involving the temples Enryaku-ji and Onjo-ji. The hall was cluttered with people and stacks of document boxes in various states of completion. In fact, Akitada's own desk nearly sagged under towering stack of paperwork that had been gathered for his information or study.

He and Kosehira stood for a moment at the entrance, regarding the place in despair.

"I should be at work here." Akitada stated the obvious.

"We'll cause all sorts of confusion," Kosehira said.

For a moment they remained undecided, then Kosehira found his archivist, who had been lending a hand to the guests, and directed him to find documents relating to trials some fifteen to twenty-five years ago.

The elderly man bowed and led them to shelving where dusty boxes had been resting in possibly permanent peace. He dusted off the first stack with an old rag he carried and remarked, "The most notorious case involved Taira Sukenori. It happened in the Echi district and . . ."

"That's the one," Kosehira and Akitada cried together.

The archivist paused and looked at them in surprise. "Just that year and none of the others?"

"Just that case," said Akitada.

A moment later, they both sat on the floor with a single document box. As an economy, the filing system required that only the basic facts of major cases be kept. The box contained documentation for other murder trials, as well as for two cases of arson and a trial for piracy on Lake Biwa. Even so, the Taira murder consisted of an impressive number of sheets.

Kosehira read, passing each sheet to Akitada when he was done.

"Something wasn't right with this case," Akitada remarked. "Did you see where Hatta tried to withdraw his confession?"

"It only says that the condemned prisoner protested his sentence. So, apparently, did his son. Who was this Hatta?"

Akitada shuffled through the pages. "It says he was Sukenori's *betto.*"

"Perhaps he was angry that Sukenori did not help him?"

"Hmm. The case seems clear enough. The victim, a rice merchant, was staying at the Taira manor as a guest. During a hunt, to which this Fumi Takahiro had been invited, Hatta shot him with his bow and arrow. Apparently there had been an argument over Hatta's daughter being dishonored by Fumi the night before. He shot him close range. There was no question about this being a hunting accident."

Kosehira frowned. "It seems straightforward enough."

"Did you note the names of the two witnesses?"

Kosehira took another look. "They were two beaters. Oh! Juro and Wakiya. Yes. But I still don't see it."

"No, but there is a hint here that Hatta may not have been guilty. Add that to the rumors about Sukenori, and it looks very much as if Hatta confessed to protect his master."

"And regretted it."

The archivist cleared his throat. They looked at him.

"There was another case involving a Hatta, Excellency. In the following year. Shall I get that box, too?"

"By all means," said Akitada. He turned to Kosehira and said, "I think we've got it. I think we've solved the mystery. What do you think?" He rubbed his hands in his eagerness to prove the point.

Kosehira looked happy, too. "You know, I should remember more about this story. Of course, I was preoccupied with my own affairs. Graduating from the university, trying for my first post, a new marriage. But I do recall talk about Sukenori. Something about a business quarrel over debt. You think that Sukenori bribed his way out of a murder charge? He was supposed to be in financial trouble."

"Excellent! Now we have a motive."

"It would take a lot of money to make another man confess to murder," Kosehira said dubiously.

The archivist returned, blowing dust from another old box. He set it down, saying, "It involved a relative, I think. The Hattas must have been a violent family."

Akitada reached eagerly for the box. Together with Kosehira, he scanned the content until they found the name again.

"Here it is. Hatta Takashi." Kosehira pointed. "Must be the son. There's not much here, is there?"

The incident that led to the arrest and conviction of Hatta Takashi was the young man's attack on Taira Sukenori, during which Sukenori suffered a serious knife wound. Apparently Sukenori had pressed the judge (Nakano) for a quick judgment that would remove this violent youth from the area. Hatta Takashi was sent into exile and hard labor, just as his father had been the year before."

Akitada asked the archivist, "Is there any further news of either Hatta?"

The old man shook his head. "Not to my knowledge. Perhaps their family is still in the area, though their property would have been confiscated after the murder conviction. That information would be in the land surveys. Do you want me to look?"

Yes, they did.

What they found confirmed the archivist's assumption that the property had been confiscated. The victim's family had been paid off and the rest, all but a small parcel, had become government property, but now belonged to Enryaku-ji.

Kosehira commented bitterly, "Soon those monks will own all of my province."

The second case against Hatta's son caused the confiscation of the small parcel left to the children. This property was given to Taira Sukenori as recompense for the serious wound he had suffered at the hands of the younger Hatta.

Kosehira said, "So both the father and the son were sent into exile and hard labor. After all this time, they are most likely dead. That leaves the mother and a daughter. What happened to them?"

But the archivist had no answer this time.

Akitada sighed. "We must go back and talk to the older peasants in the area. That old man serving in the stables at the Taira manor knew something he didn't want to talk about. I bet he has the answer."

"I cannot possibly leave again," Kosehira said. "Work has piled up while we were hunting."

Akitada glanced over at his desk. "Neither can I. The clerks are almost done. I need to look at their reports and then write up my own."

There was another reason for his wish to finish his assignment. He knew he had to leave Kosehira's house.

Staying even one more day after what had passed between him and Yukiko was impossible.

They sat silently for a few moments. Then Kosehira asked, "Do you think he will kill again?"

"I don't know. Is there anyone left alive who had a hand in the trials of the two Hattas?"

"What about the original victim. Do we know anything about him?"

They bent over the documents again. Even the archivist inserted himself to help. Akitada was amused. For once, they had managed to rouse the curiosity of a man who only cared about keeping his boxes filed in the proper order.

"There it is," cried Kosehira, finding the page. " 'The Otsu merchant Fumi Takahiro, in his fortieth year.' Fumi? Now I wonder. . ."

The archivist cried, "Yes, sir. There is a rice dealer near the harbor. His name is Fumi. A very wealthy man."

"Well, he cannot be the same." Akitada smiled. "A son perhaps?"

"I don't know," said the archivist. "He's quite old, I think."

"Hmm." Akitada pondered for a moment. "I think I'll pay him a visit later tonight after we deal with our duties."

Kosehira gave a sigh of relief. "I cannot tell you how much work awaits me. I'll have dinner here and go back late."

Akitada was helping the archivist return the papers to their boxes. He nodded. "I'll have a bite in the city. Don't wait up for me. I'll see you in the morning."

Much better than risking another meeting with Yukiko. But he could not help the pain this thought brought with it.

∞

Akitada walked to Otsu Harbor. He wished he could have told Takechi what they had discovered, but it was too late. The chief had gone home to his family.

Not having any family to go to, Akitada had a quick meal in a busy restaurant catering to travelers. The food was barely edible, but he had little appetite anyway. He paid and asked directions to the business of the rice merchant Fumi. He was told that Fumi Tokiari lived in a substantial home close to the harbor. It turned out to be one of several such properties belonging to wealthy merchants and ship owners. In this case, there was still a sort of business in the front of the large building where people could purchase rice for their households, but Akitada had been told that most of the family's business was in shipping large amounts of rice to the capital and that part of the business operated from warehouses close to the port.

Still, given the Fumi wealth, Akitada approved of the modesty that still acknowledged humble beginnings when many another rich man had already moved to an estate in the suburbs. He passed into the shop, where he was greeted politely by two clerks, and asked to speak to Fumi Tokiari. A clerk dashed off to announce him, and a moment later a heavy-set elderly man in a sober black silk robe emerged from the back.

"I am Sugawara," Akitada introduced himself, "and temporarily attached to the governor's office. His Excellency has asked me to look into some troubling local crimes. You could be most helpful by giving me some information."

Fumi looked surprised and uneasy, but he bowed deeply and led the way to the back of the house. There, in the well-furnished office where he conducted his business he offered Akitada a seat and refreshments.

"Nothing, thank you. I'm not altogether sure what your relationship to Fumi Takahiro is, but my interest concerns him rather than you."

"He was my brother."

Akitada thought the man's nervousness had increased and wondered at it. "I understand he was the victim of a murder on the estate of Lord Taira Sukenori?"

Fumi compressed his lips. "Yes."

It was clear that Akitada would have to work for his information.

"The man who confessed to the crime was Lord Taira's *betto*, a man by the name of Hatta. He was sentenced to life in the mines in the north. Apparently his son later attacked Lord Taira. Do you happen to know why he should have done such a thing?"

"I know very little about the case, sir. My brother had some business with Lord Taira and, since he enjoyed hunting, he had been invited to the Taira estate. Lord Taira was a great hunter. The murder happened during a hunt. Lord Taira at first claimed it was an accident, but the arrow tip protruded from my poor brother's back and the authorities decided he must have been shot by someone very close and facing him. This caused a lot of rumors and I pressed for an investigation. It was then that the man Hatta confessed."

"But what was his motive?"

Fumi made a face. "The man had the nerve to claim that my brother had attacked his young daughter sexually."

"That would constitute a strong motive. A father has a right to protect his children. You clearly did not believe this. Why wasn't Hatta given consideration during the sentencing.?"

Fumi had reddened with anger. "Because it was a foul lie! My brother would never have laid a hand on the girl."

"It does you credit to defend your brother," Akitada said dubiously.

"Of course I defend my brother, but in this case there was proof that my brother was innocent."

"How so?"

"My brother preferred men to women. He was unmarried and had never shown any interest in females." Fumi paused. "That's why I am his heir. He never had any children."

"Ah!" Akitada nodded. "That is very interesting. You must have wondered at the time who would make up such stories."

"Not at all. Hatta lied."

"Yes, perhaps. What sort of business did your brother have with Lord Taira?"

The look of uneasiness returned to the rice merchant's face. "My brother had advanced his lordship some funds from time to time. It was good business. The money earned a satisfactory interest. Lord Taira had a great estate to administer and a certain manner of living that required a good deal of money."

"I see. When you came to settle your brother's estate, had all the debts been paid?"

Fumi fidgeted. "No. And I never got the money either. Lord Taira claimed there was no debt, that he had paid my brother before his death. I tried to collect from his son after he died, but he also refused."

"Was it a large debt?"

"Very large. I almost lost the business."

Akitada studied the merchant with interest. Fumi certainly had no love for the Taira family, father or son. He might well have a good motive for murdering Sukemichi. Sukemichi had never fitted very well with the other victims. But after a moment, he discarded the notion, thanked Fumi, and left.

It was getting dark by then and he was tired, but instead of returning to the villa, he stayed on in the tribunal for several more hours, working on the legal documents on his desk. Only a servant was still in the archives, and he felt guilty for keeping the man from his bed. But he felt a great urgency to finish this assignment and return to the capital. The children would be disappointed that they would not attend the great shrine festival after all, but he would try to make it up to them.

When he finally closed the last document box and stretched, the servant was fast asleep leaning against a pillar. Akitada looked with satisfaction at the pile of pages that constituted his notes. Tomorrow he would draft his report, discuss it with the members of his group, and then give it the final polish. The clerks would make copies, he and the others would sign, and they would all return to their homes.

For a moment, he recalled her image as he had seen her last, a slender figure in blue surrounded by the golden light of the rising sun. He had made his farewells on that occasion, telling her that he would always remember her just like that.

He doubted it was enough to live on in the future.

27

The Wood Shed

The path leading up the side of the mountain was rough and stony. The rain had stopped, but everything was wet. They slipped and scrambled as they climbed. Tora was getting very tired and wondered how Saburo, for whom this was the same climb in less than eight hours, managed. The track took them back into dense woods and into a twilight that persisted even though the sun must be well up. After quite a long time, Tora asked, "How much farther?"

Saburo paused and looked back. "It was dark when I came this way before. I'm not sure. I'm not sure where we are or if we are on the right path. I'm moving by instinct only."

Tora cursed. His head still hurt and the physical exertion made the pain worse. "Let's stop to check. There must be a clearing somewhere." He looked around and pointed. "Over there. Maybe we can get a glimpse of the valley and you can fix on the direction."

Saburo grunted his assent, and they left the path to clamber along the steep slope toward where light appeared between the trees. Not for the first time, Tora cursed his sword which managed to get in his way in this thicket. Saburo, who did not have a sword, but who carried secret weapons hidden in the sleeves and linings of his clothes and inside his boots, was better off.

The outlook, when they reached it, showed them that they had climbed quite a way, but there was no sign of any dwelling. Forest stretched along both sides of the valley and below there were only glimpses of a small stream and an occasional section of the narrow road.

"Well?" Tora asked.

Saburo frowned. "Maybe a little more to the east. We should have stayed on the path."

Tora leaned forward to peer toward the east. "Is that smoke or mist?" he asked.

"I can't make it out, but it could be them. Cooking their morning rice."

"Let's go!" Tora said grimly and turned back.

"Wait!"

"What now?"

"You sound pretty touchy, brother. And you don't look well, if you don't mind my saying so."

"I do mind. Let's get this over with and kill the bastards."

"We have to be careful. We don't know who else might have come since I last saw them. And when we get close, we have to creep through the trees. It will be better if we surprise them."

"Right, but if we wait around talking about it, they may find us before we find them."

Saburo said no more. Together they reached the path again and followed it for a short while until the trees started to thin and light could be seen.

"All right," Saburo said in a low voice. "From now on we creep." He left the path and Tora followed. With great care, they reached a promontory, and there just below them, was a fair-sized wooden hut with a wooden shelter a little farther along the road . Smoke rose from an opening in the roof of the hut. The shelter contained stacked firewood. The narrow road passed in front of these buildings, probably the same one that also passed the hermit's dwelling at the other end of the valley. The road disappeared around another rocky outcropping like the one Tora and Saburo lay on.

There was no sign of life other than the smoke, though the sun was already high. They watched in silence for a while, then Tora said, "Are you sure they're all there?"

"They were yesterday."

"Maybe they left?"

"It's possible."

"Shall we go down to check?"

Saburo hesitated, then nodded. "Careful. They could be coming out."

"Right." Tora got to his feet, checked his sword, and rubbed his sore head. Even his eyes hurt. What was wrong with him? He had had the headaches for more than a year now, but they had never happened as often or been as long-lasting and severe."

"Wait," Saburo hissed.

Tora turned and looked.

A couple had appeared on the road. They were poorly dressed and both had large, woven baskets slung over their shoulders. The man also carried a toddler.

"Wood gatherers," said Tora.

"More like wood thieves."

The couple halted by the shed. The man put down the toddler and both took off their baskets and carried them to the wood piles in the shelter where they started loading them. The toddler staggered to his feet and explored his surroundings.

"This isn't good," Tora observed.

"We can't get down there fast enough to warn them."

They watched with growing anxiety as the child made its circuitous and frequently interrupted way to the door of the hut. His parents had cast an occasional glance his way but seemed unconcerned.

"They don't know anybody's there," Saburo commented.

Tora said hopefully, "Maybe they're right."

"You forget the smoke."

The child crawled up the steps to the door and sat down on the small porch. For a while nothing else happened. The parents had almost filled their baskets.

Tora gritted his teeth. "They have enough. Why don't they leave well enough alone, get the kid, and head home?"

But they stacked their loads precariously high. Then the man helped the woman put on her basket. Its heavy load bent her almost double. The husband crouched, slipped on his own basket, and rose.

They could not hear it, but one of them, or perhaps both, called out to the child to come. The toddler was an obedient boy. He got up, climbed laboriously down the three steps, and turned to run to his parents.

At that moment, the door of the hut flew open and one of the *sohei* appeared on the threshold.

"Too late," groaned Tora.

Things happened quickly after that. The *sohei* alerted his companions who came out, armed with swords and *naginata,* and started after the couple, viciously kicking the toddler out of their way. There were five of them.

"Come," cried Tora, and started down the side of the mountain.

It was a long way down. They slipped and slid, holding on to branches, cursing, vaguely aware of the violence that was playing out below them. Once Saburo tumbled past Tora, who caught him before he fell.

There was no point in being quiet any longer; the warrior monks were otherwise occupied and paid no attention to the hillside. As Tora and Saburo got closer, they could hear pitiful screams and the bawling of the child. They could no longer see the scene when the screams stopped and only the child still whimpered. They were now in some woods on the valley floor.

Tora drew his sword and ran, dodging trees and shrubs, aware of Saburo's rapid breath behind him.

When they reached the road, they saw a pitiful scene. The child was softly whimpering where he had fallen while his father lay much too still between the two baskets of wood that had spilled their contents all across the road. The *sohei* and the woman had disappeared.

Tora bent to check the child. His eyes were open but blood was coming from his mouth and nose. He was breathing in gasps and making an enervating mewling sound. Saburo was ahead, bent over the man.

"How is he?" Tora asked when he reached him.

Saburo straightened. "Dead. The kid?"

"Bad, but alive." Tora stared at the body. The young man lay on his stomach. A puddle of blood was slowly spreading under him. Tora started to bend down, but Saburo stopped him.

"Leave it. They slashed his throat."

Of one accord they turned their eyes toward the shed. From this position they could not see much of the inside, but they heard voices and a woman's pleading.

Tora made a move, but Saburo caught his arm. "Careful," he warned.

They crept up to the wall of the shelter from behind it.

Inside, one of the *sohei* shouted, "Give it to her! That's right! Punish the thieving bitch good!"

Someone laughed. Then another cried, "Harder! The bitch is enjoying it too much." More laughter.

"Slowly!" hissed Saburo, and they started for the corner.

Just about then, the woman screamed shrilly. A burst of laughter followed, and Tora pushed Saburo aside and jumped around the corner.

The scene was familiar. The old woman had described it when she had told them about the gang rape of the porter's wife. Tora rushed past the nearest *sohei* and used his sword to slash the bare buttocks of the animal who was belaboring the woman under him.

It was an almost fatal mistake. He heard shouts and the hissing sounds as swords slid from their scabbards. Desperately, he jumped aside, falling down among pieces of firewood. A *naginata* whistled past his thigh.

After this there was only chaos. Tora tried to get up, slipped on a log, saw the blade of the *naginata* coming at him again. Raising himself on one knee, he used his sword to deflect the blade and felt the blow all the way to his shoulder. His arm went numb and he fell again. Somewhere a man screamed, and he gave Saburo a fleeting thought. But the *naginata* was not done with him, and this time he knew he could not manage to block it with the sword. In a desperate leap he jumped past the blade and seized the shaft with both hands. He tugged, and the *sohei* stumbled forward. Tora gave him a vicious kick in the groin, then pushed his short sword into his belly. The *sohei* screamed and fell.

Before Tora could get a clear picture of the situation, two other *sohei* came for him with their swords. His sword arm was still numb, but he grabbed the fallen *naginata* and swung it at them. They retreated. Tora dropped the weapon and found his sword, seizing it with both hands. He charged them, aiming at their bellies. As he had expected, they separated, thinking to slash at him when he missed them, but he ducked, swerved, and buried his sword in the belly of the man to his right. With no time to retrieve it, he kept moving. How many were left? Two were down, one was coming after him. Where was Saburo?

Then he saw him. He lay near the front of the shed. No time! He had to get out of the way of that sword.

Unarmed, he stumbled over the *naginata*. Its owner was still curled up and groaning, but he snatched at Tora's leg and made him fall. Tora's hand caught the *naginata* and seized it. He kicked out at the *sohei* and stumbled to his feet just as a sword missed his left shoulder and struck the *sohei* instead. The *sohei* on the ground screamed only once but so horribly that his fellow froze just long enough for Tora to put some distance between them and turn.

He was not trained in fighting with a *naginata*, but guessed it was not so different from the heavy oak staffs used in stick fighting and he was very good at that. Swinging the weapon out in a wide arc he then reversed into the opposite direction while running at the two remaining *sohei* who were coming for him with their swords. He saw their eyes widen in shock, saw that one was Kojo, saw him jumping aside, and the other raising his sword to deflect the halberd's blade. But Tora's force was too great. The sword went flying, and Tora slashed his belly. The man fell, clutching himself.

Turning on his heel, Tora saw Kojo running out of the shelter and followed. A violent fury had seized him at what they had done to the wood gatherers, and this red-hot energy had not left him throughout the battle. He seemed to fly across the rough ground, down the rutted mountain road after the fleeing figure.

He caught up with Kojo where the road made the turn and roared, "Coward! Stop and fight like a man!"

The other, not having much choice in the matter, did stop soon after. Kojo still had his sword and the courage of despair.

Kojo! The one he had wanted to kill with his own hands.

Too late Tora realized that the *sohei* had stopped among trees and shrubs. The *naginata* was of little use here because he could not slash with it. This battle would have to be fought close up, and Tora no longer had his sword.

Mere details, he decided in his fury.

Holding the *naginata* straight in front of himself, he charged. Kojo jumped aside and laughed. But he was now at the very edge of a ditch. Hoping that he did not realize this, Tora changed his grip and charged again. This time Kojo slashed at the *naginata* with his sword and severed the wooden shaft. He laughed again, stepped back, and fell.

Tora was on him instantly. Using the splintered end of the *naginata* shaft on Kojo's neck to pin him down, he watched the *sohei* choke out a gurgling scream and drop his sword to claw at his neck. Tora snatched up the sword and hacked off Kojo's head.

Then he took a couple of steps and his knees buckled. He collapsed, and sat on the ground, hunched over, breathing heavily, and waiting for the pain. There must be pain. He felt sure he had been wounded though he did not know where or how badly.

The pain came, but it was in his head. It pounded viciously so that he held on to his head for fear it would come apart.

When the throbbing eased a little, he recalled Saburo. He had last seen him stretched out lifeless in the wood shed. He was either dead of badly wounded. And Tora had left him there with at least one *sohei* still alive.

He staggered to his feet. Carrying Kojo's bloody sword he headed back.

All was quiet around the hut and shed. Tora heaved a sigh. How would he explain Saburo's death? What could he say to his mother, unlikable though the woman was? What would his master say? He had been disobedient once too often. Perhaps he, Hanae, and Yuki would become homeless and masterless.

He cast a glance around in case one of the *sohei* was lurking. Seeing nobody, he went to the shed.

The smell of blood was strong. Saburo's body was gone, but four others lay about. The ground was wet and slick with blood. Tora checked them. All *sohei* and all dead. Two had died from the wounds he had dealt them, but the other two had been merely disabled. Now they had their throats cut.

He looked around, half hoping. If Saburo had killed them, then he might not be too badly hurt.

"Saburo?"

An answering shout came from the hut. He walked across. The door stood open. Clutching the sword, Tora looked in.

Saburo sat on the floor. Beside him knelt the wood gatherer's wife, her face bloody and bruised, but her hands busy bandaging Saburo's left thigh. The bandage was leaking blood, and Tora guessed that he had been slashed badly.

"How is it, brother?" he asked.

"It will do. Did you get that bastard Kojo?"

"Yes."

Tora's strength gave way again, and he flopped down.

"Are you wounded?" Saburo asked anxiously.

"I don't think so. Just very tired. And my head hurts."

"Sorry, brother."

"It's nothing." He looked at the young woman. "I'm very sorry," he told her. "We saw, but we were too far away. Are you all right?"

She looked back at him with dull eyes. "No," she said. "But it was my *karma.*" She glanced over to a corner of the room. Tora saw that she or Saburo had put her child there. The boy was much too still. "He was a very good boy," she said. "He always did what we told him." She bowed her head, then looked back up at Tora. "Why?" she asked him. "Why did they kill such a good little boy?"

Tora sighed. "I don't know, love," he said heavily. "I don't know why terrible things happen. I'm very sorry we couldn't stop them."

"Not your fault," she said listlessly and finished tying Saburo's bandage.

"What will you do?" Saburo asked.

"Go home and ask my neighbors to help me bring my husband home. I'll carry Kaoru myself."

"You're not hurt?" Tora asked.

"I'm strong," she said and go to her feet.

Tora said, "We have horses, back in the woods." It was a long way and uphill, but he would have to go and get them. Saburo could not walk.

"No. I want to go alone." She lifted her dead child to cradle him in her arms and kiss his bloody face.

Tora started to his feet, but Saburo said quietly, "Let her go. She needs her grief."

28

A Strange Case

Akitada reached his bed long after Kosehira's household had retired. A sleepy porter had admitted him and taken his horse. Akitada was thankful that the sure-footed beast had known its way home on its own. His bedding had been laid out by Kosehira's servants, and he flung his robe over the clothing stand, pulled off his boots, and fell asleep as soon as he lay down.

The next morning promised another sunny day. Akitada woke late, avoided the garden, washed, dressed, and ate the gruel provided by another servant, then headed for the stables. Kosehira joined him shortly and they rode to work together.

"I'm almost finished with the temple investigation," Akitada said casually on the way.

"Ah. What will you do next?"

Here it was. Akitada smiled at his friend. "I must return to my duties in the capital."

This clearly distressed Kosehira, who said nothing for a moment.

"You have been a kind, generous, and patient host. I shall always remember this visit fondly," Akitada added.

He would always remember it for quite different reasons; for that matter, he had used almost the same words to bid her goodbye.

Kosehira said, "I'm sorry." His tone was almost funereal. He added for good measure, "Sorrier than you'll ever know."

Akitada could not let this pass. "Why? I shall not be far away, and we shall meet again in the capital. I hope you come often."

Kosehira looked into the distance, a distance that consisted of the great lake, shimmering in the sun and surrounded by green mountains. "It's just . . . I had hoped . . ." He paused, then asked, "But what about the Great Shrine Festival? You were going to stay for that and have your children join us."

Ashamed, Akitada muttered something about not having reckoned on finishing quite so early and not having permission to stay away from the ministry. It sounded lame, but Kosehira did not argue.

At the tribunal, they went their separate ways, and Akitada returned to the archives to discuss his report with the others.

Essentially, both temples had engaged in quasi-legal land transfers to themselves by offering landowners tax free status. Since Akitada disapproved strongly of these attempts to evade fair taxes, he had made a careful list of all the cases during the past decade, with the recommendation to disallow them. Nothing would come of this, but he thought those who complained all the time that taxes had shrunk and demands on the government grown should see one reason why this was so.

More complicated were cases where temples had appropriated land without the approval of the owners. In some situations, this involved land grabs of unimproved acreages belonging to the emperor with the promise to turn the land into productive rice fields. This option was granted to tax-paying landowners, but it had been the temples that had accumulated vast acreage this way.

Lastly there was the matter of disputed land, that is, of land claimed by both temples. All of these cases had been carefully traced through the documents, and the outcome showed that Onjo-ji had legal rights in nine of the cases, while Enryaku-ji could claim only one disputed tract.

"Enryaku-ji won't like it," the tribunal archivist remarked, smiling with satisfaction.

Kunyoshi, the imperial archivist, was quick to dash such hopes. "We can assert the correctness of our findings, but getting them to hand back the land is another matter."

Akitada said, "It doesn't matter. I shall write my report and urge strongly that the various abuses be stopped immediately and that Enryaku-ji be assessed a penalty for its strong-arm methods. Following upon the attack on the tribunal, we may, for once, see some small measure of success."

They nodded their agreement.

Akitada thanked them for their work, adding, "The rest of the chore is mine. I shall remain to write my report. You will want to wish to return to your families."

They did and left quite happily.

Akitada stayed behind to work on his report. The archives were disconcertingly empty. Only Kosehira's archivist and a clerk were still present, and they worked at returning all the documents to their proper places. Their voices reached his ears from time to time, as did noises of moving ladders and, once, of dropped boxes.

But it was not this that kept him from concentrating on his writing. Neither was it the complex nature of the case. He had prepared his notes carefully and could work quickly from them.

Yukiko he put firmly from his mind.

The matter of the murders troubled him, however, as did the fact that he would have to leave things in the hands of Chief Takechi. He expected to be gone from Otsu the next morning. True, Takechi was a capable man and it was his case after all. But even so he felt that he was letting him down—and Kosehira, too—by withdrawing from the investigation at this point.

As for Yukiko: he no longer saw his departure as a cowardly flight. Their relationship had reached the point where his continued proximity was embarrassing and painful for her. No, he must leave. And so he worked industriously until midday when thoughts of the murders intruded again and his stomach growled. Rinsing out and putting down his brush, he stretched his stiff back, and got up. He would have another meal with Takechi and settle matters between them.

∞

Takechi greeted him eagerly. "I'd hoped to see you yesterday. Any news?"

"Yes, there is some, but I'd like to share another of those delicious bowls of soup with you, if you can manage it."

Takechi could manage it. "It's my turn," he said cheerfully as they walked to the noodle restaurant.

"Takechi," Akitada said apologetically, "allow me the privilege since it will be the last time I'll have the pleasure,"

Takechi stopped. "What? What happened?"

"Nothing that wouldn't have happened in any case. I'm finished with my assignment and must return."

"But the murder case—did you solve it?"

"No. But, Takechi, it was never my case. It was yours, and for the deaths in Echi district, the local prefect's."

Takechi looked at him as if bereft of words. "Yes," he said finally. "That's true enough. Still . . ." His voice trailed off.

"Come, cheer up. I know you'll do fine. And I do have one more piece of news."

They had reached the restaurant where an eager waiter greeted them at the door and guided them to good seats. They placed their orders and then looked at each other.

Takechi said, "I have enjoyed working with you again, sir. This is a real blow."

Akitada bit his lip. He would also miss the easy friendship that had sprung up between them and felt guilty that his private concerns should affect a man he had a strong liking for. "I, too, regret it very much," he said. "I've come to consider you a friend." He smiled at Takechi. "But I don't forget my friends and will make a point of stopping by your office when I can, and I hope you will come to my house whenever you are in the capital. We have one or two decent eating places ourselves, you know."

Takechi, clearly pleased by the invitation, chuckled. "I have no doubt, sir. It's our capital after all. Everything's better there."

"Not really," said Akitada soberly, thinking of his lonely life. "But let me tell you what we've found in the archives." He explained how he had begun to focus on the rumors concerning the late Lord Taira Sukenori and the murder that had happened more than twenty years earlier."

Takechi listened, spell-bound. Their soup arrived and stood steaming before them. After some time, the waiter approached nervously to ask if anything was wrong. He was waved away. Finally Akitada reached the end of his account and lifted his bowl.

Takechi stared at him, lost in thought.

"Eat," Akitada urged, smacking his lips. "It's very good. Perhaps the best yet."

"I'm thinking," protested Takechi, but he began to eat, sipping and chewing the noodles slowly. Nodding his head from time to time. When he set his bowl down empty, he said, "It fits. It all hangs together. You think the son has come back."

"If he did not die in exile, I think he would have. He was younger and stronger than his father. Some people live an entire life in a prison colony."

"The problem is, we aren't sure, and we don't know where he is and what he looks like."

"Precisely."

A silence fell while they both pondered the issue. After a while, Takechi asked, "Could it be someone else? Someone who is also part of the Hatta family? I suppose I need to find out who they are. I expect their property was confiscated?"

"Yes. In the immediate family there were only the father, the mother, and two children. The other child was a daughter." Akitada paused. A thought had just occurred to him. But it seemed far-fetched.

Takechi had watched him. "You had an idea?"

"It's probably nothing. I'm trying to recall something someone said." Akitada shook his head. "From the start we've had too many people involved in this. It's difficult to place them properly. But that reminds me that there is someone else of interest. I had a talk with the brother of the victim."

"Which victim?"

Akitada chuckled. "Quite right. We have too many murders, too many suspects, and too many investigations. I meant the brother of the original victim. His name was Fumi Takahira. He was a wealthy merchant here in Otsu."

"Oh, you talked to Tokiari. What did he have to say?"

"Something wasn't quite right about that conversation. Tokiari knows something he's not talking about. He confirmed that his brother was a guest of Taira Sukemichi when the *betto* killed him during a hunt. Fumi was shot point-blank with an arrow. An attempt to claim it had been a hunting accident failed, because the local prefect—a good man apparently—saw that he had been shot at close range. After that Hatta confessed, claiming that Fumi had raped his young daughter."

Takechi said angrily, "If he did, then to my mind, he had a perfect right to shoot the animal!"

Akitada shook his head. "Apparently the prefect didn't believe the tale, and Hatta was denied extenuating circumstances. Fumi's brother rejected the charge adamantly. He claims his brother preferred men and would never have raped a woman."

"Ah! What a tale! Go on."

Akitada chuckled. "Sorry. That's all I have. You'll have to find out the rest."

Takechi threw up his hands. "Where do I start? If it's Hatta's son who did all this, why did he do it? If his father was guilty, I mean."

"Yes, that's the biggest puzzle of all. But I recall in the *Sung-Chi*, a rather strange Chinese book of famous legal cases, there is a tale of a murderer bribing another man to confess to the crime. I seem to recall he promised the man that he would look after his children by having his son marry the man's daughter, and by giving his daughter to the son with a very generous dowry."

Takechi pursed his lips and whistled. "So you suspect Taira Sukenori was the real killer. But if there was a deal, the son should have honored it."

"Not if Sukenori never paid off."

"Ah!" Takechi's eyes lit up. "By the gods, that would explain it all. You've done it again, sir."

"I have no proof," cautioned Akitada, "but it suggests an investigation into possible legal improprieties. Given Judge Nakano's murder, you can ask some questions about old cases."

Takechi grinned widely. "I will," he said. "Oh, I shall enjoy this." He clapped his hands in glee.

The clapping brought the waiter. Akitada took the opportunity to pay for their meal.

They walked back together, Akitada mostly silent, but Takechi excitedly reviewing all the facts and proposing ways of proving them.

At police headquarters, they stopped. Akitada said with a smile, "You will let me know, won't you?"

29

Another Murder

His departure from Otsu, and more especially from Kosehira, was an embarrassing and painful one. Having returned very late the night before, Akitada slept only fitfully and was up at dawn, getting dressed and packing his clothes into saddle bags. Then he sat around, waiting for sunrise. He wished more than anything to go into the garden, perhaps to catch a final glimpse of her.

When he thought the time right, he ventured to Kosehira's room. His friend was up, looking serious and drawn.

"Well," Akitada said with false cheerfulness, "I suppose it's time to bid you goodbye, my friend."

Kosehira nodded. "You got everything finished then?"

"Yes. Late last night. There is still the matter of the Jizo killer, but I met with Takechi yesterday and told him everything we knew. He's a very capable man. He'll solve the case."

"I shall miss being your assistant in your murder investigation," Kosehira said wistfully. "Come and sit for a little and share my morning gruel."

Feeling guilty again, Akitada sat. He told Kosehira of his visit to the merchant Fumi and his suspicions regarding the old murder case.

Kosehira nodded. "I know that old Chinese tale. I bet Taira Sukenori knew it, too."

"Even if he didn't, he could have arrived at some such offer. Their children were the right ages and genders."

"Yes. I see."

They fell silent as a servant brought in the food. Neither ate with much appetite.

Akitada put down his bowl first and gave Kosehira a beseeching look. "You have been more than kind, you and your family. I'll never forget this visit." There was a greater truth to that than Kosehira would ever realize. "Will you please make my goodbyes to your ladies and the children?" He choked a little, and added quickly, "You are a very lucky man."

Kosehira looked at him sadly. "Thank you, Akitada. I know it well. It was my hope that you, too . . . well, it was my intention of taking you out of your sadness. Perhaps I have succeeded a little. But, Akitada, you need a wife. You cannot at your age continue like this. It isn't fair to your children or to yourself. I hope you'll forgive me for speaking so frankly. I *am* your closest friend and have your best interests in mind."

Akitada glanced away. "I know. I don't know what to tell you. I'm no longer young. And Tamako is still too much with me."

"Well," said Kosehira briskly, "so be it. You'll take your time, but I insist that you come back here frequently. My tenure as governor will be up in another year and I may be sent to the ends of the earth then. So please come to see me often while we are close, and I'll stop by your house also when I'm in the capital."

They both rose. Akitada said, "I will, brother," and embraced Kosehira.

On the way out, Kosehira said, "I'll convey your farewells to Yukiko. She'll miss seeing you before you go."

Akitada stopped. "I . . . I had occasion to speak to Lady Yukiko. In the garden. The other morning." Recalling the impropriety of that meeting, he added, "We met by accident. Briefly." He knew his face had turned red and hoped Kosehira had not noticed.

Kosehira's lip twitched. "I see. Well, then." He took Akitada's arm and they walked outside. "Have a safe journey."

Akitada saw that an armed escort of mounted guards waited. He stopped. "Not for me, I hope?"

"Of course they are for you. Really, Akitada, you're too important a man to travel alone, especially when carrying a report of the type you have prepared for His Majesty."

Akitada saw the sense of that and expressed his thanks. Mounting the horse they brought for him, he thanked Kosehira again and rode away in great pomp and circumstance.

∞

The Sugawara home, slightly shabby and ever in need of repairs, received him, if not with the luxuries he had become accustomed to, at least with the warmth of familiarity and the joyful cries of the children. Akitada passed around some silver to his escort and dismissed them.

Then he dismounted, returned Genba's happy smile, waved to Tora, and scooped up his children for a hug. They were full of questions and stories, but acquiesced when Tamako's little maid came to take them away. Tora waited to greet him.

Akitada searched his face and decided that the rest had done him some good. He still looked drawn and tired, but his eyes were less dull and he flashed his usual smile.

"Welcome, sir. We didn't expect you until the end of the week."

Yes, that had been the plan before his foolish desire for a lovely young girl had sent him rushing away. "We finished yesterday," he said in explanation and without mentioning that he had worked long hours to be done so soon. "I've missed my family," he said, hoping to cheer himself up.

"What? His Excellency, the governor, and his lovely daughter haven't been able to detain you?" Tora teased.

Akitada turned away. "I have work to do here. Where's Saburo?"

"He's coming. Twisted an ankle so he's a bit slow these days."

Akitada looked and saw Saburo making his way toward him on two crutches. "That looks bad," he said. "Are you sure it's just a minor thing?"

"Oh, yes."

Akitada hastened to meet Saburo to save him some painful steps. "Are you going to be all right, Saburo?" he asked, searching his face. He thought he looked feverish, but with all that facial hair and makeup it was hard to tell.

Saburo grimaced. "Welcome home, sir. Sorry, I twisted my foot. It will make me a tad slower than usual. I'll be ready to go over the accounts or take down any letters you may want to send."

"Yes. Actually I do have some business to take care of. Take your time. I'll have a bath and change first.

Saburo hobbled off in the direction of the main house. Akitada shook his head and remarked to Tora, "How will he manage the stairs?"

They watched as Saburo made his way up, hopping on one leg and holding both crutches in one hand while the other clutched the stair rail.

Tora released a breath. "There. He made it. You can trust Saburo to do what is needed."

"Yes, but he seems very badly off for just having twisted an ankle." Akitada shook his head again. "How is everything else? Has anything happened I should know about?"

"All is well, sir." Tora smiled. "We're glad you're back."

∞

The rest of the day passed uneventfully. Akitada spent time with the children and exchanged a few words with the women. Hanae was her old cheerful self, and Mrs. Kuruda had her usual complaints.

"I don't know, sir," she said almost immediately after greeting him, "I do my best to keep my eye on things, but it isn't easy. Yoshi fell out of a tree and scraped his arm, Yasuko doesn't seem to take any interest in learning to sew, and my clumsy son twists his ankle and won't let me put hot compresses on it. Sometimes I think nobody pays any attention to what I tell them."

Akitada said soothingly, "I'm sure they all benefit from your wisdom, Mrs. Kuruda."

She sniffed and bustled off to see about his dinner, no doubt much to the dismay of the cook.

In his study, Akitada went over the accounts with Saburo. His salary had continued during his special assignment and his people had managed so well in his absence that he had more money than when he left. He praised Saburo and then dismissed him to rest his leg.

After a midday meal, which he took with the children, he changed into his good robe and carried his report to the *Daidairi* where he delivered it to the prime minister's secretary. Afterward, he called on Fujiwara Kaneie in the Ministry of Justice.

The minister was very pleased to see him. No doubt work that was beyond Kaneie and any of the others in the ministry had stacked up in his absence. But Kaneie had the good manners to enquire about Akitada's work in Otsu and received a copy of the report with great interest.

"Well," he said with a smile, "I knew you'd put a stop to the greed of those monks. I hope you made your comments suitably strong. They have too many supporters at court."

Akitada nodded. "I agree and I think I made it quite strong enough. Though it was mainly their misdeeds that made my case."

"Excellent." Kaneie eyed the fat report with a slight frown. "Good work as always. And we'll be very glad to have you back, but no need to start today. Take the weekend off. You deserve a rest."

It was afternoon by then and weekends were always days of rest, but Akitada expressed his thanks and departed before Kaneie could change his mind.

His next visit was to his friend Nakatoshi in the Ministry of Ceremonial. Nakatoshi cocked his head and eyed him. "I notice a new energy in your bearing. Is this entirely due to a chore well done or have you by chance met a pretty lady?"

Akitada laughed and blushed. "No, no," he lied. "But I did come across some interesting murders."

Nakatoshi was easily distracted and listened with interest to Akitada's account of the killer who left Jizo statues on his victims. "Will you go back to identify the murderer?" he asked.

"No. Kaneie has work for me here. The Otsu chief is a very good man, though. He'll get him."

They parted, promising to meet soon for a meal at Nakatoshi's house.

Akitada's next and final call was to Superintendant Kobe of the Metropolitan Police. After years of strained relations between the police official and Akitada, the justice ministry official who dabbled in crime, the two men had become good friends. Like Akitada, Kobe was alone now, but with a difference.

During his political troubles, he had lost his heart to a blind shampoo girl, and his wives had taken things very badly. One had become a nun rather than to live with a man who had offended both his superiors and society, and the other had taken the children and retired to Kobe's country estate. Neither she nor his children wanted to see him. Kobe had regained his position, but he now lived alone in his house in the capital.

As it was still daylight, Akitada went to police headquarters and found Kobe in, busy as usual, but very pleased to see him.

"Akitada!" he cried. "Back already? Was Otsu not to your liking or did those cursed monks drive you away?"

Akitada smiled. "On the contrary. I finished my report and have just delivered it to the prime minister. Still, they have caused us some trouble." He told Kobe about their attack on Tora and how he had managed to free Tora and arrest the ringleader, only to have a large group of *sohei* attack the Omi tribunal and set their prisoner free.

"Those godless thugs are a menace," Kobe snarled. "I recall the last time they descended from their mountain into the capital. They were carrying the *mikoshi* of the gods, but they were armed and ready to fight. I had to call up all of my men, and the court sent the imperial guard, useless though those youngsters are, and we would have had a bloodbath and a burning city if the chancellor hadn't made concessions."

"I remember. I regret very much that Tora's attacker escaped. He and others had been torturing and raping the populace for months. But our report gives the government enough evidence of their dangerous behavior that both Enryaku-ji and Onjo-ji will trim their fighting forces in the future."

"Good work! And you look much better," said Kobe.

Akitada wished to return the compliment, but Kobe looked tired and older. On an impulse, he invited him to dinner at his house. "I think they are planning a special meal. It would give me great joy to have you share it with me."

Kobe seemed moved by the invitation and accepted. They chatted a while longer. Akitada told Kobe of the case of the Jizo killer and caught a spark of the old enthusiasm in Kobe's eyes. Kobe said, "I'm very glad you're back, Akitada," and embraced him when they parted.

Akitada returned home and made arrangements to entertain Kobe. Then he looked in on the children again. They had planned to share the meal with him, and he found himself again disappointing them. Yasuko said nothing, but Yoshi burst out with, "You're always too busy for us."

Akitada looked at him and nodded. "Yes, I have been so busy, too busy. I'm very sorry."

Yoshi was not done. "You said we could go to the shrine festival."

"I know."

Silence fell while both children looked at him accusingly.

"Look," he said finally, "perhaps we can still attend the shrine festival if we leave here very early and return the same night."

"Oh, yes!" Yoshi shouted and embraced his knees.

Yasuko was laughing with pleasure. "Yes, please, Father! It would be such an adventure! May I tell Yuki?"

Akitada nodded. They would have to go like ordinary visitors and hope that word would not reach Kosehira, who would be deeply offended. He debated sending his friend a message so they might meet at the festival but rejected it. Kosehira would insist that they stay at his villa.

Kobe arrived and seemed in better spirits. Cook had outdone herself and Akitada and Kobe dined on a delicious meal of fresh prawns, stuffed dumplings, fried tofu, boiled eggs, grilled sea bream, and rice balls stuffed with pickled plums and wrapped in seaweed.

During the meal, Akitada asked how Kobe was getting along on his own.

Kobe looked down at his tray of food and said glumly, "We live as simply as we can. With one old servant. Sachi is saving money for my children."

"But surely that's not necessary. Your wives and children are well provided for."

"Yes, they are. I want to see my children, but my wives have made that impossible."

Akitada pressed no further. He was appalled. Had Kobe been such an ogre in his household, or had he married three ogres?

"How is Sachi?"

Kobe's tired face broke into a smile. "She's expecting our child. I cannot tell you how much joy she has given me."

"I'm very glad. Congratulations! How soon will you be a father again?"

"Three more months." Kobe paused, then asked, "When will you marry again, Akitada?"

His heart twisting, Akitada said, "I don't know. I miss Tamako. And I'm not sure it would be fair to bring another woman into my settled family life."

"You've always been good at it. Marriage, I mean. Tamako was a great wife. I was half in love with her myself. I think you should take another wife. Children need mothers."

Akitada thought of Yukiko, nineteen years old and not long past childhood herself. She had been very good with her younger siblings, but would she have taken to his own, much quieter household? Would the children have taken to her?

Such thoughts led nowhere. Fleetingly he remembered that other woman he had loved deeply. She was closer to his own age and had children of her own, but she had rejected his offer. Should he seek her out and ask her again?

There was an interruption at this point. Tora brought in a letter.

"A messenger from Otsu, sir. It's from Chief Takechi. I thought you might want to see it right away."

Apologizing to Kobe, who looked interested, Akitada opened the letter.

Takechi reported that the merchant Fumi Tokiari had been found bludgeoned to death. A small Jizo had rested on his chest.

30

Otsu Again

akechi had not requested his help, but Kosehira did in short order. He sounded upset in the letter delivered by an official messenger from the tribunal. Phrases like "shocking murder of an important businessman," "rumors abound that a killer is loose," and "the shrine festival is in two days" suggested that he was at wits' end and in need of help.

With the free weekend ahead, Akitada had his horse saddled and, taking Tora with him, set out for Otsu again.

One benefit of his stay in Otsu had been a marked improvement in his physical health. He was no longer tired out by long rides and felt stronger in every way.

But his conscience troubled him again. Another man had died because he had not stopped a killer. He had liked the merchant Fumi, a modest, unassuming man who was soft-spoken and quiet until roused to anger by a foul accusation against his brother. And now he was dead also. Akitada could not grasp the reason for this killing and wracked his brain all the way to Otsu.

Perhaps there was no reason any longer. Perhaps the killer had learned to enjoy killing. They said there were such men, men who were not by nature brutal but who got a thrill from the fact that they had killed and got away with it. Murder made them feel invulnerable, almost godlike in their powers over life and death. Akitada noted that Fumi and Sukemichi, unlike the other victims, had not been bad men. Surely their only offense had been that they were loosely connected to the fate of Hatta Hiroshi, the Taira *betto*.

A very dangerous man, this killer.

In front of the tribunal he found an unruly crowd. The big gates were closed and guarded by a contingent of armed soldiers. Akitada made his way through, hearing to his dismay shouts of "There goes another one," "Got the killer yet?" and "Lazy officials!"

Fear will make people believe all sorts of tales. No wonder, Kosehira had sounded concerned in his letter.

Admitted to the tribunal, Akitada turned his tired horse over to a groom and walked up to the main hall. Kosehira was in his office, dictating to a clerk. Other clerks were wielding their brushes, making copies.

"Akitada!" cried the governor, jumping to his feet. "You made very good time. Thank you for coming. You saw the state of affairs?"

"Yes. It seems rather sudden. Could the rumors have been started by someone in order to make trouble?"

Kosehira looked astonished. "But who would do this?" He paused. "You don't mean that this is Enryaku-ji's revenge?"

"Perhaps not. That would have been directed against me. It just seems strange that the rumors spread so fast. Unless you have other plans, I think I'll go talk to Takechi and have a look at the body."

"Yes, that might be useful. Not much doubt who did it, is there?"

"No. Though I don't understand why. But clearly we must find him fast."

"Yes. The festival is in two days. Any disturbance then would bring the entire court down on me."

Akitada nodded.

"You will stay tonight?"

"If it becomes necessary. Thank you, Kosehira."

∞

Takechi received him with similar relief. Akitada wished people did not place so much confidence in him. Disappointment was sure to follow.

Takechi outlined what he had learned. Fumi Tokiari had been alone in the house, his family and the servants all having gone to a neighborhood shrine at the end of the street. The merchant had stayed behind to work on his books, but had promised to join them later. When he did not show up after quite a while, his son sent a servant who found his master dead in his office.

"With a Jizo," Takechi added dryly.

"Yes. And I take it there was another shrine fair."

Takechi nodded. "Just a very small one, but it was their family shrine."

Let's have a look at the body."

Fumi Tokiari had been brought to police headquarters for the coroner to have a look at it. They found Doctor Kimura washing his hands after his examination.

"Same as the others," he said when he saw them. "Knocked unconscious, fairly violently, and strangled. He managed to break the neck this time. I'd say the attacks are becoming more severe."

Akitada nodded. Another hint that the killings were no longer just personal and that the killer was changing. The crowds outside the tribunal and Takechi's office were not far wrong in their fear.

They left police headquarters—to more jeering shouts—and walked to the merchant's house. On the way, they passed the small shrine at the corner where remnants of the fair still littered the street. Torn paper flags, bits of rice straw, discarded fans, and a few paper umbrellas, broken and left behind, gave a colorful impression of the activities that had distracted everyone's attention from an old man being murdered a few houses up the street.

Takechi confirmed this. His constables had interviewed all the neighbors and servants and none had seen or heard anything.

THE OLD MEN OF OMI

They were admitted to the merchant's house by a servant in the hemp clothing of a family in mourning. The shop part of the building was shuttered. Inside it was dim and silent, but when they had followed the servant to the back of the house, they could hear children's voices.

The Fumi family were all together in the large room. A middle-aged man Akitada did not know rose to bow them to pillows that a woman placed for them. Takechi introduced him as Fumi Tabito, the son of Fumi Tokiari. The woman was his wife. There was also another, younger, woman with two small children. These were the daughter and grandchildren of the couple and had come to support the family.

Akitada expressed his condolences. They received his words with polite bows. The daughter hurried to bring wine and refreshments, while her mother gathered the two little ones to her. It was a typical, peaceful family of industrious and well-to-do people, and Akitada regretted their loss again.

The son talked about his father's murder, wiping tears from his eyes. "I blame myself. We should have stayed with him. Or at least left a servant behind. But who would have thought that such a thing could happen on our quiet street? In the harbor now, that's another matter."

"I did not have the pleasure of meeting you when I called on your father recently," Akitada said.

"I run the shipping side of the business. Usually I'm in my office near the harbor."

Akitada commented on the good health of his grandchildren.

His wife bowed her thanks and said, "It was for the sake of the little ones that we went to the fair. My daughter had come for a visit. She lives with her husband in the capital."

At this point, feeling all eyes on himself, the little boy, who was perhaps five, said, "I saw the dolly man."

His grandmother hushed him, but he was persistent. "I wanted that dolly. I wanted the monkey dolly."

His mother said, "He means the puppet man. From the fair."

Akitada thought of all the fairs and of his own children, disappointed once again. He asked the merchant, "Did your father have other children?"

"No, sir. And we have only a daughter, but now there are grandchildren, and it may be that one of them will run the business some day. Who did this, sir? My father was old, but he was very healthy. First my uncle and now my father! Who hated him so much?"

Takechi cleared his throat. "Have you received any threats? Say from people who borrowed money from you or your father?"

The merchant bristled. "No. We are fair, and we don't lend money to untrustworthy people. My Uncle did more lending than we do now. My father rarely advanced funds. He hated that business. He said it brought my uncle death. Does this have anything to do with my uncle?"

Akitada and Takechi exchanged a glance. Akitada said, "Perhaps, but we cannot be certain. Did your father ever mention anyone watching the house?" He looked around the room, but they all shook their heads.

"You think someone was watching us?" asked his wife. "Are we in danger?"

"Probably not," said Akitada. "But I think you should keep your eyes open for a while and not go anywhere alone."

"Amida!" cried the merchant. "They are right. A maniac is loose in Otsu and he's after my family." The women cried out in dismay, his wife pulling the children closer to her.

"Please calm down," said Akitada. "There is probably no reason to be afraid, but it couldn't hurt to be careful for a few days. We are close to getting the man responsible for these deaths." It was a hopeful lie, because he hated having put them into a panic.

They left after this, and Akitada returned to the tribunal to report to Kosehira.

Kosehira was dismissing a citizen's delegation with some reassuring words and a smile. As soon as the door closed behind them, he waved Akitada to a cushion and asked, "Well? Anything?"

"I'm not sure," said Akitada. "This business made me realize that there have been fairs in all the other cases."

"Oh, Akitada, it's the time of year. It's spring, rice planting season. All the shrines put on fairs to bring people in to pray to the *kami* for a good harvest and to collect donations. The temples are also behind it. Enryaku-ji sponsors many shrine fairs as well as the big one coming up that you won't bring your children to see."

Kosehira's reproachful face made Akitada smile. "I told them we might come up just for the day of the procession."

"You won't stay with us?"

Too late Akitada realized he had made an error. He did not know what to say and muttered something about work at the ministry.

Kosehira recognized this for prevarication. His face set, he demanded, "What happened at my house to send you away in such a rush and make you refuse to come back?"

Akitada just shook his head and muttered, "Nothing, Kosehira. Nothing at all?"

"This has something to do with Yukiko, right?"

"No, no." Akitada was aware that he had flushed. "Kosehira," he begged, "let it go. Nothing happened. I'm just in one of my moods."

For a few moments, Kosehira did not speak. Then he said, "I was wrong to push my daughter at you. It was not respectful of either of you. Now I have made her desperately unhappy, and you refuse to accept my hospitality. I beg your pardon."

Akitada gazed at him. He thought he must have misheard. "What?"

Kosehira wrung his hands in distress. "I'm sorry, Akitada. Believe me, I thought it would help you to have someone to love again. And Yukiko, well, she's my favorite, though I'll deny it if you mention it to anyone. I wanted her to have a happy marriage. Like Tamako's."

Akitada found his voice. "You wanted me to meet your daughter because you wished us to be married?"

"Yes. That's why I arranged your stay at my house."

"But Kosehira, I'm too old for her and certainly not a good prospect in terms of rank and influence."

Kosehira waved a hand to disperse such objections like gnats. "Who cares? I know you and I know you would be kind to my child."

Weak with the shock of this revelation, Akitada burst into laughter. "Oh, Kosehira," he gasped. "With you for a father-in-law, no son-in-law would dare mistreat Yukiko."

Kosehira did not smile. "You don't understand. It doesn't matter. I'll try to look after her. The trouble is she's been talking about becoming a nun. Yukiko a nun? Think about it."

Akitada thought about it and stopped laughing. "I thought she planned to marry the prime minister's son?"

"She doesn't like him."

An awkward silence fell, while thoughts chased each other in Akitada's mind like agitated *koi* in Yukiko's fishpond. "Kosehira," he finally said, "I left because I'd fallen in love with your daughter."

Kosehira's jaw sagged for a moment. Then he jumped up, laughing out loud, and performed a little dance. Grasping Akitada by the hands, he pulled him up, embraced him, and then made him dance about with him. They were both laughing.

When heads appeared in the doorway, they stopped.

Kosehira waved his clerks away. "Never mind," he called out. "Just some very good news."

They left, and Kosehira looked as if he might start dancing again. Akitada, deeply embarrassed, though quite ridiculously happy, cleared his throat. They resumed their seats and looked at each other, smiling.

Akitada said, "I'm too old for her."

Kosehira countered with, "*She* doesn't think so."

"You mean she would really agree?"

"Of course. You nearly broke her heart."

They fell silent. Akitada sat, shaking his head, smiling, suddenly impatient to see her, to be certain she really wanted this.

Kosehira guessed his thoughts. "No time like the present. You'll stay with her tonight?"

"Dear gods," protested Akitada, "you cannot rush such a thing. I have not had any time to court her. She has not met my children."

"Yes, but hurry up, will you?"

Akitada promised.

Kosehira next insisted on discussing his daughter's dowry. Akitada was reminded that Tamako had brought him nothing but herself and an empty lot where her father's house had stood. His ears were ringing by the time Kosehira was done. He said weakly, "It shall all be hers and her children's."

Kosehira rubbed his hands. "It's all set then. I'll have the papers drawn up tomorrow."

31

The Wild Geese

As soon as they reached Kosehira's villa that evening, Akitada went into the garden, hoping to find Yukiko.

Kosehira had spent the ride home chattering gleefully about his daughter. It was clear he loved her dearly, and Akitada had the uncomfortable feeling that his friend would remain alert to her welfare even after she had become his wife and lived in the Sugawara home.

Custom prescribed that a son-in-law live in his new wife's home and become a part of her family. It was not a notion Akitada found appealing. There would be no privacy for the couple, and he treasured his privacy. In his first marriage, the possibility had not arisen because Tamako had become both fatherless and homeless on the same day. In this case, it was surely understood that Yukiko would come to him, but clearly there would be strings attached.

More worrisome was that all of these plans had been presented to him so quickly and completely. Apparently, Kosehira had expected Akitada and Yukiko to step unprotestingly into their ascribed roles. And so he now wanted to see her to assure himself that she would come to him willingly and without reservations. He was no longer at all sure of this.

Alas, the garden was empty, and after waiting quite a long time, wandering back and forth between the promontory and the *koi* pond, Akitada returned to his room to change. There would be another family dinner tonight in celebration of the engagement, and he dreaded it.

It was young Arimitsu, the youngest of Kosehira's sons, who met him on his way to the main house. He came running, all smiles, and stopped before Akitada with the words, "You are to be my brother-in-law. Father said so. I'm very glad!"

Greatly moved by this artless welcome, Akitada laughed and swung him up into his arms to hug him, saying, "I'm very glad, too, Arimitsu. Thank you."

They walked hand-in-hand to the main house, Arimitsu quiet now and proud to be leading the guest of honor. When they entered the reception room, chosen for this meal in honor of the occasion, Akitada's heart misgave him again. It was all happening too fast. He had not had time to think. What would Kosehira's wives think of this odd match?

He glanced around nervously, but saw only smiling faces. Yukiko was absent, and that gave him a new worry.

They seated him between Kosehira and his first lady, Yukiko's mother. This was perhaps traditional. The presence of all the children though, was surely not. He was grateful for it, especially when Arimitsu gave him a broad grin. The other youngsters were more reserved, but seemed quietly pleased.

When all eyes turned toward the door, he saw Yukiko. She wore a gorgeous robe of shimmering gauze over pale green silk with touches of red and pink peeking forth at her full sleeves and at the hem of her skirts. She looked beautiful and remote. Not once did she lift her head to look at Akitada as she went to her place on her father's other side where Akitada would be unable to catch her eye throughout the meal.

He wished himself elsewhere. Back at home in his study, far away from people and obligations, from having to make conversation when his heart misgave him. Dear gods, how was he to get through this meal?

And through the other formalities yet to come?

Somehow they consumed the first courses, served by two pretty maids, while talking about the weather.

"Today, I saw geese flying north again," said Arikuni, Kosehira's second son. "Spring is almost over. What a pity. All those fairs are so much fun. Will you be here for the Great Shrine Festival, Cousin Akitada?"

"Yes. That is, if I can get the time off. My superior indicated that he has a good deal of work waiting for me." That had sounded stilted and awkward, and he added, "Yasuko and Yoshi have been begging to come, and I did promise them."

They asked more questions about his family and home next, all easy to answer. Yukiko's mother wanted to know about the children's ages and their upbringing. Kosehira supplied anecdotes from his visits to Akitada's home, carefully avoiding references to Tamako.

Akitada felt grieved by this. He said, "I have neglected my children. It was very wrong of me, but the death of their mother was deeply painful. I hope to make up for my neglect." This, alas, struck a funereal note on what should be an auspicious occasion.

To dispel the somber mood, Kosehira said, "You have good people who look well after your children. I recall seeing Genba jumping about the courtyard with young Yori on his back, and Tora used to teach him how to fight. I'm sure they also look after the other two very well."

Seeing some blank looks, Akitada explained, "Yori was my first son who died in the smallpox epidemic." The women sucked in their breath and gave him pitying glances, while Kosehira bit his lip. Clearly the topic of tragic losses was undesirable. Embarrassed, Akitada added quickly, "You are right. My people love the children, and so do their wives. Tora has a son who is a year older than Yasuko. They all study and play together. And now Genba also has a little daughter."

He felt awkward talking about his family and wondered what Yukiko thought. This new worry caused him to fall silent.

Kosehira changed the subject to the troubles in Otsu. "Akitada has been helping Chief Takechi with those murders that have people so upset," he said. "It's a difficult case, and I'm very glad he's here to help."

This brought more questions which Akitada and Kosehira answered cautiously, leaving out details that might frighten the women and give the smaller children nightmares.

And so the meal finally ended. Yukiko left quickly with the other women. She had not spoken once. Neither had she looked at him.

He walked back to his room dazed and miserable, wondering what was expected of him next. Was he to slip into Yukiko's room under cover of darkness and make love to her?

Probably. But he had no idea where her room was. A younger man would have found out such an important fact long before now. He grimaced at the contrast between himself, a staid government official with a growing family, and a young lover. Poor Yukiko.

Clearly he could not force her to submit to him. It would be insensitive and brutish. The bedding of the bride had been easier in Tamako's case, though there, too, he had been afraid to make his move. But he had been younger then, both eager and ardently in love, and that had overcome all his scruples. Now he had acquired a host of feelings of inadequacy.

He reached his room, looked at the bedding spread out by servants, and knew he would not be able to sleep. Turning around, he went back into the dark garden.

Half hoping.

It was already quite dark at the *koi* pond, and no one was there. Disappointed, he walked on to the promontory. Daylight lingered on the shining mirror of the lake, but a pale moon had risen, and the land lay dark beneath the starry sky. Only a few lights glimmered like glowworms in the city below.

Was the killer sleeping down there somewhere or was he watching another victim's house? He had surely been watching the rice merchant's house, waiting for the family and the servants to leave for the shrine fair. Then he had gone inside to kill Fumi Tokiari. This killer was a man of enormous patience.

So many fairs! A memory nagged at him, the words of a child. Yes, it had been the little boy at the rice merchant's place wanting a puppet. Could he have seen the killer?

A rustle among the shrubs, a soft step, the scent of almond blossoms.

He turned slowly. Yukiko stood on the path. She wore the same blue robe as the last time they had met here—when he had believed he would never see her again.

"I thought you might come here, Akitada," she said softly.

"Yukiko," he murmured, extending his hand to her. "Oh, my dear. Are you pleased?"

"Yes, Akitada. I'm well pleased. And you?"

"Come here, my love!" he begged.

She came and he drew her close, and after a moment's hesitation he cupped her face in his hands and put his lips to hers, tasting her sweet breath, and then kissed her again. His hands found their way under the loose blue robe to the merest wisp of silken undergown and the warm skin beneath. He caressed her lightly and kissed her again, feeling her soft gasp and the way she swayed against him.

Releasing her reluctantly, he gestured at the moon. "Last time, the sun was rising and you were bathed in golden light. I thought you the most beautiful sight I'd ever seen and grieved my loss. And now, by the light of the moon, I find you again, far more beautiful and dearer to me."

She took his hand and placed it against her cheek. "It nearly broke my heart, your leaving."

They stood, their arms around each other, looking up to where the moon was riding on a bank of silvery cloud. The Milky Way, that magical river in the sky had been crossed by the herdsman to embrace the weaver maid. Akitada was enchanted that he, too, should have found love again.

Just then a flight of birds crossed the sky. He murmured, "Not magpies, surely."

"Geese," she said with a soft chuckle. "My brother was right. They *are* flying north."

They followed the arrow of their flight as they passed across the moon. It was a beautiful sight and surely a good omen.

Yukiko took his hand. "Come!" she said.

32

The Puppet Man

kitada spent at least part of the next day in a
dream.

He intended to work with Takechi, to talk
again to all the people connected with the crimes, but
this time asking them a specific question. This would
be time-consuming and frustrating, but there was a
sense of urgency now, and the danger of riots was rising
in the city. People were frightened by rumors of a mad
killer and had become angry with the authorities. Even
the constables were not safe. In one street, a crowd of
boys had pelted them with horse droppings and stones
and called them names.

But his thoughts were with Yukiko. He was as hungry for her as a young man in his teens and could not stop thinking about their night together. Feeling foolish, he reminded himself that this unaccustomed passion was due to long abstinence—or if not abstinence, then those quick and loveless unions he had purchased with silver. Yukiko, beautiful, young, utterly desirable, was his wife. He was barely able to comprehend it yet. Every thought of her filled him with a strange mix of tenderness and lust.

After spending the night with his daughter, Akitada's first meeting with Kosehira was awkward. Fortunately, his friend was similarly embarrassed, and the situation in the city was the topic of the conversation. Akitada told Kosehira what he had remembered. Kosehira looked dubious, but said, "Well, since we have nothing else, I suppose you and Takechi had better look for the man."

It was easier said than done.

His next embarrassment stemmed from Tora's reaction when he told him what had happened. Tora's jaw dropped in utter surprise. Alas, his shocked silence was temporary. After boisterous congratulations accompanied by backslapping, he bombarded Akitada with advice. You would have thought he, Akitada, had never bedded a woman or—which was more galling—that he was well past the age where he was able to function in the marriage bed. Tora insisted on regaling him with his experience in sexual matters.

"Remember now, sir, hot passion cools easily. Take it slowly. The young ones like it that way. Else you might frighten her."

That one got Tora a stern warning, "How dare you, Tora. Mind your own business."

Tora merely grinned, and Akitada was too happy to pursue the matter. But Tora was not done yet. He next advised, "Be careful how you look to others today, sir. It's hard to conceal one's thoughts of love-making." Caught out in a lustful memory, Akitada flushed and shot Tora an angry look.

"I suppose you've been writing a hot poem this morning," Tora observed with a grin. "Nice custom. Among the rest of us, women prefer something a bit more substantial."

"Enough!" roared Akitada. "If you cannot control your tongue, you can go home and stay there. I don't need you."

A stricken look on Tora's face caused him to relent. "Oh, never mind. The Grand Shrine Festival is the day after tomorrow. I promised the children they could come. Under the circumstances, you'd better ride home and tell everybody what has happened. I'll give you a letter for my sister." He paused a moment to consider Akiko's reaction. It was altogether predictable. She would be enchanted and immediately start planning. He sighed. "Hanae will need to prepare for my new wife. Yukiko will have Tamako's pavilion, and that means Yasuko will need new quarters. Have Saburo take whatever funds he needs and get things ready. I don't want him to spare money this time. And you may return with the children tomorrow."

This time, Tora obeyed without further comments.

As for the morning-after poem, Akitada had, in fact, returned to his quarters before dawn and taken up his brush to write: "*Did you come to me or I to you? Your gown, like mist dispersed by wind, revealed my heart's desire. Am I asleep or awake?*" It was a poor effort, but he had never been a poet, and while the image of the wind was quite improper, he hoped she would see how great his passion for her was. He had slipped the note under her shuttered door.

Many years ago, he had labored longer over Tamako's morning-after poem, eventually sending her a pretty verse about wisterias, tied to a wisteria branch from her father's garden. This was different, frank and passionate. He was no longer the young lover.

His matrimonial duty done, he eventually turned his thoughts to catching a killer. In Otsu, he and Kosehira drafted letters to be sent to Prefect Ishimoda of Echi district and to Masaie, the warden in Okuni. Both were to ask more questions of witnesses near the victims' homes. A special messenger was sent post-haste and told to return with answers that night.

Then Akitada went to see Takechi and told him of his idea. "I want to go back to the merchant's house and talk to the child again," he said. "And after that, we need to see the judge's servants."

Takechi's expression suggested that he was as doubtful as Kosehira had been. But like the governor, he was desperate. "Let's go," he said.

The merchant's shop was open for business. Fumi Tokiari's son said apologetically, "People need to eat. We had to open up."

Takechi nodded. "Better this way. For them and for you. Work keeps your mind on the living."

The merchant nodded.

"We'd like to have a word with your grandson. Is he still here?"

"My grandson? But he's only five. He knows nothing."

"Nevertheless," said Akitada impatiently.

"Yes, they are here. For the funeral." He led the way to the back of the house which seemed a good deal more crowded today. Akitada spied the boy playing with another child and went to speak to him.

Crouching down to the child's level, he asked, "Do you remember me?"

The boy stared and nodded.

"And do you remember going to the shrine festival."

Another silent nod.

"You told me you saw a puppet man. A dolly man I think you called him."

The child's eyes brightened. "Yes. I saw him. I wanted the monkey, but mother said I couldn't have it."

"Right. Now think, because it's important. Where was the puppet man?"

"Outside."

The boy's mother inserted herself into the conversation. "He means at the fair."

"No," said the boy, "he was outside on the street. I saw him. He showed me his dolls in the box. I liked the monkey. He asked if I was going to the fair."

Akitada rose and looked at Takechi. "He was watching the house," he said," waiting for the family to leave."

The mother gasped and drew the boy closer.

Turning to the rest of the family, Akitada asked, "Did anyone else see the puppet man outside?"

They shook their heads.

"You did not even see him at the fair?"

They looked at each other and shook their heads again. The boy said stubbornly, "He wasn't at the fair. He was outside."

Akitada gave the child a shiny silver coin and told his mother, "He's a bright boy. Keep an eye on him."

∞

The judge's servants, Kiyoshi and Tatsuko, were still living in his house. They had no place to go, and the heirs had allowed them to stay to keep an eye on the property. Kiyoshi worked at the harbor and Tatsuko looked after her children and kept the place clean.

She was home when they got there and recognized them. A look of fear crossed her face. "Has anything happened? Is it my husband? Do we have to leave?"

"No, nothing like that," Takechi reassured her. "Lord Sugawara wants to ask you a few more questions, that's all."

She smiled with relief and bowed to Akitada.

"Do you recall," Akitada asked, "that you told me the judge did not even pay you enough to take your son to see a puppet play?"

She blushed. "I shouldn't have complained. The judge's heirs have been very good to us."

"I'm glad to hear it, but I wondered what made you think of puppets that day."

"Oh, it was nothing. There was this puppeteer in front of the house, and I was thinking how my son would like to see a puppet show. He was just an ordinary puppet man with a box slung around his neck, the kind that walks around at fairs. They take their puppets out and make them move and talk. It only costs a few coppers to watch, but we didn't even have that to spare."

"Ah. You have an excellent memory. Can you describe the puppet man?"

She blushed at the compliment. "Well, as I said, he had this box—"

"No, I mean what *he* looked like. How old was he, was he tall or short, did he have any distinguishing marks?"

She frowned. "I didn't look at him very long and he was on the other side of the street. He was a big man. Not young, I think. He had on a colorful cap, but his face looked old. I'm sorry, that's all. Oh, and he had a limp."

"Thank you. That was very helpful." Akitada gave her a piece of silver, and they left.

Outside, Takechi said with a good deal of admiration, "I'm beginning to think you're right, sir. However did you hit on a puppet man?"

"It took me far too long, Takechi. I went to a shrine fair with the governor's children and saw a puppeteer there, but my interest was in the sellers of Jizo figures. There have been several mentions of puppets, mostly by children, who have an eye for such things. I suddenly thought of all the vagrants who wander from town to town to perform or sell their skills at fairs. It's a perfect cover for a convict who has escaped and intends to avenge his family."

Takechi nodded. "And this is the perfect time for it. Omi is known far and wide for its spring festivals. I bet he'll be at the Grand Shrine Festival, too. They are already setting up the booths and grandstands at the Hiyoshi Taisha shrine. We'll be sure to get him then."

"It would be safer if you could find him sooner. Where do such people stay in Otsu?"

"We have a lot of hostelries for travelers near the harbor. Some cater to *hinin* like him."

Hatta would be an outcast now, though he had once belonged to the respectable family of a senior retainer. A terrible change for a man! All of the homeless migrants of the country, entertainers at fairs and private houses, jugglers and dancers, prostitutes and soothsayers, belonged to this non-class of people. They were almost invariably poor and at the mercy of the authorities who arrested them frequently for stealing and loitering, for causing trouble and for prostitution.

Akitada said, "Let's have a word with that very observant neighbor of the jailer. If she saw him, she may remember another detail. And if the people in the Echi district also report seeing a puppet man near the murder scenes, you will have enough for an arrest."

Takechi nodded. "We'll have to be careful, or he'll smell what's afoot."

Tokuno's neighbor welcomed them eagerly. "Any news?" she asked. "Have you got him yet? Everybody's afraid around here. Some people barricade their doors and won't come out."

She was evidently made of stronger stuff because a mere knock brought her to the door. Takechi asked his question, and she said immediately, "The puppet man? You mean he's the one that killed Tokuno and that merchant? And the judge?" She put a hand to her head. "Amida! He might've killed me. I talked to him." She swayed a little, and Takechi caught her arm.

"He wanted Tokuno, not you," he told her. "And you can tell people they are perfectly safe. Now tell us about him."

She told, eagerly and with great detail. He had walked down the street, looking at the houses on either side while she had been outside sweeping the path to her door. He had stopped and asked her where the jailer Tokuno lived. "Of course, Tokuno wasn't a jailer anymore. I told him so. He was just a sweeper now. He seemed pleased by this. I pointed out Tokuno's house." She raised a hand to her mouth. "Oh, merciful Kannon! I sent the murderer to Tokuno."

"He would have found the house without you," Akitada said. "Can you describe him?"

"Oh, he was a tall man. Gray hair. It was long and he tied it in back. And he was really sun burnt, like he'd been traveling. I asked him what he had in his box, but he wouldn't tell me and walked away."

"Was he limping?"

"Yes. I guessed it was from all that walking they do. And I knew very well he was a puppeteer even if he wouldn't say."

And that was that.

Akitada and Takechi parted, Takechi to organize his search, and Akitada to return to the tribunal to report and to await news from Echi.

33

The Grand Shrine Festival

Word from Echi district arrived late that night. The news was mixed. No puppet man had been seen near the Taira manor at any time, but the fair attended by Wakiya and Juro had indeed had a puppet player on both days of the fair.

"It doesn't matter about Sukemichi's death," Akitada said to Kosehira. "I myself passed a sizable fair within walking distance from the manor. Hatta was there, I'd swear on it."

They had taken to referring to the puppet man as Hatta, assuming he was Hatta Takashi, the son of the Taira *betto* Hatta Hiroshi, who had confessed to killing the rice merchant Fumi Takahiro and had died in exile. The son had attacked Sukemichi's father and had also been sent to work in the mines in the north. They had no proof that he had escaped and become a puppeteer to avenge his father's death and his family's ruin, but no other explanation would account for all victims. They hoped that, once arrested, the puppet man would confirm their assumptions.

But in spite of the most thorough searches of every hostelry in Otsu and the surrounding countryside, the puppet man had not been found.

Kosehira grumbled, "It may all have been in vain. He could have left right after killing Fumi Tokiari. His work was done and he went home, wherever home may be. We'll never solve the murders, and the people will call us inept."

Akitada, who was also worried, pointed out that the Grand Shrine Festival was the next day, and that Hatta would not miss such an excellent chance to earn enough money for his journey back.

Kosehira grimaced. "Can you imagine what will happen when the constables try to arrest him in the middle of the event?"

Akitada could imagine it, but he preferred to remain hopeful. "The fair grounds are not part of the procession route, and you can position constables in ordinary clothes there to keep a look-out for him."

Kosehira brightened. "Hmm. Yes. That may work."

Toward evening, Tora arrived with Akitada's children and his son Yuki. Akitada greeted them nervously, having no idea how they had reacted to the news of his remarriage. He should have gone home to tell them himself, but that could not be helped now. The children had come on their own horses, smaller versions of Tora's mount. It gave Akitada considerable pride to see that they could ride so well.

When Yoshi saw him, he cried "Father! Father!" and slid unaided from the back of his little horse to run to him. Akitada swept him up and swung him around, laughing out loud. "Welcome, my son! What a very fine horseman you've become!"

"I came all the way on my horse," Yoshi informed him. "Tora said I was doing very well!"

Akitada put Yoshi down and went to help Yasuko. His little lady also sat her horse well but evidently felt it was appropriate that she should be assisted. She was smiling. Akitada muttered a prayer of thanks to the gods. The children were not angry with him for taking a wife.

Yasuko let him lift her down, arranged her gown, and straightened her straw hat.

"Welcome, my daughter," he said with a smile. "How very ladylike you look!"

"Thank you." She peered up at him. "Where is your new lady, Father? I want to see her. Tora says she's *very* beautiful."

He glanced across at Tora and Yuki, who grinned back. "Yuki," said Akitada, "I'm very glad to see you, too. Come join us while your father takes the horses away."

Yuki obeyed and came shyly, handing Akitada a letter. Tora gathered the reins of the children's horses and took them to the stables.

The letter was from Akiko. Akitada tucked it away for later. "Come," he said to the children. "You shall see my wife. Her name is Yukiko, and she is indeed very beautiful."

A little later, he gave another prayer of thanks, because Yukiko and the children seemed to like each other. He waited on her veranda while she introduced them to her brothers and sisters.

Tonight would be their third night together, the night that sealed the marriage contract. Of course, he had never had an option in the matter, but neither had he wanted to escape. He put aside any quibbling doubts about this match and reminded himself that he was a man in love. Now, if they could only find the killer, he would be a completely happy man.

Then he opened Akiko's letter.

It was worse than he had expected. "You sly fox, you," she wrote. "Here I was worried about finding you another wife, and you engage yourself to the daughter of a high-ranking Fujiwara! I'm making all the preparations here. You need not worry about anything. Oh, what a time we'll have, your little bride and I. And you are set on a great career. Well done, Brother!"

∞

The morning after the third night broke with the noise of festive preparations all around them. Akitada had been awake for a while, watching the sun gradually make its way through the slats of their closed shutters.

Yukiko beside him slept in a tangle of quilts and disordered undergown that revealed a smooth thigh and leg. He caressed this limb with his eyes and debated whether to wake her. Her long hair partially covered her face. It struck him that she slept as deeply as a child, and once again he felt that terrible tenderness for his young wife.

He had lost Tamako to childbirth, and for all he knew his new bride, this lovely young creature beside him, was already embarked on that same final journey.

In the corridor outside Yukiko's room there was a rustling sound followed by whispers and a giggle. Yukiko stirred, stretched like a kitten, yawned, and then turned to smile up at him.

"Good morning, wife," he said.

"Good morning, husband." She covered herself, then stretched out a hand to touch his face. "You need a shave," she said.

He kissed her anyway, feeling the surge of desire returning, but suppressed it. They would be embarrassingly late for the congratulations if he delayed.

He got up and found the traditional wedding offering left outside the door. A tray with elegantly arranged rice buns waited there. When he returned with it, Yukiko was sitting up, twisting her hair into a knot. She seemed to him the most exquisitely lovely woman he had ever seen, and she was his. He knelt to offer her the tray.

She smiled, took the top bun, and offered it to him. Looking at each other, they ate the sweet, honey-flavored treats.

"May the gods smile on this day," he said formally.

Yukiko blinked. "Oh. I almost forgot. It's the shrine festival today. And the sun is up already. We must hurry, Akitada." Already she was up, looking for her robe that he had carelessly tossed aside last night to make love to her.

A little disappointed, he said, "I meant it is the day of our marriage."

She paused, looking stricken. "I'm sorry, Akitada." And then, "I know I shall make many mistakes."

He got to his feet to find the robe, placed it around her shoulders, and held her. Burying his face in her scented hair, he murmured, "In my eyes, you can do no wrong. And you're quite right. We must hurry."

∞

The preparations for the Grand Shrine Festival took most of the awkwardness from their first appearance together as man and wife. Everybody was far too busy to stare or tease or burden them with best wishes and good advice.

In the courtyard, two ox-drawn carriages stood ready to carry the women and children down to the lake shore. The men would ride. Kosehira, as the governor and a guest of honor, had an escort. Akitada, Kosehira's sons, and Tora trailed behind. Tora wore his half armor and a sword.

When they reached the lake, they separated. Kosehira was greeted by Abbot Gyomey on behalf of the sponsoring temple, Enryaku-ji, and by the shrine priest of the Hiyoshi-Taisha shrine. Seven *mikoshi*, the portable shrines containing the *kami* of the sacred shrines of the mountain, had gathered at Hiyoshi-Taisha in preparation for their boat journey on the lake between Sakamoto and Karasaki. Shrine ceremonies preceded this departure.

Akitada and Kosehira's sons supervised the arrival of the women and children—who took their places behind screens—and then found their own seats on the grandstands nearby. Tora departed to search the crowds for the puppet man. Takechi and his men were also about.

After the shrine service, the ornate mikoshi began to make their journey to the lake. The procession was solemn and colorful. Shrine priests in red, white, and black attire carried large paper lanterns , shrine maidens, *miko*, in their traditional red and white jackets and trousers, tossed paper flowers, little boys in court dress performed small dances as they walked, and the *mikoshi*, very handsome in red lacquer and gilt, each carried by twenty strong, bare-chested young men, passed one by one. The Buddhist priests walked in their black robes, accompanying the image of Monkey, the messenger of the Mountain King and guardian of Mount Hiei.

Akitada had seen the festival before, years ago. It was a strange mix of Buddhist and Shinto observances and divine beings. Today his eyes searched for a killer. Tora reappeared briefly at his side to report that Takechi's men had found no puppet man in the city. They were now stationed among the crowd here and in the area where the fair was taking place. There had been no sign of him there either. Chances were good that he had indeed left Omi to return to whatever northern province he had found a home in. In was extremely unsatisfactory.

Fortunately, Akitada had other, more pleasant, things to occupy his mind. As soon as the procession had passed, Kosehira and his sons joined it on horseback. The crowd of onlookers dispersed to follow. Akitada remained to look after the women and children.

He found that Kosehira's wives wanted to return home, and Akitada saw them safely into one of the carriages. Yukiko and the children were to stay with him and return later in the other carriage.

He left his horse with the servants, and they walked the rest of the way to the lake shore. The children, both Kosehira's and his own and Yuki, skipped ahead excitedly. He and Yukiko followed.

His wife looked very fetching in a pink gown with a white embroidered Chinese jacket. She was dressed for the outing and her long hair was gathered and tied with a white silk bow in back. He thought her enchanting and told her she resembled the cherry blossoms on the trees that lined the road. She thanked him and blushed.

The ceremony of carrying the *mikoshi* on board a barge festooned with straw ropes and colorful bunting was nearly complete by the time they reached the lake. Crowds had converged here, and they had to slip in between people to find a place where the children could see.

What with all the pushing of the crowd, Akitada was afraid of losing one of the children, though Yukiko had told them to hold hands with each other so they would not get separated. Then he almost lost Yukiko as a fat man pushed past him, followed by an equally large family. He looked about frantically and finally found her. After this incident, he kept his arm around her for the rest of the ceremony.

By the time, the barge had been rowed out into the lake, the crowd was headed back toward the fair. They were still all together, for which Akitada gave silent thanks, but he now worried about the fair; it was much larger than the last one where they had temporarily misplaced young Arimitsu. And now they had three additional children to watch.

The fair presented a cheerful picture with its many-colored awnings of fabric stretched between bamboo poles. Kites flew overhead, causing the boys to point and plead. Paper lanterns swung in the breeze, and music came from all sides. Delicious food smells hung in the air, and everywhere vendors shouted their wares.

They were very busy for the next hour and blessedly lost not a single child. Coppers passed from the children to vendors of sweets, more coppers from Akitada to the children. There was a puppet show, but its master had a regular stand for his stage, and he did not limp. A story teller enthralled the children for a while, until they discovered dancers in elaborate lion and dragon costumes dancing on a stage. Akitada took every opportunity to draw Yukiko close, or at least hold her hand. They laughed a good deal, and he was as deeply happy as he had been in many years.

And then he saw the man.

He was ordinary looking, gray-haired and deeply tanned, and he stood watching the puppet show. Something about his expression had caught Akitada's attention, a sort of sneering intentness. As if he could feel his stare, the man suddenly turned his head and looked at him. For a moment their eyes locked, and Akitada knew he was looking at the killer. Then the man turned abruptly and disappeared into the crowd.

Akitada was shaken by the encounter. Instinct told him to follow the man, but he could not leave Yukiko and the children. He scanned the crowd and eventually thought he recognized one of the constables. Waving him over, he described the man and sent him after him.

He was beginning to tire of the entertainment and long for a peaceful rest on Yukiko's veranda, when he saw the man again. This time he was walking away from them with a pronounced limp.

Akitada decided to take the risk. "Yukiko," he said to his wife, "can you manage the children for a little? There is something I have to do."

She raised her brows and giggled. "Certainly, my husband."

He did not correct her mistake and dashed after the limping man.

34

The Little God's Message

"Stop!" he shouted, and when this brought no results, "Stop that man!" Of course, people ignored this, scattering instead in panic. Where were the constables when you needed them? Akitada was hindered by his clothing which, while not the paralyzing court dress, was still not made for running after fugitives. He also had no weapon.

The man was getting away from him in spite of his limp.

Stubbornly, Akitada persisted. His prey vanished from sight once or twice, and eventually Akitada found himself lost, confused and out of breath behind the vendors' tents. He retraced his way to his family, hoping he had not lost them, too.

Then he found the man again in the crowd and simultaneously saw Yukiko and the children, still waiting near the spot where he had left them. He debated his priorities for only an instant, then ran to them. He must make sure they were safe before he could hunt for the killer.

Arriving somewhat out of breath, he told Yukiko, "Come! We must leave. It isn't safe for you or the children." He saw a flash of understanding in her eyes, and took her arm. Turning to gather the children, he found himself once again making eye contact with the killer.

Akitada was certain now that this was the killer. It was also clear that the man knew he had been unmasked. His face was filled with a hate so intense that Akitada was shaken by it. "Come, children," he said. "Hold hands. We must hurry."

They obeyed for once, though Arimitsu protested, "But we haven't seen everything, yet."

Yukiko took her brother's hand. "You have seen enough."

They were headed back to their waiting carriage, but Akitada had reckoned without the killer. Instead of fleeing, Hatta rushed after them, flinging himself between Akitada and Yukiko to seize her by her hair, pulling her head back. He placed the point of a knife against her throat.

"If anyone lays hands on me, she dies," he snarled at Akitada.

Akitada froze. All around him the scene exploded into chaos. The children shrieked, people cried out in fear and scattered, but for Akitada time stood still. He saw only the knife at his wife's throat.

Finally and too late, two red-coated constables appeared, and Akitada knew the danger had just escalated. The madman's mind would snap completely if he was attacked.

With every fiber of his body Akitada wanted to snatch Yukiko from him, but that knifepoint at her throat stopped him. The tip was placed where even a slight cut would prove deadly. He had seen a soldier die in a few moments when a sword had nicked him in that precise spot. His blood had gushed forth and it had been all over.

His voice trembling, he asked, "Are you Hatta Takashi?"

"So you know my name. No matter. She dies unless I leave a free man."

Akitada caught sight of the constables closing in and shouted at them, "Stay back! Don't touch him."

Dear God, he thought, not Yukiko. Not Yukiko also, his just-found love, his poor, dear young wife. She was as pale as snow and her eyes were tightly closed, but tears escaped from under her lashes. A bead of blood formed where the blade pressed into her neck. If she dies, he thought, I shall also die.

"Don't do this," he begged in a shaking voice. "I promise to try to help you. What Taira Sukenori did to you and your family was abhorrent. I understand your wish for revenge, but my wife has done nothing to you."

"You think I care about you courtiers and your spoiled wives? You're all alike. You cheat everyone, and when you're found out, you kill and make some other poor man pay for it. If you know who I am and what Taira Sukenori did to us, you know I could not forget or ever trust one of you again."

Akitada's eyes were on the drop of blood as it slowly coursed down Yukiko's white throat. Her eyes were still closed, and he was still as helpless as before. All he could do was to keep talking. "I don't know all the facts, but your father, I believe, witnessed a murder. The victim was the rice merchant Fumi Takahiro, and he was killed by Taira because he owed Fumi a great deal of money. I don't know how Taira convinced your father to take responsibility for the murder." Akitada prayed that he could distract Hatta by talking about the old crime, and that a single moment of inattention might give him a chance to disarm him. But even as he thought this, he despaired. Hatta would not hesitate to kill Yukiko if he saw himself attacked.

There was a slight movement in the crowd behind Hatta. His heart pounding, Akitada said quickly, "You had a sister. What happened to her?"

Hatta's face darkened. The hand holding the knife trembled and Yukiko gave a small moan. Hatta said, "He killed her, too. He killed that merchant, he killed my father, he tried to kill me, and then he killed my sister. He's the monster, not I."

Tora had silently moved into position behind Hatta and drawn his knife.

Akitada swallowed down his nausea. In the space of a single breath, both Hatta and Yukiko might be dead. Seeing Yukiko in Hatta's clutches with tears on her face, reminded him of the weeping maid being man-handled out of the Taira compound. This was yet another mystery, and somehow it, too, must link to Taira Sukenori. He said as gently as he could, "There's a young girl in Okuni. She was born on the estate. She may be your sister's child."

For the first time, Hatta's grip on the knife faltered. "My sister died. She died in childbirth. That monster made her a slave and gave her to his son. The son raped her and made her his mistress." He bared his teeth. "That's why I killed him."

"The girl—she is your sister's child, hers and Sukemichi's."

Hatta's eyes narrowed. "How do you know this?"

"Sukemichi raised her like his own children, but because he loved her mother, his wife hated her and drove her out of the house after his death."

"You saw—?"

He did not finish his question. Arimitsu suddenly shot forward, screaming, "You let my sister go!" and delivered a mighty kick to Hatta's shin. Akitada and Tora moved simultaneously, Akitada to snatch Yukiko from Hatta's grip and Tora to bring him down from behind.

Akitada did not care what happened next to Hatta. He held Yukiko, who clutched him, weeping softly.

"My dearest," he murmured, "Forgive me, I would gladly give my right arm to have spared you that. Are you all right? Let me see your neck."

He heard a small giggle. "In public, Akitada?"

He sighed his relief and held her a little closer. "I love you, my wife," he said, "and I don't care who knows it. I was terribly afraid."

She sniffed, stepped away, and smiled at him. "Well," she said, "I can see that my life with you will be a great deal more lively than it has been."

Kosehira rushed up at this point. "Yukiko," he cried, "Are you hurt?" The wound was inspected and found trivial. Having satisfied himself of her safety, he turned angrily on Akitada. "How could you let this happen? Are you mad? That animal might have killed her."

That animal lay on the ground, his face in the dirt, and Tora's knife at his neck.

Yukiko stepped closer to Akitada. "No, Father. This wasn't Akitada's fault. I'll not have you speak this way to my husband."

Kosehira was taken aback for a moment, then he laughed weakly. "I told you, brother. She has a mind of her own. Let's go home."

∞

It was in the tribunal jail that Akitada and Takechi interrogated Hatta later that evening.

After his violence at the fair, Hatta appeared to be at peace now. His face bore some scrapes and bruises, and he was chained, but he sat upright and answered their questions calmly and with considerable dignity.

He had already admitted being Hatta Takashi, son of Hatta Hiroshi, but Takechi painstakingly elicited more detail about the old case. As Akitada had guessed, tempted by Sukenori's wealth, the *betto* had agreed to plead guilty to the murder of the rice merchant. The crime happened during a pheasant hunt, and Lord Sukenori had first claimed it was an accident, but when this was proved to be impossible, the *betto* had come forward and confessed.

Taira Sukenori had promised he would make Hatta's children rich. Specifically, he would arrange marriages between the children of both families. Young Hatta Takashi would take the Taira daughter in marriage, along with a very large dowry, and Takashi's sister would marry Lord Sukenori's heir.

The terms were extremely generous and the Hattas owned little but some poor land and a good name. The Tairas were a powerful family. The elder Hatta agreed and confessed to the crime.

The first indication that Lord Sukenori had no intention of keeping his word came when he told the authorities that the rice merchant had raped Hatta's daughter. Hatta had not liked it but was convinced that such a claim would get him a lighter sentence, or perhaps none at all. In the end, however, he was convicted of murder and sent to the north to work in the mines. He died there.

But things got even worse for the Hatta family. Neither marriage took place, and the Hatta home was confiscated and sold for blood money. In his fury over his father having been duped and condemned for something he did not do, Hatta Takashi attacked Taira Sukenori, stabbing him so severely that he nearly died.

Thus Takashi traveled the same path as his father before him. And his mother died soon after and Takashi's sister went into service in the Taira household as part of the reparations for the attack. She became a Taira slave.

It took Takashi nearly twenty years to flee the mines. By then, he had become a trusty, lived outside the mine, and had a family. But he had never given up on his vengeance. One day he left his family, and went on the road, where he fell in with a troupe of itinerant performers.

Nothing in all of this was unexpected, though Akitada thought the tale shocking enough and wished there were some way to find justice for what had been done to the Hatta family. Alas, after committing six murders, Takashi could not hope for mercy.

"Why did you kill so many?" Akitada asked, frustrated by the situation. "Why those two old men in Okuni?"

"They were witnesses," said Takashi. "And they lied."

"You mean they saw the murder committed?" asked Takechi.

"They were beaters during the hunt. I don't know if they saw what happened, but they agreed to lie and say my father shot the merchant."

"And the others?" asked Takechi.

Takashi shook his head. "What does it matter?" For the first time, he showed frustration. He sagged, resting his chin on his chest. "Leave me alone now."

"The truth matters, even after all these years," Akitada said. "You should know that better than anyone."

Takashi sighed. "The judge refused to listen when I protested my father's sentence. When Father withdrew his confession, he ignored him. He was in Taira pay."

"Hmm," said Takechi. "Can you prove that?"

Takashi just gave him a look. "The jailer Tokuno beat my poor father when my father tried to deny his guilt. He was an animal and deserved to die."

"Taira Sukemichi was not an evil man like his father," Akitada pointed out. "It may be that he bedded your sister without making her his wife, but he raised their child like one of his own. And why kill Fumi Tokiari? He had done nothing to you?"

Takashi glowered. "He collected the blood money. We lost everything; my mother died and my sister became a slave."

"It doesn't really matter what everybody else did or didn't do. The only man who really harmed your family was Taira Sukenori. Everything else followed from his murder of the rice merchant and the plot he fabricated to escape just punishment with your father's assistance. Your father was as culpable as he."

Takashi reared up in sudden fury and tried to throw himself at Akitada. Only his chains stopped his violent lunge, and he fell back, sobbing. "You dog-official," he shouted. "Dog-official like the Taira dog-officials! May the gods destroy you all! May a thousand devils flay you alive in hell! May you burn forever. You use people and throw them away like so much filth. You take our land, rape our wives and daughters, and kill us when it suits you." He choked and collapsed into incoherent curses, tears running down his face.

Takechi touched Akitada's arm. "Come, sir," he said. "We have all we need."

Akitada nodded, but he had one more question. "Why did you leave a figure of Jizo on the bodies of the men you killed?"

At first, the prisoner did not answer. Then he muttered, "I'm a traveler in a dark and dangerous world, a world where all roads lead to death. I needed his protection until I had my revenge."

∞

Outside the jail, Takechi said, "So it meant nothing. We've been racking our brains in vain."

"Not quite nothing." Akitada had felt a great depression settle over him during the interview. Like some huge dark cloud, it managed to blot out the joy of springtime, love, and hope. " 'A dark and dangerous world,' he called it. Jizo was his talisman. After each murder, he left it behind as a token that he had fulfilled an oath he made to his dead father."

"Jizo is a kind spirit, a spirit of protection for the weak. It's a shocking insult to ask his help in the killing of innocent people."

"Well, not quite innocent in several cases, but you're right." Akitada sighed. "We'd better report to the governor."

∞

Kosehira heard their account silently. In the end, he only said, "Well, he'll be condemned to exile again and sent back. For all we know, he'll step right back into his position as trusty and live out his life with his family. We have a very inadequate system of justice."

Akitada felt compelled to protest. "Hatta had very great provocation. It should have been Sukenori who was sent to work in the mines."

Kosehira thought this funny. "Such a thing would never happen, Akitada. Send a Taira nobleman to the mines? The notion is mad."

Akitada snapped, "Yes, and that is what causes men like Sukenori to behave the way they do: they know they can't be touched. The only thing Sukenori feared was the loss of a lucrative position he craved."

Kosehira gave him a sharp glance, perhaps to warn him that Takechi was with them. Akitada looked at Takechi who looked back. At that moment Akitada felt a greater bond with Takechi than with Kosehira, even though he was his best friend and father-in-law.

As if he had read his thoughts, Kosehira said, " *You* are one of the good people, Akitada, and you'll soon surpass men like Sukenori. Consider this a good fortune for those without power."

∞

In spite of all the happy preparations around him, Akitada could not shake his depression or the nagging thought that he, too, might succumb to the poisonous lure of power some day. Then a small consolation arrived in the form of a message from Warden Masaie. Young Masaie had married the maid Mineko. This news went a long way toward lifting Akitada's spirits as he prepared to bring Yukiko home to a house that had been too long without joy or hope for the future.

Historical Note

The city of Otsu was an important port and business center during the Heian period. Having briefly served as capital once, it never lost its importance because of its location at the southern tip of Lake Biwa near the place where the Seta River emerged from the lake and flowed southward to become the great Yodo River, thus linking shipping from the lake to the Inland Sea. In addition, two important highways connecting the capital to the provinces passed through Otsu; here the Tokaido, the great eastern highway, and the Tosando, the great northern highway, met to continue to the capital and thence to the western provinces. The city thus became a center of travel and commerce.

In addition, Otsu was home to two powerful Buddhist temples, Enryaku-ji on Mount Hiei, and Onjo-ji, in the city. Saicho, the founder of Enryaku-ji, was born in Otsu. By the eleventh century, Enryaku-ji is said to have owned sixteen valleys, three major temple sites, and three-thousand buildings housing priests.

During the tenth century, quarrels between major Buddhist institutions resulted in the militarizing of the great religious institutions. These hired mercenaries or trained young monks in the military arts in order to defend their properties, as well as to attack opposing temples. These warrior monks or Buddhist mercenaries were the *sohei.* For their historical significance, see *The Teeth and Claws of the Buddha* by Mikael S. Adolphson.

The issue of religion in the eleventh century requires a brief explanation. There were two faiths: Shinto and Buddhism. Shinto is the native religion that worships *kami,* gods that are manifestations of the world around us. Buddhism, on the other hand, is an import of the Indian religion which came to Japan via China and Korea. Shinto is of the greatest significance in Japan, because the emperors are descended from the gods and represent them during ceremonies involving the rice culture. The rice culture, however, meant life or death to the Japanese people of the time. For this reason, Buddhism never attempted to oppose Shinto. Rather, it adapted to it, making the native gods Buddhist avatars. This explains why Enryaku-ji is involved in the many spring-rice-planting celebrations by the Shinto shrines. The *Sanno-Sai Matsuri* in the novel is still celebrated by both Shinto and Buddhist priests.

Religious observations and rituals attracted fairs that catered to crowds by selling religious objects, amulets, memorabilia, etc, and by entertaining people with acrobats, dancers, musicians, storytellers, and various other performers, such as puppeteers. These fair performers were members of the *hinin*-class, the so-called non-persons of society. They traveled the highways of the land and had no homes. The *kugutsu-mawashi* were traveling puppet operators who performed at fairs or by special invitation at country estates. Like other itinerant people, these strolling players of Japan subsisted on what people were willing to pay. Like others, such as the *asobi*, women who danced and sang and sold their bodies, they were considered undesirables by the authorities. Travelling puppeteers usually carried their puppets in a box that would become the stage on which the puppeteer let the dolls perform. They were the forerunners of *Bunraku*, the Japanese puppet theater.

The continuing prevalence of hunting as a sport is another example of old customs surviving in spite of Buddhist teachings against the taking of life or the eating of animals. Hunting with bow and arrow and with falcons was well known in Japan before the advent of Buddhism and was practiced by emperors and the nobility. An imperial reserve, where pheasants were protected and harvested for the imperial table and special court observances existed at the time of this novel in Omi province and had a Taira administrator. Falcons were trained and treasured throughout Japan's history. There are many screens from later centuries that depict collections of falcons displayed in the manner described in this novel.

Last but not least, something must be said about wedding and marriage customs in the Heian period.

Most marriages were arranged between families, and husbands lived with their brides in the wife's parents' home. This, no doubt, assured the young woman's safety and comfort but may also have allowed her father to influence politics by controlling her husband. Something of the sort is described in Lady Murasaki's *Genji*, where Genji, an imperial prince, moves into his father-in-law's house after marriage. The matter of the consummation of a marriage not being binding unless performed on three consecutive nights assured the bride and her family that the suitor was committed to the match. He could, of course, walk away before the third night. He could also divorce his wife by merely telling her so. In general, sexual relations tended to be casual and no special importance was attached to virginity or to the husband's faithfulness. Noblemen traditionally had more than one wife and also kept mistresses. A noblewoman's security lay in her producing sons, in her family's protection, and in owning her own property. And finally, to clear up a misconception: the Japanese did indeed kiss. It appears that a Western misconception, possibly caused by Lafcadio Hearn's assertion that Japanese lovers never kissed, has been accepted as historical fact. Thus, I offer the evidence of the *Ishimpo*, an ancient medical text used in Heian Japan, which describes kissing as part of its instructions for love-making. The custom of kissing certainly did not die out either, for later examples may be found in the *shunga*, those graphic woodblock depictions of lovers.

About the Author

I. J. Parker was born and educated in Europe and turned to mystery writing after an academic career in the U.S. She has published her Akitada stories in *Alfred Hitchcock's Mystery Magazine,* winning the Shamus award in 2000. Several stories have also appeared in collections, such as *Fifty Years of Crime and Suspense* and *Shaken.* The award-winning "Akitada's First Case" is available as a podcast. Many of the stories have been collected in *Akitada and the Way of Justice.*

The Akitada series of crime novels features the same protagonist, an eleventh century Japanese nobleman/detective. *The Old Men of Omi* is number thirteen. The books are available on Kindle, in print and in audio format, and have been translated into twelve languages.

Books by I. J. Parker

The Akitada series in chronological order

The Dragon Scroll

Rashomon Gate

Black Arrow

Island of Exiles

The Hell Screen

The Convict's Sword

The Masuda Affair

The Fires of the Gods

Death on an Autumn River

The Emperor's Woman

Death of a Doll Maker

The Crane Pavilion

The Old Men of Omi

The collection of stories

Akitada and the Way of Justice

Other Historical Novels

The HOLLOW REED saga:

Dream of a Spring Night

Dust before the Wind

The Sword Master

The Left-Handed God

Contact Information

Please visit I.J.Parker's web site at www.ijparker.com.

You may contact her via e-mail at heianmys@aol.com. (This way you will be notified when new books come out.)

The novels may be ordered from Amazon and Barnes&Noble as trade paperbacks. The electronic versions for Kindle are at Amazon. Several short stories are available for both Kindle and Nook. Please do post Amazon reviews. They help sell books and keep Akitada novels coming.

Thank you for your support.

Made in the USA
Lexington, KY
02 January 2015